Praise for *Clinging to the Moon*

"*Clinging to the Moon* is an extraordinary story. It tackles the biggest hurdles we humans must face—love, change and death—with such tenderness and intimacy that you will be both illuminated and comforted. This is a story that will transform your notions of how we love, how we change and how we die. This is a story that will stick with you long after putting it down, indeed perhaps for the rest of your life. Clinging to the Moon is Cogan's masterpiece."

—Dr. Wendy Parciak,
Award-Winning Author of *Requiem for Locusts*

"Priscilla Cogan's writing draws in the reader as only a master storyteller can. Within a few short pages I was drawn into the lives of two people plunged into the living hell of traumatic injury, and the strange old woman who helps them find humor and comfort despite their injuries. And readers of Cogan's earlier novels will be happily reunited with Meggie and Hawk who bring their compassionate wisdom to the healing process."

—Jennifer Barker, Coauthor of *The Goddess Within*

"A masterpiece that can be read purely for pleasure as well as for the spiritual teachings it embodies. This very wise, beautifully told, love story weaves together many threads into an emotionally satisfying whole. It reveals how life's tragedies create opportunities for growth and healing. The book will reach inside and touch your soul."

—Dr. Lesley I. Shore, Founder of Harmony Ctr., Medfield, MA

"As a Christian, I always come to Priscilla Cogan's novels with a great deal of curiosity, because I know she will always delve deeply into the spiritual aspects of her characters' lives. *Clinging to the Moon* stands as a poetic tapestry of beliefs, pain, and the deep soul needs of redemption and love."

—Sue Harrison, Author of *Mother Earth, Father Sky*

"Resilience of the human spirit shines in Priscilla Cogan's new novel *Clinging to the Moon*. Her expertise is evident in the psychological musings of her two main characters who struggle for dignity and survival in the face of adversity. They form an unlikely bond with their damaged souls and the battered bodies that hold them. A tale of profound disability becomes an even deeper fable of healing."

—Evelyn Wolfson, Author of *Roman Mythology, From Abenaki to Zuni*

ALSO BY PRISCILLA COGAN

WINONA'S WEB

COMPASS OF THE HEART

CRACK AT DUSK: CROOK OF DAWN

DOUBLE TIME

THE UNRAVELING THREAD

CLINGING
TO THE
MOON

A NOVEL BY

PRISCILLA COGAN

TWO CANOES PRESS
Hopkinton, Massachusetts

Two Canoes Press
PO Box 334
Hopkinton, MA 01748
www.TwoCanoesPress.com

This book is a work of fiction.
Names, characters, places, and incidents
are products of the author's imagination
or are used fictitiously.

Jacket and book design by Arrow Graphics, Inc.
Watertown, Massachusetts
info@arrow1.com

Jacket illustration by Aramais Andonian
Author's photograph by Duncan Sings-Alone

Manufactured in the United States of America

Publisher's Cataloging-in-Publication
(Provided by Quality Books, Inc.)

Cogan, Priscilla, 1947-
    Clinging to the moon : a novel / by Priscilla Cogan.
    p. cm.
    LCCN 2012955591
    ISBN 978-1-929590-19-3

    1. Brain damage—Patients—Fiction. 2. Paralytics—Fiction.
3. Indians of North America—Fiction.
4. Catholic Church—Fiction. 5. Healing—Fiction.
6. Lovestories.   I. Title.

PS3553.O4152C55 2013   813'.54
                      QBI12-600242

Acknowledgments

•◆•

A NOVELIST IS A LISTENER and collector of personal stories, begged, borrowed, and begotten, all of which are then stitched into the larger fabric of a novel. Characters invariably pop out of the writer's imagination and psyche, enter the landscape of the novel, then pronounce their independence and are off and running. Often the writer knows the end of the story, has to discover the beginning, and then tries to corral the characters in the right direction.

For their stories and their courageous struggles, my appreciation and admiration go to Dr. Nancielee Holbrook, Matthew Maguire, William Fuller, and Carol Whitlock.

For her fine editorial work, thanks to Rebecca Chown.

For fine book design, Alvart Badalian, and the beautiful book cover art, Aramais Andonian.

For information on label fraud, Diann Heming of Good Harbor Winery.

For legal advice on divorce in Michigan, Dona Laskey, Esq..

For the workings of a psychic, Robert Stevens.

For a wonderful grading system, Dr. Bardwell Smith.

And last, but never least, thank you to my best reader, friend, husband, and source of constant support—Duncan Sings-Alone.

Dedication

❖

For Dr. Nancielee Holbrook
&
the late Matthew (Magoo) Maguire

*L*OVE IS LUNAR, sometimes full and bountiful, casting light upon dark shadows and bathing the world in a glorious, magical gold or a pale, poignant dawning white; sometimes pointed and sharp at both ends, signaling a coming or a going, a potential or a decrease, a promise or a withholding; sometimes hidden or disappeared, leaving the self to a blackness both inside and out, a despair, a time of waiting, a hope that the day will arrive with another partner so large and brilliant in scope that we shall soon forget the shifting tides of love's lunacy.

But night follows day as intractably as day follows night, and without the magic and mystery and risk of love, we would all choose to walk in the blinding sun.

—Priscilla Cogan

Tess

Chapter 1

• ◆ •

FOR FORTY DAYS AND FORTY NIGHTS, I wandered in the seductive sea-deep wilderness of the dead, speckled with distant, hollow voices, wavering flashes of surface, sunless light, and the steady sounds of a beating heart.

"Help!" I screamed, but no sound issued forth.

Once I heard a woman's watery voice echo back, "Wake up, Tess."

But all I could do was float among other pale, human forms, guardians of the deep, their arms and legs rocking back and forth in the oceanic depths, their faces unknown, their eyes shut.

A man with long curly hair and seaweed for a robe silently urged me to close my eyes, release into the fathomless sleep. He drifted toward me, his translucent arms fluttering out to engulf me in a dark, moonless embrace.

My lungs gasped for air. I was drowning.

This is the end, I thought.

Panic surged through me like an electrical jolt.

Thrashing and flailing, I pushed myself off the bottom of the mud-blackened depths into layers upon layers of aching cold, my heart thumping wildly, my arms and legs beating the water, until finally I crashed through the glassy skin of the sea and awakened to the suck of sweet, pure air.

Breath had propelled me back to life.

My eyes popped open to the glaring lights of a hospital room and the sight of a team of doctors bending over me, their mouths agape. At the end of the bed swayed my handsome husband, tears streaming down his cheeks.

Oh Nick, I thought but could not say. *I'm alive! I'm alive!*

Little did I know that my darling Nick had finally given permission for the doctors to shut off the ventilator. "It is what she would have wanted," he had told them.

All expectation was that I'd sigh, perhaps a rale or two, then slip into a peaceful death. Instead my battered lungs seized and gasped at life.

Breath.

I was going to live.

The sterile room in the ICU exploded into activity; the doctors murmured, momentarily crowding Nick out of view as the white coats swarmed over me with their instruments and comments. My eyes tracked him as he retreated to a corner spot, leaning against the wall, the back of his hand erasing the last tear.

My head throbbed under the lights. My eyes could not properly focus. The rasping sounds in the room buzzed over me. My throat ached. I closed my eyes and, for a moment, almost wished myself back down in the muffling sea.

The voice of a male doctor bombarded me with questions: "How many fingers am I holding up?"

I opened my eyes again.

"Two," although the pudgy fingers overlapped into four.

"Name?"

"Tess."

"Last name?"

I looked at Nick, shadowed in the corner. He answered, "Outerbridge."

"Age?"

"Twenty-nine and holding," I answered.

The doctor didn't laugh.

What is the value of a life without humor?

"Thirty-six," I squawked.

"What month is it?"

I shook my head and squinted. I simply did not know. I looked at Nick again, hoping he'd answer.

"What's the matter with me?"

Why does my head hurt? Why am I in a hospital bed?

"Lift your right hand to touch your nose."

I dutifully complied.

"Now your left hand."

The physician then commanded me to wiggle and lift my feet. He tested foot reflexes. Then he pulled out a slender pencil-thin light to examine my eyes.

I blinked.

"President of the United States?" he asked, as he focused on my pupils. His breath smelled of stale coffee.

The black guy.

"Obama," I said, pleased that I knew that much.

"What city and state are we in?" He flicked off the light and deposited it back into his lab coat pocket.

"Cambridge, Massachusetts." That was easy. I was an English teacher, with a Ph.D., at the exclusive Buckingham Browne and Nichols School.

From the corner I could see Nick shaking his head, a concerned and puzzled expression crossing his face.

The older doctor exchanged knowing glances with the younger ones who encircled my bed. He addressed them. "Mrs. Outerbridge experienced a moderately severe traumatic brain injury. She was brought into the ER forty-one days ago with brain swelling, so we medically induced a coma, but she stayed overlong in that state. As you can see, she's currently experiencing some disorientation."

He turned back to me, giving his best professional smile. "You're very lucky to have survived that car accident. There was considerable doubt that you were going to make it."

He placed a consoling hand upon my shoulder, then with a nod to the medical students, led them out of the room to examine other unfortunates who had also landed in the ICU.

What car accident?

I looked again toward the corner, but Nick was no longer there.

Did I simply dream his presence?

A young female physician had remained behind.

"What happened?" I asked.

"A terrible car accident," she said. "Rainy night. You hydroplaned into a telephone pole."

"My head . . ."

"Your brain jolted forward, then backward. In the process there was quite a bit of shearing of neurons. You've had a severe traumatic brain injury. As Dr. Ogilvy said, we weren't sure that you were going to make it."

To be or not to be, that is the question.

A great fatigue washed over me, like the wave of an inviting sea, yet I didn't want to drown again in the watery depths. If I returned, the Dead might not release me this time.

As if intuiting my thoughts, the doctor said, "It's okay to take a nap. This must be very confusing for you. You're going to need to take lots of naps during the healing period."

To suffer the flings of misfortune. Flings?

"Was there anyone else in the car with me?"

"No. You were alone," she answered.

"Can you stay with me until my husband returns?" It was hard to talk. My brain was sparking, not making meaningful connections.

Her eyes shifted to the corner of the room, the empty spot where I had last seen Nick. A puzzled look wrinkled across her brow for a fleet second before she erased it and turned back toward me with a comforting smile.

"Of course," she answered.

I slept and awoke, slept and awoke—every time startled to find myself in an alien room, hooked up to a drip of who knows what. At first there was a nurse, then a nursing aide, followed eventually by a plump, elderly woman seated in a brown vinyl chair near my bed, reading a dog-eared romance novel. She said her name was Cassie McDermott. I was relieved that she didn't ask me any questions. I had no answers. No memory of the accident and too much of the unconscious, murky world. I couldn't even tell night from day in the room's artificial light. My brain grappled at old poetic lines, but everything seemed jumbled and in fragments.

The doctors prodded, probed, and asked me to perform routine tests. On the third day, they had me stand up as the crowd of medical students took notes, the johnny robe barely covering my butt. The world spun around like a carousel.

"I'm falling down a rabbit hole," cried Alice.

They quickly restored me to the solidity of the bed. They talked about me as if I weren't there, using numbers and medical terms I'd never heard before, their focus on misbehaving reflexes, spasmodic eye movements, MRIs, CAT scans, blood chemistry, and the initial med-flight and ER findings. I detected a certain undercurrent of pride in their interventions and the astonishing fact of my survival. When they trooped out to examine another patient, Cassie returned and said, "It was by the grace of God and your seatbelt that you survived. As for that coma, you chose to wake up."

Tess, wake up!

Yes, it had been Cassie's voice that I'd heard.

"You were here when I was . . . away," I said.

She looked up from her book and nodded. "They told me there was this patient who might not emerge from a coma, so I took that as my own personal challenge. You just needed to know that someone was here pulling for you."

"Where's Nick?" I asked.

"Nick?"

"My husband."

How do I love thee? Let me count the days. No, the ways.

Cassie shrugged her shoulders, picked up her book, then put it down, and looked over her half-glasses. "Good question," she muttered.

After four days, they transferred me out of the ICU to a regular floor. I was no longer in danger of dying, but I was still confused and disoriented.

"Where are you?" the doctors kept asking me.

I insisted, "Cambridge, Massachusetts."

They'd smile a patronizing smile, shake their heads, and consult among themselves. Apparently I had severed my connections to the last seven months.

It was Cassie who informed me that I was in the hospital trauma center in Traverse City, Michigan. Nick had informed the hospital staff that we had moved from Cambridge, Massachusetts, to his old family house in Traverse City seven months earlier.

"He told them you had found it difficult to leave your friends on the East Coast and that you were depressed," said Cassie.

If you had just returned from the land of the dead, wouldn't it make sense to think you had landed back in your old home?

It was not a thought I dared verbalize. I wasn't functioning on all cognitive cylinders, and I didn't want them to think I was a total wreck.

Cassie sat there quietly reading her romance novel, turned a page, and without looking up at me, added, "I think your husband suggested to the doctors that the crash might not have been an 'accident.'"

I frowned, trying to understand what she was saying.

"That, maybe on that rainy night, you chose to hit the telephone pole," she continued.

A telephone pole, for God's sake. Can you hear me now? Can you hear me now?

I snorted, then started laughing. My brain was on full revolt, tossing me comedic lines at the most inopportune time.

Could I really have been suicidal forty-three days ago?

A social worker with the ridiculous name of Jane Smith arrived to gather basic information. In her twenties, she was dressed conservatively, a brightly colored scarf the only splash of color on a dull grey sweater dress.

"What kind of work do you do, Mrs. Outerbridge?"

"I'm an English teacher at a private school in Cambridge, Massachusetts."

Jane Smith's eyes twitched.

I said something wrong, incorrect.

"No, no that was last year." I forced my delinquent brain to work. "I'm unemployed right now." I tapped my forehead. "Everything's still muddled."

"What does your husband do?"

"He's a clinical psychologist, but . . ."

"But what?" she asked.

"I don't know where he is."

A loud knock upon the door startled me, hurt my ears. My head echoed like a boom box, magnifying every sound.

A sallow man with a dark, thin mustache stuck his head into the room. "Is this the room of Mrs. Tess Outerbridge? Am I interrupting anything?"

"Yes and yes," scolded Jane Smith who, obviously, did not welcome the intrusion.

He pushed open the door even farther. "Well, I won't take any of your time then. I simply needed to give you this, Mrs. Outerbridge." He dropped several sheets of paper on the bed, then abruptly turned to leave. When he shut the door behind him, I could swear it was a slam.

"What is it?" I asked, my head reverberating with the sound.

The social worker picked up the papers and rifled through them, then sighed. "Your husband, Dr. Outerbridge, is suing you for a divorce. This is a summons and a copy of the complaint for divorce."

"What? No, it can't be true," I insisted. "There's been some mistake here. Nick loves me. I adore him."

Jack and Jill went up the hill.

Shut up!

I dug my fingers into the sides of my face to hush the inner rebellion of my thoughts.

"Where's the telephone? Let me call him. Maybe that guy got my name mixed up with someone else."

Jane Smith shook her head as if she didn't know what to do. She pulled out her cell phone, checked her fact sheet, dialed my home number, then handed me the phone. Three times it rang, before it was picked up.

"Hello?" Nick's tenor voice.

"Nick, it's me. Tess. Where are you?"

"I'm home, Tess." Annoyance underscored his voice. "That's the number you dialed on the phone."

In the background, I could hear a woman's voice, asking, "Honey, who is it?"

"Nick, it's weird. A man came, left me divorce papers. What's this all about? When are you coming to get me and bring me home?"

I heard the click of another receiver coming online. A female voice. "Tess, this is Sandy. We never thought you were going to make it out alive. I know this is a big shock to you, but . . ."

"Sandy?"

Nick's old high school girlfriend, a crystal healer or something like that.

"Yeah, well, sometimes these things happen. When the spiritual energies mesh, you've just got to go with it," she continued. "It wasn't like an overnight thing."

"Sandy, get off the phone," ordered Nick.

I could hear the click of a receiver being hung up.

"Look, Tess," he said. "It's over. Sandy's moved in and that's that."

"But . . ."

"The old family house is in my name. Let's be civil about it. The hospital isn't ready to release you, but when they do, I'll help you find an apartment and move your stuff over there. I'm sorry I haven't been up to visit you, but I've been working my ass off. Your hospital bills are costing me an arm and a leg."

"But Nick, we've been married for thirteen years. Doesn't that count for something?"

I felt like I was pleading for my life, my old life. We'd gone to graduate schools together, gotten our first professional jobs, had the normal arguments over money and chores, and had even started talking about the next step—having children. Nothing that suggested divorce.

"We haven't been on the same wavelength for a long time, Tess."

"But . . . is this because of the accident? I know I'm confused right now, that I have trouble processing stuff, but it'll get better. My brain will heal, I'm sure of it. I'll be just like I used to be. The old Tess."

"No, that's not the reason. Of course, you'll get better. What you didn't know, Tess, was why I insisted we move to Michigan. I had to find out if this connection with Sandy was real. I wasn't honest with you, and I'm not proud of that fact."

The high school reunion over a year ago, when he returned to Massachusetts, cold and withdrawn. And dummy me thought the move to Michigan would help him feel better about himself!

Two and two still didn't make four or, in this case, three. My brain literally felt like it was going to explode on one side. As I choked down my feelings, my throat began closing up.

"The accident just kind of simplified things," he added. "I've got to go. Look, I know this is rather sudden for you, and that you have a lot of feelings to process, but you've always been a strong woman, Tess. A survivor. You'll adjust and move on with your life. We'll talk about it later."

Click. He hung up.

I sat there in the hospital bed, the receiver cradled under my chin, tears welling up in my eyes, unable to comprehend what was happening. A headache was killing me; my heart was breaking. I grabbed the bedside button for the nurses' station and thumbed it hard. "They better bring me something soon to stop all this pain."

Jane Smith reached out, took my hand in hers, her voice honeyed with compassion and irony. "He sure has a helluva sense of timing."

Right then and there, the nightmarish world of the dead didn't seem so bad after all.

If I hadn't chosen to return, I never would have known such pain. I could have died, blissfully ignorant, still in love with the man with whom I had sworn to spend my whole life.

Oh, Nick. When did you, the real you, disappear from me?

My child brain answered:

When Jill came tumbling after.

Sonny

Chapter 2

"You kind of look like that black Jesus on the wall there." The ninety-five-year-old woman pointed to a framed painting above her worn sofa. "You're Dora's boy alright. I remember her showing me pictures of you." She shuttled a toothpick back and forth along the thin line of her lips. The black skin on her face folded back in on itself, wrinkles marking years of hard work.

Slowly, she eased herself up off the rocking chair, a worn cotton dress reshaping itself to gravity's purpose. She stood there, neither moving forward nor to the side. "Gotta wait until the knees know where they is and where they's going." She chuckled at that, before shuffling forward toward her little apartment kitchen. "Sure you don't want another cup?"

I felt the indigestion bubbling up from my stomach, fired by that first bitter cup of coffee.

"No, Ma'am," I said. "Do you know where's she gone?" It had taken me far too long to track down Mama's relatives.

She poured herself another cup and pulled out a box of tea biscuits from the cupboard. "Good for the digestion," she said, offering me one.

I accepted the cookie. I could see that I needed to pace myself to the old woman's sense of time.

"Don't get many visitors," she added, ambling back into her small living room. "Gets lonely around here. Sunday's the big day for socializing. You go to church regular?" She carefully eased herself back down into the rocking chair.

"I was placed in a Catholic boarding school."

She scratched her head. "Yes, I remember that now. They wouldn't let her see you. Not really Christian of them, was it? Seems to me them Catholics could learn something from the Baptists, you know?"

I certainly didn't want to get into any theological arguments with an old woman, but I couldn't help thinking: *A pox on all of them: Catholics, Baptists, Lutherans, Jews, Muslims, and all the rest. Everybody claiming to possess the TRUTH, hugging it to themselves and saying everybody else is going to hell. Who needs the insanity of religion to live?*

I kept my mouth shut, chewed quietly on the cookie.

"Dora sure loved you. Nothing brightened her up 'cept to talk about you." The old woman smiled. "I tole her, 'Dora, you best forget that boy. He ain't coming back.' But she just couldn't do that."

She rocked back and forth, back and forth, tapping her small shoes down on the wooden floor. "Said that at least you was getting a good education from them Catholics, but I tole her they were gonna teach you how to be a white boy." She leveled her sharp, rheumy eyes at me, scanning for any bleaching in my mulatto skin.

But there was no denying my ethnic background with brown dreadlocks framing the thinly etched features of my face. I had once wished for a tall, basketball player's body but instead inherited a wiry body and the looks of a Caribbean hippie. I would have settled for a big, powerful body like that of Mama. She carried herself forward into a crowd with a sense of dignity and power, a body with sensual curves, big bust and hips, a bulwark of safety for me to hide behind.

"It was a classical education. Got offered a scholarship to Harvard," I answered with a tinge of pride.

Her eyebrows raised. "You going?"

I nodded but added, "Only after I find Mama."

"Harvard. That would make her right proud of you. Maybe even worth the sacrifice."

"That's why I want to find her. To thank her."

"You gonna come back, help your people then?" The old lady squinted at me like an alligator surveying potential prey. She didn't really trust the color of my skin or my intentions.

"My mind's okay. My body's strong enough, but . . ." I stammered. "I have to find her to become whole again. You understand?" My voice cracked with suppressed feelings.

I felt like I was talking to a deaf woman. Not like me to let slip my emotions. I'd learned those lonely nights in the dormitory to cry quietly in my pillow.

And then, it was like something eased in that old woman's spine. Her face softened into warmer lines. She reached out with bony fingers and grasped my hand between cold palms.

"Haven't seen Dora for over five years now, but last I knew, she was headed up north."

I waited for more.

"Seems to me," she said, "that Dora mentioned Traverse City, Michigan. Tole me it was by the 'little finger' on the western side. Said she had heard there was work up there. Sara Lee, I think it was. She always did like their coffee cakes."

A memory suddenly flooded my brain. Sunday mornings and the smell of heated apricot coffee cake. Mama had always made Sundays really special. "A time to celebrate the Lord's Day," she would say.

Sara Lee and Traverse City. It was the first lead I'd gotten in months.

I smiled and politely took my leave.

She walked me to the door. "You gonna look for Dora now?"

"I'd even follow a trail of bread crumbs to find her." I smiled, enjoying the image of Mama and the apricot coffee cakes.

"Well now, that fairy tale of Hansel and Gretel didn't turn out so good, did it?" The old lady squinted up at me. "You best be prepared for wherever that path takes you."

But I was pretty damn sure that after all these years, the trail of crumbs would finally lead me home, a way of ending one journey before beginning another.

Tess

Chapter 3

◆

NICK, OH NICK . . .

It was an unfinished sentence to the refrain running through my mind. I was calling out to him in my dreams, pitiful, begging him to make my world all right again. When day finally arrived, I peered into the hand mirror on the table. A red and blotchy face appeared, a crying face, eyelids swollen like some reptilian creature.

The doctors passed my bed in the morning but had the decency to keep their concerns to themselves. Or perhaps they were hoping Jane Smith, intrepid social worker, would somehow clean up the emotional sop I was rapidly becoming.

First to arrive was Cassie McDermott with a cup of strong coffee for me and a giant blueberry scone for the two of us to share. "I heard," she said, as she handed me the coffee. "You need this."

"I look like hell warmed over," I said, stifling the tears.

"Honey, you look like a woman scorned." She broke apart the scone and actually fed me a piece, as if I were a baby bird in need of sustenance. Truth to tell, I needed someone to feed me at that moment.

"The fury will come later," she added, placing yet another piece on my tongue.

A light knock on the door, and Jane Smith entered the nest.

"I'll leave the two of you to talk," said Cassie, gathering up her rumpled bag of crossword puzzles, knitting, and romance novel. "I'll be back."

Jane waited until Cassie had left. "How are you doing this morning?"

"No job. No money. A husband who has suddenly decided that he doesn't want me anymore. No place to live. And let's not forget my scrambled brain. Other than that . . ." I forced a smile.

While jotting notes on a yellow pad, she didn't seem to notice that tears were once again forming in my eyes.

"Headaches?"

"Yes, killer ones." I rubbed my eyes.

"Has the physical therapist come around yet?"

"Oh, they have me up and moving with a walker, but my balance is worth shit."

Without warning, the tears crested my eyelids and dribbled down my cheeks.

"You're going to find that your emotional balance has taken a hit as well," Jane said, handing me a tissue.

"Great. Not only can't I think straight, I'm an emotional mess as well. Maybe a mental hospital will take me when I get out of this place."

Jane didn't smile.

Not a good sign.

"Talking about discharge, your husband's insurance company wants us to transfer you to a rehabilitation center."

"An institution for invalids and the brain-damaged?" Things were going from bad to worse.

"There are programs for people with traumatic brain injuries to help you get back most of your previous functioning. Physical therapy, speech therapy, occupational therapy. True, most people go to these programs on a daily basis while living at home."

"And I'm homeless." It sounded so pathetic.

"Right, and you can't live alone at this point. So, I will research the best alternatives. Is there anything you need right now?"

"Yes," I answered.

Jane Smith smiled, because in the midst of my despair, she might actually be able to do something helpful.

"Could you get me some hemlock?"

"Is that some kind of herbal remedy?"

"Yes, it's a drink," I answered, realizing that she didn't know it was a poison. "It simplifies things."

She stood up, straightening her linen skirt. "Could you get one of your friends to pick it up at a nutrition shop?"

"You forget. I don't have any friends here. Except Nick who turns out not to be a friend at all."

Jane frowned. I was pitching pathos at her with an undercurrent of building rage, like a sulky summer day with the distant rumble of thunder. Should she pay attention to the sun, the clouds heavy with rain, or the menacing storm?

"I'll tell the physicians that you need something stronger for your headaches." She fled the disaster I was rapidly becoming.

As Jane opened the door to leave, Cassie brushed by her, a cold fruit smoothie in hand.

"Bad news?" she asked, after waiting for Jane to close the door. She brushed my stringy hair away from my face in a motherly gesture.

"They want to dump me into some rehab facility, as I have no place to go. I can't walk straight. I can't think right. And I feel dead inside. Thank you for the smoothie." I slurped it right away, food serving as my last resort.

"So, what do *YOU* want to do?" she asked.

"Kill Nick. Kill Sandy. Then jump off a bridge or something like that. Only . . ."

"Only what?" Cassie leaned forward, taking my hand in hers.

"Only I have a thirteen-year-old Sheltie at home. Her name is Imp, and I can't bear to think that Sandy would replace me in her affections."

"You have responsibilities."

"Yes. Do you find that strange?"

"Okay," said Cassie, shaking her head as if she had just made up her mind. "Okay. I can take a dog."

I frowned, puzzled by her response.

"I'm seventy-three years old," she continued, "and I live alone in a very large house. When I talk to myself, I hear the echo of my voice. I don't know much about dogs, but I think I can accommodate one."

"You mean while I'm recovering in a rehabilitation unit?"

"It's lonely being in that house all by myself. That's why I volunteer at this hospital."

She paused, waiting for me to respond, forgetting that my brain didn't track right anymore.

Cassie tried another tack. "Look, we're born in one family. As we get older, we fall in love and make another family. Sometimes that works out. Sometimes it doesn't. People love, then leave you. Or else they up and die suddenly. So then you learn to create a different kind of family, one based on friendship. One where you can create a sanctuary for each other, a refuge when the world batters and beats you to a pulp."

"A sanctuary," I said, savoring the sound of that word.

"Yes," she said. "Now you understand."

"I think so."

She patted my cheek before pushing herself off the chair. "Okay. I'll go let that Ms. Jane Smith know that you and Imp will be staying with me for as long as is needed."

"Are you sure?" I couldn't believe that someone would spontaneously open her home like that to a stranger. Hell, she didn't even know me from before. When I was normal. Competent. Strong. Happily married.

"Yes, I'm sure." Cassie patted my arm. "Now is there anything else you want me to tell the social worker?"

I thought a moment, then added. "Tell her . . ."

"Yes?" Cassie stopped.

"Tell her I won't be needing that hemlock after all."

Cassie shook her head and rolled her eyes.

Sonny

Chapter 4

⋅◆⋅

I DROVE FROM CHICAGO up the western side of Michigan in a Honda Accord that had seen better days. Mama had never taken me to Michigan. In late June, the traffic consisted mainly of retired elders trekking up north to their summer cabins along Lake Michigan and the smaller, inland lakes. The pickups and SUVs dragged boats of all varieties: sailboats, elaborate fishing rigs, long-snouted cigarette boats, jet skis, and sleek kayaks. At Holland, Michigan, I veered over toward Grand Rapids, wanting to make my way to Traverse City as fast as possible. It was delightful to pass through long stretches of unspoiled wood and farmlands after the hustle and bustle of crowded city streets.

"I'm coming, Mama," I whispered. Excited that after all these years, we'd finally reunite as family again. The last time she'd seen me, I was only eight years old, screaming my head off as they dragged me away from her.

What will she think when she sees me now, at five feet, nine inches, and eleven years older? Will she even recognize me?

The farther I got from Chicago, the whiter grew the pedestrian faces. Some Mexicans, but that was about it for diversity.

Nearing the town of Cadillac, a white guy in sandals, torn jeans, and scruffy t-shirt stood, thumb out, hitching a ride with one hand and clutching a paper bag with another. I slowed and pulled over. He ran over and jumped into the car.

"Thanks, Dude," he said, slamming shut the car door. "Headed up north?"

"Traverse City."

"Ditto. Don't see many black folk around these parts." He then reached into his pocket and pulled out a joint. "Wanna smoke?"

I shook my head and unrolled my window. "Be my guest."

His eyes glazed over as he finished the joint. Real relaxed. "Tell me when we get there," he said, promptly closing his eyes.

I turned on the radio, got some Upper Peninsula station featuring Finnish humor, then switched over to Interlochen Public Radio with classical music. In apparent sleep, my passenger let out a snort or two. I turned off the radio and switched on the CD player to listen to Snatum Kaur's ethereal voice chanting:

"Oh, my soul, it comes and it goes
Through paths of time and space.
In useless play, you'll not find your way
So set your goals and go."

"What's that?" My passenger slowly opened his eyes and nodded toward the speakers.

"She's a Sikh who sings prayer songs."

"Got anything else, rap or something?"

I switched off the CD player and shook my head. Obviously my temporary companion hadn't spent the last eleven years in devotional studies at The Most Precious Blood Academy.

"You gotta job in Traverse City?"

I shook my head.

"Wanna make some money? I got a good business contact there. Mind you, not exactly legal. I don't have a car, and you do."

Oh God, what did I pick up here? A drug dealer?

Again I shook my head, wondering how soon I could get rid of my passenger. The brothers at the Catholic school had always told me to give people the benefit of the doubt.

Dumb, dumb, dumb.

He shrugged his shoulders and returned to his nap.

As dusk gave over to the moonless night, we pulled into Traverse City.

"Where can I drop you off?" I said, hoping sooner than later.

He directed me down a back alley, unlit, but with cars parked in haphazard fashion. He got out of the car, announcing, "I'll be right back."

I should leave now, make my getaway.

Instead I watched him as he entered the rear of a store, paper bag clutched in his hand.

Moments later, he busted out the door, yelling at me, his hand waving something black, solid, and metal. It took me a few seconds to realize it was a gun. I flipped the car locks, turned on the key to back up, and in my peripheral vision saw other guys running after him.

Boom!

A loud explosion, glass splintering around me, the warm feeling of wetness on my face but nothing else.

I don't remember the police, the ambulance, the emergency room.

Everything disappeared into the darkness.

When next I opened my eyes, a pretty blond nurse greeted me. "Well, hello there."

I started to say, "Where am I?" but there was something in my throat. No sound came out.

She put her hand on my shoulder and said, "You've been shot. You're on a ventilator. They did a tracheotomy on you."

The weirdest thing: I don't feel any pain. So I'm going to be okay, I thought. *I'm going to live.*

The nurse took a washcloth and announced she was going to give me a sponge bath. It's a man's dream to have a beautiful woman touch him all over his body. I was afraid I'd get an unwanted erection. She raised the sheet and proceeded to sponge off my body.

My mind is playing tricks on me.

At least that was what I thought, because nothing made sense.

As I watched her hand traveling over my skin, I couldn't feel a thing.

Not the dampness of the washcloth.

Not the touch of her hand.

Not the penis rising.

Nothing.

Tess

Chapter 5

THE DOCTORS DISCHARGED ME in the care of one Cassidy McDermott. As I inched along to her car, pushing the walker ahead of me on the damp sidewalk, I felt the humiliating stares of people my age looking at me as if I were some goddamn sort of freak. All my life I had been athletic, in good shape, and here I was, grasping the bars like a lifeline. My vision was still screwy, and I couldn't keep the world from shifting on me. The doctor had insisted that I wear sunglasses to protect my overly sensitive eyes.

Cassie's car, a blue Subaru station wagon, had seen better days. A few dents and scraped paint suggested that she might not have the best eyesight either. As I angled into the front passenger seat, she held the door for me, then folded up the walker and laid it in the trunk.

My memory was coming back in bits and pieces. It had been chilly in early May, the trees still barren before the accident. Now green was sprouting everywhere. Winter no longer possessed the land, and I had somehow slept through the short spring.

An in-between time. An uncertain period, pregnant with possibilities. Time had begun to tuck itself back into my life. At least I knew the month now: June.

Forty days and forty nights.

Time enough for a wintry season to steal away and a worthy marriage to implode.

Cassidy slammed her door.

I jumped.

"Sorry. I forgot how loud everything sounds to you."

"Supersonic," I said.

She turned on the motor. "Ready?"

"Do you mind if we swing by my house, I mean Nick's house?" I expected that both Nick and Sandy would be at work.

She nodded, careful not to let the automobile suddenly accelerate.

"Does it frighten you to be in a car?"

I shook my head. "I don't remember the accident. Maybe that's a good thing."

I wasn't prepared for the swell of nausea as the landscape whipped by me. I held my breath. It helped to look down, silently praying, *Please, please, don't let me puke in her car.*

Twenty minutes later, we pulled into the short driveway of the weathered Outerbridge summer house, nestled under pine trees and fronting south Lake Leelanau. In the side yard, next to the gate of the chain link fence, lay Imp, resembling a miniature collie, her beautiful long, mahogany coat, unbrushed and dry looking, her sweet face resting on two front paws, looking forlorn and abandoned. She stood up as the Subaru pulled closer to the house and began barking.

"Oh Imp," I said, tears suddenly cresting and dripping down my face.

Cassie took one look at me and asked, "Do you think anyone is home?"

I shook my head.

Imp sniffed the air, unable to get a whiff of our identity through the closed car windows.

"Give me the keys," Cassie demanded.

I handed her the door key.

"Tell me what to get," she said, "and make it snappy, because I don't want to be accused of home invasion."

"The bag of kibbles and two plastic bowls are in the kitchen, the leash is on a nail by the front door, and her bed is upstairs on the bedroom floor."

I opened the car door.

"No, you stay there," she ordered. "I don't want you in the way."

"But," I hesitated, "could you unlatch the gate?"

"Just so long as she doesn't bite me." Cassie edged toward the fence and the Sheltie.

Imp growled in warning, and Cassie gave me a look of concern.

"Imp! Imp!" I shouted.

Immediately Imp's ears shot up, high and alert.

Cassie raised the metal latch.

"Imp, come," I commanded.

She shot out of the yard, scrambling madly toward the car and the sound of my voice, throwing herself into my lap.

Wiggling at both ends, wildly licking my face, Imp whimpered and moaned in sheer ecstasy. Mama had come for her at last.

"Oh Imp," I laughed, letting her tongue slurp all over my face.

Meanwhile, Cassie nervously rushed about the house, gathering up Imp's bowls, bed, food, and leashes. She had to make three trips to get everything, the last one with her hands full of plush toys. No sooner had she locked the front door and slammed down the car trunk when a black Ford Escape pulled up alongside us in the driveway.

Nick and a brunette.

Probably Sandy.

Nick got out, took one look at Cassie, and asked, "What are you doing here?"

Cassie nodded toward me in the front seat, then slipped into the driver's side of the Subaru.

Nick peered through the backseat window, taking note of Imp on my lap, her bed in the trunk. Sandy emerged from the Escape but kept a safe, uninvolved distance.

"You can't take the dog," Nick said.

"You've got the house. You've got the girlfriend. I get the dog." I hugged Imp tightly and slammed shut my door, giving Nick the meanest look I could muster.

Nick walked around the Subaru and yanked open my door. He reached in, about to pull Imp right out of my hands, as Cassie started the car.

In an instant. Imp comprehended what was at stake. The very moment Nick touched her, she whipped around and bit him.

"Ouch, damn it," he bellowed, yanking back his hand.

"Go," I yelled at Cassie. I grabbed the door handle, swung the door shut, and locked it. Cassie hit the accelerator, and we roared backwards, as Sandy rushed over to examine Nick's bitten hand.

We sped down the street, away from this little scene of domestic violence. I gave Imp a big kiss on her wet, black nose.

"Good girl. Good girl. You know who's your Mama. Honestly," I said, turning toward Cassie, "Imp's never bitten anyone before."

After a few minutes, Cassie slowed down and began laughing. "Tess, I hope you don't give me a heart attack, but I gotta say one thing."

"What's that?"

She reached over and tousled Imp's furry head. "This dog is a good judge of character."

A long red tongue darted out, leaving a soppy trail across Cassie's palm.

"Oh," she said, wiping her hand on the bottom of her blouse.

"That's her way of telling you that you're now part of her pack."

Cassie said, "Just so's I don't have to lick her back."

Sonny

Chapter 6

THERE WAS A TROUBLESOME ITCH on my face to the side of my right nostril. I wiggled my nose, but the tickle did not go away.

How I wanted to scratch it with my hand, but as I lay there, nothing below my neck was moving. Not a toe, a finger, a penis, an elbow, or an ankle. All was still, as if no longer part of me.

I turned my head and rubbed my nose against the pillow, but my neck constrained the range of movement, the body a heavy counterweight.

When will the rest of me wake up?

Sighing and clicking out of my sight was a machine pushing air in and out of me. Not a good sign that I wasn't able to breathe on my own.

A rising river of panic in me.

How badly am I hurt?

The rubber of time stretched out, it seemed hours, before someone checked on me, yet perhaps no more than fifteen minutes. It was a man in a white lab coat, stethoscope dangling like a metal necklace from his neck.

His eyes widened. He seemed surprised to see me awake, a bit discombobulated, as if it would have been more convenient to find me asleep.

I stared at him, willing him to answer my unasked questions.

"I'm Dr. Miller." He rubbed his chin, caught in the moment of awkwardness. "I know you can't talk right now, but you can communicate through eye blinks. Later on, you'll learn how to move your lips and speak on the exhale of the ventilator, but it can be a bit painful. So one blink for yes, two blinks for no. Do you understand?"

One blink.

"Do you remember what happened?"

I didn't blink.

"Okay, how about three blinks for 'I don't know?'"

I gave him the three blinks.

"A bullet impacted your spinal cord. In our vernacular, we call it a high break, one of the worst I've ever seen. It effectively means you are a quadriplegic; there's no way of sugarcoating that fact. Nor are we at a stage of being able to use stem cells or reconnect what has been severed. I wish I could promise you a miracle, but I've yet to see one."

I closed my eyes.

"Have I said too much too fast?"

I opened my eyes and blinked twice. What I really wanted to do was to tell him to go away and leave me with a shred, a morsel, a fragment of hope.

I blinked again, once, but he didn't see it while fiddling with the stethoscope.

He placed it on my chest and listened.

How can the heart go on beating to sustain a body disconnected from a mind?

Who am I without a body?

He nodded, obviously satisfied with the heartbeat. "When everything is stabilized, we'll move you out of the ICU. Eventually therapists will come and work with you, to help you learn how to talk and how to use your head and mouth to work a computer and a wheelchair, but right now, we're watching to make sure there aren't any added complications to the wound on your neck. In a few minutes, a nurse and I will position you onto your side so that I can change the bandages and see how well you're healing."

He gave me a professional smile, probably thanking the gods that he wasn't in such a dreadful condition.

An older nurse, built like a linebacker, entered the room, and together the two of them rolled me over like a plastic mannequin and proceeded to examine the damage. After the doctor snapped on his latex gloves, she handed him bandages and a disinfecting lotion of some sort. I was simply a lump, a piece of driftwood in their hands, tossed up on their shore.

He picked up a tablet of paper and asked, "Do you have any family that we may contact?"

I blinked once out of hope, then three times out of reality. "In this area?"

Again once, followed by three times.

"The social worker, Jane Smith, will be by before long to get that information from you. She has a board of letters and numbers to help with the communication." He then put a hand on my non-feeling shoulder and said, "You're lucky to be alive, given the nature of that wound."

Lucky?

In truth, I'd rather not know such luck.

When Miz Jane Smith arrived, it was a slow and torturous hour, but I got out the information that Dora Augusta worked at Sara Lee. A mousy, young woman with nice legs and long fingers, Miz Smith tapped the letters on the alphabet board. I was to blink when she got the right one. Of course, the first piece of information had to do with medical insurance. I had none.

She said I would have to apply for Medicaid. While efficient, she seemed to have difficulty looking at me for any sustained period of time.

I thought, mistakenly, it was due to my condition. I was beginning to suspect that quads are like lepers. Don't get too close or the condition might be catching. But, no, that wasn't it.

"You know," she said, right before leaving the room to call the Sara Lee office. "You really look like . . ." She stopped, perhaps sensing she was crossing boundaries or maybe would say something I didn't want to hear.

But I knew what was coming, so I smiled at her.

"Like Jesus," she said.

Before leaving Chicago, I had even grown a slight beard, hoping it would turn on the women. What resonated with people was a certain commercial painting of a dark, Semitic Jesus, hung up on countless living room walls. Perhaps that was why the brothers and nuns who taught at The Most Precious Blood Academy tended to favor me above the other students.

In no other way was I the living embodiment of Jesus. When in their care, I smoked. I drank. I tried pot and hallucinogenic drugs, but they never caught me. Perhaps that was why the other students, all boys, called me "Wily Coyote."

It was pleasant thinking back to my school days. Something to occupy my mind, a dam to the cresting flood of fear.

I'll get better. I'll walk again. I'll make love to a dozen women before settling down to one. I can do anything.

I stared at the bland, blank hospital ceiling, reciting to myself, "Yes, I can. Yes, I can."

Tess

Chapter 7

THE MIST INTENSIFIED as Cassie neared Lake Michigan. The wind shuffled across the tops of trees. She slowed down before turning off into a dirt driveway set between two wooden signs, a white "Private Road" and a green "Hagen's Heaven." Off to the right, I could make out a lone maple tree in a large field. The sky above was turning into a bruised, angry, blue-black.

"Gonna have a storm," said Cassie.

We drove through a bower of shuddering woods: huge pine trees, cedar, elms, oaks, birches, ash, and maples, their leafy arms swaying in the gusts.

Imp's nose traced squiggly lines on the car window as the Subaru bumped along the driveway.

At a bend in the track, a large oak tree sported a smiling face of plastic eyebrows, a nose, a mouth, and a mustache. An old wood sprite to welcome visitors.

"I put it up the other day," Cassie said. "Got the pieces out of a catalogue. I had one of them Imelda Marcos moments."

"Huh?"

The car took its third curve, coming too close to a side ditch of tangled brush. I held my breath, but Cassie seemed unconcerned.

"You know, when you get that urge to buy stuff you don't really need. I'm trying to live within my means, but there's a little voice in me that says, 'Why Cassie, you deserve it.' It's probably what Mrs. Marcos said when she bought her 2,700 pairs of shoes. Well, here we are."

The car stopped.

I couldn't believe my eyes. From Cassie's modest presentation, I had expected a vinyl-sided ranch house. Instead, at the top of the hill, overlooking Lake Michigan, stood a huge cedar log house, all wood and window with wide overhangs, an open front porch with a large cedar swing hanging from suspension chains, a cluster of green Adirondack chairs and black metal side tables. At the very top of the house perched a round tower with a view to green fields, dark woods, white-capped water, and the distant Fox Islands.

"Beautiful, isn't it?" said Cassie, pulling the walker from the trunk.

I opened the car door and let Imp jump out. She put her nose to the ground and tore off, following some animal's scent.

"My, oh my," was all I could say. There had been nothing about Cassie's frumpy appearance to suggest such wealth.

She handed me the walker, then grabbed the lone suitcase Nick has so thoughtfully dropped off at the hospital. "Will the dog run away?" Cassie asked. "Because there's a black bear that's been leaving poop on the driveway."

I shook my head.

Imp was busy establishing her own sense of territory, peeing here and there, letting the wild animals know that she, too, had arrived. But she was smart and didn't venture too far.

Cassie walked slowly, letting me gallump my awkward way with the walker.

"I picked up all the rugs on the first floor, so they wouldn't trip you up," she said.

Silently, I began to cry again. I stopped to wipe my eyes on my sleeve when Cassie turned and asked, "What's the matter, Tess?"

"I'm not used to people being so kind to me."

I grabbed the side rail to climb the porch steps. The effort made the world spin at bit, so I stopped and took a breather. When I got to the top step, Cassie said, "Welcome to my little bit of paradise."

"Little?"

"Well, it's kind of grand, even for me."

She opened the front door. A stuffed female coyote with a malevolent attitude greeted newcomers in the front hall with yellow glass eyes and an underslung jaw.

"That's Bernadette, the butler," Cassie said. "Native Americans say you've got to recognize the coyote spirit in all of us, else you'll take yourself too seriously."

After depositing my bag in a first floor bedroom, Cassie insisted on showing me around.

The interior of the house was open, one room flowing into another. Only the bedrooms and bathrooms sported doors. Native American blankets covered the sofas and stuffed chairs with the colors of the southwest: burnt oranges, adobe reds, yellows, and desert browns. Punctuating the rooms was the smooth sheen of cedar walls, lofty ceilings with skylights, large windows, and fieldstone fireplaces.

An eclectic collection of oil, water, and acrylic paintings hung on all the walls, obviously expensive artwork –– paintings of hidden streams, mysterious woods, predatory birds, domestic animals, and people caught in the middle of an unfinished story.

Large stately portraits and professional photographs of a tall, graceful woman in the many stages of her life decorated the living room walls accompanied by two portraits of a scholarly-looking, portly man with round glasses, plus a host of ancient relatives photographed and perched in black frames, none of whom resembled the squat frame of my hostess.

Display cases featured intricately carved, blown glass paperweights, bronze sculptures, and Native American artifacts. The dining room sported a long mahogany table with twelve matching chairs, a chiffonier for silverware, and a glass case for gold-rimmed dishes. The house reeked of new wealth masquerading as old wealth.

"Hagen's Heaven," explained Cassie. "Can I make you a cup of tea?"

She led me to a moderately-sized kitchen with dark granite counter tops and microwaved me a cup of chamomile. "It'll relax your tired brain."

I was fatigued but also intrigued. "Who's that beautiful woman on the living room walls?"

Cassie handed me the tea and poured herself some coffee from a thermos. "Black as sin," she answered.

Outside, I could hear the wind whipping around the house. Rain started pelting the windows.

"Natalie," she finally said.

"What?"

"Natalie Hagen. This was her house. She designed it and had it built. Obviously married to a very rich man."

"A relative of yours?" My brain was feebly trying to make sense of how Cassie came to own this mansion.

A melancholic expression flickered over Cassie's weathered face but vanished so quickly I doubted I'd really seen it. The chamomile was beginning to fog up my senses.

"No," she said. "It's a long story. I've only lived here since March. My husband died this last winter."

"Oh, I'm sorry, Cassie."

Cassie's shoulders slumped a little bit. She drank the last of her coffee, stood up, and took our mugs over to the kitchen sink. She paused, her back to me.

"I think you'll be needing a nap now," she said, turning toward me. "I've not changed much in this house yet, because I still feel Natalie's spirit lingering here. This was her sanctuary long before it became mine. You only have to look around and know how important this place was to her. I don't think she was very happy in her marriage."

"The fat guy in the round glasses?"

Cassie nodded. "He was a successful businessman, and she was beautiful. Perhaps that's why he married her. But beauty isn't the same as companionship."

"I bet you were married for a long time, Cassie."

Again, a sadness bridged her eyes. I figured it was simply the grief, not yet finished from his passing.

"Over fifty sweet years," she said. "C'mon, time for you to take a nap."

"Tell me, Cassie, how you ended up in this place." I was too tired to sleep, and I didn't budge from my chair. A crack of lightning flashed outside the window, and the crash of thunder resounded within the house.

Imp ducked nervously under the kitchen table.

"That's probably Natalie trying to tell us her version of the story." Cassie sat back down at the table, sighed, then arranged four small juice glasses in a line next to a bottle of cream sherry.

"Here's the legal truth of it." Cassie turned over the first glass. "Edward Hagen, the businessman, died from a heart attack. He left everything to his wife."

Cassie turned over the second glass. "Soon, thereafter, Natalie tripped over something here, fell down the stairs, and broke her neck. A sudden, unexpected death. Maybe she'd had too much to drink. Who knows? Maybe it was suicide."

"Or murder?" I suggested. I loved a good mystery.

"The police decided it was an accident as there was no evidence of any robbery or a struggle. In any case, in her will she left everything to Devin McDermott. Devin was my husband."

Cassie turned over the third glass. "Strange as it seems, soon after learning about Natalie's accident, Devin fell off a bridge and drowned. Everyone also thought it was an accident." Cassie shut her eyes.

"Why did Natalie leave everything to your husband? Was she a close cousin or something?" Something about all this didn't add up.

Cassie snorted and poured a generous amount of sherry into the one glass that was still standing. "Oh, I wish that had been the case. I surely do."

Sonny

Chapter 8

I COULD TELL BY THE LOOK on the doctors' faces that my neck injury wasn't healing right. It was the way they glanced at each other, the slight downturn of their mouths, the sucking energy of despair being communicated across my immobile body. My other senses were sharpening, as I didn't have anything else to do but lie there and think about the monotony of time, the solidity of space, and the repetitive sighs of the ventilator.

A dumpy, middle-aged woman appeared in my room and introduced herself as Cassie McDermott. "I'm a hospital volunteer. They said you could do with a visitor. I can't stay long, as I just moved a young woman who had a bad car accident back to my place."

She maneuvered around all the equipment to examine the bandage around my neck, then returned to my field of vision, shaking her head.

"They told me you couldn't talk."

I blinked once.

"But I'm pretty good at lip reading, so let's try that, shall we?"

I smiled. Any change in the routine was wonderful.

"First, do you have any itch on your face that needs to be scratched?"

A blessed angel from heaven.

I blinked once, but she didn't know the code. With exaggerated expression of my lips, I articulated, "Nose." It came out as a strangulated whisper, sounding like "Noosh."

"Right, the nose. Here?" She reached over and scratched the right side of my nose.

I slowly turned my head to the left, and she scratched there as well.

Ah, what release from the torture of an itch!

Next, she lathered moisturizing lotion on her hands and began to rub it into my face.

I closed my eyes.

This must be what it's like to get a facial. If only it was a young woman at a spa and I . . .

Cassie was determined to fill up the silence with words. "They say you aren't from around here, but that you might have family in the area. Here, let me open the blinds, so you can see a little bit outside."

All I could see was sky and it didn't look all that friendly, but I smiled anyway.

"I'll be back when things are more settled at my place." She looked right at me. "I know that your neck was broken and that things seem kind of bleak right now."

I stared right back at her. The precious solemnity of truth hung in the balance.

"I am reminded of a story I once heard," she said. "On a dark, cloudy night, a man lost his way in the woods and slipped off a tall cliff. Tumbling down, he reached out and managed to snag the small branch of a tree. There he was, dangling in a precarious situation because he couldn't climb back up to the top without some help. If he let go, he would die on the rocks below. He yelled and yelled for help in the dark night for a very long time, but no one answered. He began to despair.

"Then, suddenly, the moon slipped out from behind the clouds, and its shadowy light restored his hope. He began to pray. 'God, I haven't been a good Christian, but if you can save me, I will go to church every Sunday and do anything You ask of me.'

"Out of nowhere came the baritone reply, 'Anything?'

"'God, is that really you?' asked the man. 'Will you help me?'

"'Will you do what I tell you to do?' asked God.

"'Oh yes,' promised the man.

"'Then let go of the branch.'

"The man thought for a few moments, then shouted, 'Is there anyone else up there?'"

I grinned.

Cassie patted my shoulder, and said, "Prayer can't hurt, now can it? But if I were you, I'd keep holding onto that branch."

She patted my cheek and left.

What a remarkable woman, the first one to make me laugh at my own predicament. God, are You up there for me? Do You even care?

A short while later, a young man entered the room and announced that he was a physical therapist. "I'm doing an internship here."

Give him the mannequin on which to practice.

"We'll have you up and walking in no time," he said, full of good cheer and obviously ignorant of my medical file.

But, then again, maybe he's a magician with a bag full of miracles.

"Do you exercise on any regular basis?"

Not lately.

He stared at his mute patient.

I made an exaggerated NO with my lips.

He wrote that down on his pad of paper.

"Have you been out of bed yet?"

I shook my head.

"Hmm," he muttered, probably thinking I was a recalcitrant, lazy, good-for-nothing soul. He scratched his head, puzzled.

A nurse entered the room, sized up the situation, and glared at the young man.

He nodded at her. "I'm Brad Johansson, the new physical therapy intern. This patient hasn't yet been gotten out of bed." A slight tone of criticism underscored his statement.

The nurse shook her head, incredulous. "Didn't your supervisor instruct you to read the medical records before you start making assumptions about your patients?"

Oooo, the Iron Lady speaks and casts a look of pure malevolence.

Before Brad could summon a reply, she demanded, "Who is your supervisor? Let's go find him right now."

I think she would have grabbed him by the scruff of his neck if she could.

He jumped to her command.

Round one to the nurse.

The two of them left, leaving the door ajar. I doubted that I'd be seeing the hapless Brad Johansson anytime soon.

At the very least, the conflict further awakened me from a slumbering life.

Is there anyone else out there?

Tess

Chapter 9

• ◆ •

THAT FIRST NIGHT at Hagen's Heaven I didn't sleep well. The wind howled up from Lake Michigan, but it wasn't Nature that bothered me. It was the disembodied voices and echoing footsteps in the hallway. I couldn't tell if the sounds came from inside or outside of me.

Was the house haunted by Natalie? Or were my broken synapses retying themselves into an undersea cable, rerouting misinformation to my brain? I looked at the far door to the other bedroom, cast in the shadows of night, and fear shivered through me. I didn't want to maneuver in and out of any more jagged reefs. I didn't want to swim again in any more ebony seas, unlit by the light of the day.

But when I closed my eyes, I could feel myself sinking back into the murk of the underworld.

In the dark, tattered seaweed robe, the cadaverous man once more floated before me. Neither young nor old, his face was sharply outlined with a clear, emaciated bone structure, as if his flesh no longer contained any substance.

Then I remembered: while I was in the coma, he had offered me the choice of two passageways: one to an underwater city, the other through a dismal, mucky swamp. "The one to the right will be easy, bringing you through flooded streets to the house of your parents. The one to the left is difficult, dark, and dank. There'll be no one there to greet you. Come, take my hand, for your parents are waiting."

I had answered no, that Nick needed me, and that my parents were in the grave.

But this time, while on the night stage of Hagen's Heaven, the creepy apparition conjured up a closet door, a door of many locks. He shook his head in disappointment and vanished, leaving the door behind to linger a few minutes longer in my dreadful imagination.

My eyes jerked open. I touched my face to make sure I was still alive. I picked up the flashlight Cassie had left on the night stand and clicked it on, shining it into Imp's bed to make sure she was okay. Her dark, almond-shaped eyes blinked lazily at me, unperturbed by any night specter. I aimed the flashlight at the closet door, opened ever so slightly.

Without warning, a headache slammed into me. The neurologist at the hospital had given me nortriptyline pills for the headaches and told me they'd decrease in frequency over time. He never said anything about nightmares.

I rolled out of bed, grabbed the walker, and made my way to the bathroom where I swallowed the pill and chased it down with a glass of cold water.

Modern medicine, work your magic on me!

As if that could be called a prayer.

I firmly shut the closet door, cradled my head, and lay back down on the bed. My eyes refused to close, as my mind summoned up the terrors.

"Two roads diverged in a yellow wood and I . . ." I started to recite the old Robert Frost poem.

An incantation on choice.

Cassie had left a mobile telephone by my bed, in case I needed to call her in the middle of the night.

I knew better, but still I could not resist. I picked up the phone and dialed his cell phone. How could I retain those numbers so easily, when otherwise time and space so eluded and confused me?

The phone rang three times, before Nick's sleepy voice answered.

I kept my silence.

"Hello?"

He waited a second, then said, "Look, I don't know who this is, but if you need an appointment, call my office in the morning. If you're an old client, then I'd remind you to respect my boundaries and not call me in the middle of the night, unless you're feeling suicidal."

Pause.

"Well, are you planning to kill yourself?" he asked, irritation edging into his voice.

I bit my lower lip and gingerly clicked off the phone, realizing it was a masochistic, quasi-suicidal act to call my adulterous husband in the middle of the night.

"Oh Nick," I said to myself, pulling the sheet all the way up over my head. I lay there on my back, eyes shut, arms by my side, my hands folded neatly on my belly, legs out straight. *Like a dead person.*

I am ashamed to admit that the next morning, Cassie came into the bedroom only to hear a muffled weeping in the closet. She opened the door and found me on the closet floor, knotted into a fetal position, arms wrapped around a complacent Imp, crying my eyes out.

"What . . . ?" but she didn't finish before I burst out with loud gulping sobs.

"I don't know why he doesn't love me. I don't know why it can't be like it was before. My head hurts. My heart hurts. Nothing is the same as it was."

Cassie reached in and with some grunting on her part hauled my butt up off the closet floor. "C'mon now," she said.

Imp danced around us, barking a shrill bark of anxiety.

Cassie opened an outside door and let her out.

I sucked in a noseful of snot. "He kept telling me I needed to lose weight. I'd lose ten pounds and then he'd say I needed to lose ten more. Is that why he left me for Sandy?"

Cassie guided me into a seated position on the bed, shaking her head. She passed the box of Kleenex to me.

I looked up at her, my lips trembling, "You know what really bothers me, Cassie? He kept confessing how attracted he was to this woman and to that woman, and hell, they all seemed like they were kind of fucked-up people, excuse the expression. I mean, they were needy women who didn't have a sense of their own power, you know what I mean?"

Cassie nodded, handing me a pair of jeans and a t-shirt. She fished out socks from the bureau drawer and placed them beside me. "Well, there you have it," she said. "He's one of those men who needs women to fawn over him. You're better off without him."

A predictable argument, but I wasn't buying it. No, I was thinking that maybe I should get some straight pins and a cloth doll and name it Sandy. First, I'd stab some pins into the forehead so she could feel what it was like to have a brain injury, then maybe into the left shoulder blade, the chest, and down the left arm, so she could also worry about heart trouble.

Confronted with a sick woman, Nick might return to me and apologize for his behavior and beg . . .

"Breakfast is on," interrupted Cassie. "You gotta stop tuning out the world and pay attention."

Cassie finished her blueberry scone over a second cup of coffee, dabbing her finger around the plate, picking up the last little bits. Her round cheeks were rosy against her fair skin and flighty white hair. With a little makeup, she could be a beautiful old woman, but Cassie obviously scorned such affectations. No one could call her baggy pants and oversized shirt stylish. Comfortable, yes. Fashionable, no.

Imp positioned herself between the two of us, hoping that we'd remember to give her a crumb of compassion.

"Today," Cassie announced, "we're going for a hike."

"Sure," I laughed, feeling better for the food and coffee.

Me with my walker, hiking. Ha!

Cassie stood up and produced a blue corded belt that she proceeded to tie around my waist.

"What are you doing?" I asked.

Cassie's eyebrows arched in a mischievous manner. She disappeared from the kitchen table for a second, returning with two spring-loaded German walking sticks. She thrust them into my hands.

"You've got to be kidding. I can't go anywhere without my walker."

"Stand up. You're not an invalid. Let's head down the driveway," she said. "You won't fall. My hand is tucked in the back of the belt."

"Cassie," I protested to no avail.

"Only one mile," she promised. "No more. No less. We'll move as slow as you want."

A mile to hell and back, I thought.

That was the beginning of physical therapy, first with Cassie and then with professionals who, I might say, were a bit easier on me than was Cassie. Every day, rain or shine, she forced me to walk that goddam mile, until I began to notice that her hand no longer held the belt.

I was walking on my own power.

The walker then vanished, I don't know where.

When feeling a bit off-balance, I asked her about the walker, wanting the security of something to lean on.

"Oh, it's gone to people who need it more than you."

"Eat poop," I said.

Cassie squinched her eyebrows together. "What did you say?"

"I think I said eat poop, but that wasn't what I meant."

We both broke out laughing. It was going to be a long, long time before I could resume being an English teacher.

The physical therapist in Glen Arbor was cute, at least ten years younger than me. First he taped straight lines on the floor and asked me to "walk the line," putting one foot in front of the other. Initially, he let me rest a hand upon his shoulder, lest I fall flat on my face, but then I began to walk in a more sober fashion. He increased the difficulty, having me step over cones, stand on one foot and then the other, and do squats. I got a bit dizzy on the treadmill, but that too seemed to fade rapidly. I was getting back my old balance.

"It's great that you were so athletic before the accident," he said.

If only the brain would heal as fast as the body. My mind, which used to be so quick and bright, now acted like a flickering, dim bulb.

The third night at Cassie's place, feeling the fatigue that never really went away, I watched Cassie dump out thirty pieces of a jigsaw puzzle onto the dining room table.

"I can't do it," I complained.

"Of course you can. Gotta get that brain working again," she said. No compassion there.

"Lemme see the picture then." I grabbed for the cover of the box, but Cassie snatched it out of my reach.

"It's a jungle picture."

"Why won't you let me see the picture?"

"Because sometimes you don't know what the whole picture will be until you take the first steps. Now look," she said, "in every unknown situation, you have to establish a structure. Find the straight edges." She put two of them together as an example.

Lines or colors, I couldn't figure out which way to do the matches, until Cassie began to suggest that one piece was part of a tiger, another a baboon. Why wouldn't she show me the cover of the box? Only later did she tell me that it was because the box label read "Age four and up."

It took me about ten minutes, but it felt good to complete the puzzle. I clapped my hands in delight.

The next night, Cassie set out a puzzle suitable for a six-year-old. Sixty pieces! Phew, I didn't think I would be able to do this one, a pictorial representation of a Tyrannosaurus Rex, jaws open to devour some smaller, plant-eating dinosaur.

Probably a vegetarian like Sandy.

I turned the pieces around and around, seeking the right fit, but aware this time that it was a dinosaur.

Cassie hovered over me, offering encouragement and repeating herself as if reciting a mantra. "As you fit the puzzle pieces into a whole picture, it'll be like putting the fragments of your life back together again."

Only I didn't want to end up as some sort of dinosaur or jungle cat. I simply wanted to be that aspiring poet and former competent English teacher of bright high school students, Dr. Tess Outerbridge—grading papers, reading essays, and wondering what the future held for each one of them.

Amidst all these thoughts, I got to the last piece and pounded it in with bravado. Actually, I was quite pleased with myself, because I doubted that even the most advanced baboon could have done a sixty-piece puzzle.

Cassie and I high-fived each other. Truth to tell, it was her words matching my work that instilled hope in me. I was going to piece my life back together!

Sometimes you come across old-fashioned, wooden puzzles with great landscape pictures and odd, interesting shapes of animals with broken tails or people with missing noses or even two or three absent sky pieces—yet you can still appreciate the beauty of the original work.

Maybe I wouldn't ever be able to return to the "before" Tess who contained only unbroken pieces, but at least I was moving forward, going somewhere.

Of course, no sooner do you say, "I *can* cross that bridge!" when a troll emerges to block your way. Only in this case, the ogre was Nick, probably prompted by little miss crystal-worshiping ogress in the background.

He had tracked me down via the hospital social worker and discovered that I'd relocated to a veritable mansion in the wealthiest area of the Leelanau Peninsula. I betcha that must have burned him a bit on his chinny chin chin.

"We have to meet, to talk things over," he said over the telephone.

"No, we don't," I replied in as carefree voice as I could muster.

"Tess, don't be difficult. I know you're angry at me."

"Uh-huh."

"I can understand that. But you've got to know that the doctors didn't think you would survive the . . ."

"Removal of the ventilator," I interjected.

"The accident," he insisted.

"But I did, didn't I?" A high falsetto voice.

"And Sandy thought . . ."

"Quickie come, quickie go. Alas, she must be losing her crystal-reading powers. So, what does the future hold for you, Nick?"

"I want us to work out a mutual divorce plan, so we don't get to battling like this and give all our money away to attorneys."

"An oxymoron."

"Huh?"

"'Mutual divorce.' It's an oxymoron, Nick. Nothing mutual about it."

"You see, that's one of the reasons I don't want to live with you anymore, Tess. You make light of everything I try to do. I'm trying to be civilized here, and you create a diversion into grammar. I know you're hurting, but you pretend otherwise. How do you expect to stay in a relationship if you can't even be honest with yourself?"

"I'm hurting, Nick. My husband abandoned me for another woman. So how can you help me, Nick? What can you do for me?"

Nick let out a big sigh. "You need to see a therapist, Tess."

"But you forget, I'm married to one."

"Tess, I can't be the one to help you. You've got to learn to let go, to move on with your life. It's no good being married to . . ." he hesitated.

"To what?" I encouraged him to finish his sentence.

"To someone who doesn't love you anymore."

I clutched my stomach, then slammed down the receiver. If he had punched me in the gut, he couldn't have hurt me more.

Bad enough to be brain-damaged, but far worse to be told I was unloved by a man who had lived with me for thirteen years.

The world stopped. I felt frozen, condemned forever to a life of limping bleakness.

"Two steps forward and one step back," announced Cassie who once again discovered me in the closet, hugging onto Imp. "But Nick does have a point," she added.

"What?" I growled.

The empathic Imp growled too.

"It wouldn't hurt for you to see a therapist. I found it very helpful right after Devin's accident."

"It would be my luck to end up seeing one of Nick's closest colleagues, someone who'd go to him and say, 'Boy, what a unlovable bitch you married, a real humdinger!' People love Nick, because he makes you think you're the most interesting, important person in his world at that moment. Me? I'm the aloof, nose-in- the-air English teacher, lost in her books and a bit too liberal for this part of the Midwest."

"There's nothing wrong about loving books," said Cassie. "They take us outside of ourselves, give us adventures where, otherwise we'd never dare to tread. They let us know that we're all part of the same human condition." She crouched down, trying unsuccessfully to bend her knees and fit into the closet with me.

"Oooof!" Her butt shot down to the floor, tipping her over and spilling her partway out the closet door.

I couldn't help laughing, nor could she. Who was going to pull us, the walking wounded, into a stable standing position?

Cassie rolled out from the closet onto the wooden floor, then pushed back on her hands, found purchase on one foot, and heaved her butt back and upwards. It was not a graceful move but it was effective. She straightened her blouse and her scrambled hair, then offered me a hand.

I was still laughing at our predicament.

Cassie shook her head. "You know, those people who tell you that you can defy age by simply refusing to accept it? They're so full of shit. Your body is what gives it away: the cracking knee, the aching neck, the stiff fingers. Then you forget where you left your keys or reading glasses, wonder what errand brought you to the bedroom. You lose your train of thought in a conversation. It's all part of Nature's plan to wind us down. But, and this is a big but, you can learn to accept your limitations and proceed with those things you *can* do."

She braced herself and helped me to my feet. "It's the same with the brain injury, only you'll get better and better as time goes on."

"A therapist, huh?"

Cassie nodded. "A female therapist. In the meantime, you're starting the daily rehab program next week. How about coming with me to the hospital this afternoon? I'll introduce you to the other volunteers, and there's somebody there I want you to meet."

"I don't know if I ever want to see the inside of a hospital again." That felt like a giant step in reverse direction. I was afraid I might discover myself back on the ICU floor still in a coma with that creepy, bony man wanting to be my guide. What if Cassie and Hagen's Heaven were all simply part of a dream?

I pinched myself hard on the arm, raising an instant red blotch.

Cassie frowned.

"The pain tells me I'm awake." That explanation sounded stupid even to me, unintelligible, embarrassing.

Cassie simply waited for me to gather myself together.

"Okay," I blurted. "I'll go with you."

"Good, because I've already told him that you're coming."

Sonny

Chapter 10

"I'VE GOT SOMEBODY FOR YOU TO MEET," Cassie McDermott announced, coming into the room.

From behind her solid form emerged an attractive woman in her mid-thirties, brown hair, green eyes, nice tits, and an uncertain smile.

"I'm Tess Outerbridge," the visitor said.

"Sonny," I mouthed.

The woman looked around the room, obviously uncomfortable, probably due to my condition. It would have helped ease things if I could have reached out and shook hands with her, but all I could do was lie there, immobile, a hospital scarecrow.

I told Cassie as best I could with my lip movements about the physical therapy intern. It pleased me to see her get angry.

Tess shrugged off a light jacket and pulled a chair closer to the bed. I caught a whiff of lilac scent. She nodded to Cassie in what looked like a previously arranged signal.

Cassie came over on the other side of the bed and stroked my cheek. "I'm going to leave the two of you to get acquainted while I meet and greet new patients on the floor. Okay?"

What could I say? I was at the mercy of other people's good intentions. So, of course, I did the polite thing –- smiled and nodded my agreement. But this was hard to reconcile, that my life was no longer my own. I was at the mercy of the whims of others.

Cassie departed. I turned my head back to Miz Tess.

She reminded me of a chickadee, the way her head darted from side to side, looking around the room. Nothing still or quiet within her. Her legs jiggled.

A nervous type, I surmised.

Finally, her energy settled into intention. She said, "I don't like being here."

Neither do I. So what else is new?

My inability to talk, however, had transformed me into a great listener.

"I was in a coma for forty days and woke up here, in the ICU."

Ah, the car accident victim. The one Cassie took home with her.

She laughed a sardonic laugh. "I, too, was on a ventilator. My husband gave the order to turn it off, let me go. It would have been simpler that way."

Whoa, what is she saying?

She bent her head, her eyes hidden behind her shoulder-length hair. It was hard to read her feelings.

Shame?

Then she looked up at me, bobbed her head back and forth. "He wants to marry another woman and I guess he thought I would go easy. But I didn't, you know."

Okay, you've got my attention now.

This would be the cue to sit up straighter, show a little flirtatious interest, but of course I could do no such thing. So I gave her my most compassionate smile. Later, I learned she mistook the look for one of saintly wisdom.

She leaned closer to the bed and whispered, "I can be real pitiful if I try."

That seemed to shift her to a different narrative track.

I wanted to ask, *Well, what happened next?*

Instead, she turned her attention back to my condition.

Boring. Dullsville. Don't go there.

But, of course, she did.

"Here I am, blabbing away about all my troubles, and look at you." She put her hand to her mouth. "No, that didn't sound right. I'm sorry." She sat back, annoyed with herself.

Oh, for God's sake, I don't need your pity. What I want is entertainment, something to pull me outside of my bland life of endless waiting.

"It must be awful," she continued, "not to be able to move, to speak, to even feel your body functions."

Go away, I want to tell her. *Before you embarrass both of us.*

"So . . ." she paused, "What can I do to make your life better? I'm an English teacher or I was before the accident. I could read to you."

Big smile from me and an exaggerated YES with my lips.

"Poetry would be good."

I frown.

"History? Biographies?"

Another frown.

She giggled. "Suspense novels with lots of sex."

Bingo! A big grin from me.

"Okay, next time I'll bring a book to read aloud," she announced, leaning toward the bed. "You know there's a real advantage for me in your inability to talk. I mean, I can tell you anything and I know it will be kept secret."

I nod, like a sage priest.

Confessions, especially from a woman, could prove to be very interesting. I might finally learn how the female mind really works.

"Cassie McDermott is an angel."

I already know that.

"But something is really strange about where she lives. I mean, she's obviously not a high society woman. Yet her home reeks of untold wealth. Her version of the story is kind of muddled. Would you like to know more? I don't want to bore you."

Of course.

She continued, "A rich man died and left the place to his wife, who then expired under mysterious circumstances. She then left the place to Cassie's husband, but he dropped dead in a strange way, leaving all his possessions to Cassie. It's the straight and narrow path of estate inheritances, but it's all crumbs when you come to the emotional footprints. And she isn't really talking about it to me. At least, not yet. It's a mystery waiting to be solved." Tess arched her eyebrows, a detective on the hunt.

You don't have to be a genius to know that the trail is one of broken hearts.

Ever distractible, Tess switched subjects once again.

Maybe she has Attention Deficit Disorder?

"So my husband is suing me for divorce. I'm without a job. I've got a traumatic brain injury and can't work. I'm to go to an elementary school-like rehabilitation program every morning. I'm homeless, and Cassie has taken me in. But you know what I think?"

I shake my head.

"Everything bad happens for a reason. It's not the event that counts; it's how you react to it."

New Age pablum. It may work for her, but it doesn't do shit for me.

Thankfully, Cassie returned and interrupted what probably would have turned out to be some self-reassuring motivational speech meant to restore hope, a return to normalcy, and faith in God.

Okay, I admit I'm being cynical here. But God has been conspicuously absent from my bedside.

Is there, please I beg you, is there anyone Else out there?

Tess

Chapter 11

• ◆ •

How quickly the trees had opened into full umbrellas of green, with the sun and shade playing tag in the soft summer breeze. White sailboats dotted Lake Leelanau and water skiers plowed sudsy trails across its surface. Despite the whining growl of motor boats during the day, nighttime brought out quiet twinkling stars, diamonds in a dark sky where the full moon perched like a central amber jewel in a royal crown. It was peaceful at Hagen's Heaven, and I didn't want to leave.

With great reluctance, I'd agreed to meet Cassie's newest project: the quadriplegic man shot in the back of his neck. Cassie had insisted, and I'd thought it was the least I could do to please her.

The experience left me mortified.

First, Cassie drove too fast for my comfort. You would think that at her age, she'd have the sense to slow down. It's not like the Subaru was a high performance, sports car but she sure treated it as such. She blew by a sign that said "Reduced Speed Ahead" as if it held no import.

I started laughing.

"What's so funny?"

"Didn't you see that sign back there?"

Cassie nodded. "It's for other people, the ones who don't drive very well." At that moment, the Subaru's tires protested as she took a steep curve. I bounced against the inside paneling of the door.

"Okay, okay," she continued. "I'll slow down, if it makes you feel any better."

"But I wonder if that sign means something else," I said. "Maybe, ahead of us, there's a space of reduced speed. Perhaps we're entering a time zone where everything just slows down."

Cassie crooked an eyebrow at me. "You mean like my aging brain? Anything slower and I might as well lay myself into the grave."

"Anything faster and I get left behind."

"Wait until you reach age fifty, Tess, and your short term memory goes on total disconnect. Then it starts to come back at fifty-five and goes on call waiting."

Cassie's foot hit the accelerator again, and the world streamed by. I closed my eyes, so as not to crash mindlessly into the speeding landscape or get sick to my stomach. Cassie and I simply lived in different time zones.

The hospital finally loomed large, a bulwark of stone, metal, and glass against the surprising fragility of human flesh and the brutal tenderness of the human heart.

I did not want to enter that particular time zone.

Cassie either didn't notice my dread or simply chose to ignore it. She parked the car in the hospital garage, repeated to herself the number of its space, told me to hurry up, and then locked the car with the remote. As we walked out the garage door, she stopped and took several steps back toward the car, holding out the remote to lock it again, not simply once but three times just to make sure.

I did not want to go inside the massive medical building. There's something about the smell of a hospital, the enclosed space, airless, windless, unnatural. The sound of shoes squeaking against a polished floor. The drift of a television daytime program in the waiting rooms. The bustle of a quiet crowd, squeezing past each other along narrow corridors, coming and going. It's as if Death slouches in the corner, waiting tirelessly for his daily bundle, and we, the living scurry by, afraid to tarry too long in his vicinity.

We took the elevator up to the ICU unit. The atmosphere there is very different than downstairs. Here the beeps and hums of machines work hour after hour, defying the pull of immortal sleep. There's a grim intensity to the ICU, behind all the folksiness and humor that laughs at Death. He is to be kept downstairs, closer to the ER where he can snatch the unwary. Here, the staff watch over you and count each survivor as a true victory.

"Hey, Tess, do you remember me?" It was one of the nurses who had tended me during my prolonged stay on the unit.

I smiled and answered, "Of course, I do!" But it was a lie. I remembered little of my time there.

The staff greeted Cassie with affection. She came there almost daily to talk with the patients, to see what she could do to give them comfort.

"You're looking good," another nurse said to me. "And no walker!"

Cassie interrupted the congratulations and said, "That's the problem. She looks good. She speaks good, but . . ."

"I drool a lot." I scrunched up my face in self-mockery.

"You do not," Cassie protested. "But the neurologist told you it will take years for the brain to heal." She turned toward the staff member. "Meanwhile, Tess has started cognitive retraining."

I let my tongue hang out and crossed my eyes.

The staff member began to laugh.

Cassie tossed me an exasperated look, then grabbed my hand, and propelled me into a patient's room. "I want you to meet Sonny."

Deep within my troubled brain, I had nurtured the suspicion (or was it hope?) that Cassie wanted to introduce me to a handsome forty-year old man with dappled brown and silver hair, someone to take my mind off Nick. I flashed on my brightest smile as I turned the corner around the privacy curtain only to behold a scrawny nineteen-year-old black kid connected to tubes and machines, looking strangely like a dark Jesus with his wisp of a goatee and long curly brown hair. His head didn't shift in my direction, only his eyes, but the sweetest smile miraculously appeared on his face.

His lips moved but no sound issued forth except a little popping of the lips due to the sighing ventilator. Still I could catch the meaning of what he silently mouthed.

"Welcome."

"Hi," I answered. "I'm Tess Outerbridge." I reached out to shake his hand, but no hand rose in return.

"Sonny was in the wrong place at the wrong time. Shot by a stranger," Cassie explained.

Sonny mouthed, "Broken neck."

Or, at least, that is what I thought he was trying to say.

Cassie reached over and brushed some of Sonny's long hair out of his eyes and gave him a kiss on the cheek. "So how are they treating you?"

Sonny then proceeded to lip talk at some length. I could not decipher what he was saying, but Cassie's reaction was one of smoldering anger.

"Sonny, I know that you want to get out of this bed and be on your way. You want to walk out of this hospital on your own two feet. But it's cruel for people to come in here and give you false expectations simply because they can't deal with their own fears."

Cassie then turned toward me, irritation punctuating every word. "A physical therapy intern informed Sonny that he'd have him up and moving on his own power within days. A ray of hope by someone who obviously hadn't read the case record."

She turned back to Sonny, "I'm glad the nurse was on the ball and stopped that idiot." Then Cassie charged out of the room, mission in mind, abandoning me to the inherent silence between the young man and myself.

I pulled up a hospital chair and positioned myself close to Sonny, so that I could better read his lips. My vision wasn't yet back to normal, so at times, things got really fuzzy.

I began the conversation. "I was up in this unit not so long ago. They didn't think I was going to survive. Car accident. No memory of it, but it was raining and there were skid marks on the road." I was babbling on and on. To my surprise, I felt embarrassed by my own discomfort with his incapacity to talk and my inability to understand him. I couldn't understand his lip movements, and I didn't want him to get frustrated with my stupidity.

"Anyway," I continued, "I was in a coma for forty days and forty nights and, like you, on the ventilator. Finally, Nick, my husband, gave the okay for them to pull the plug. Nobody expected me to live. But here I am. Here I am."

Sonny smiled. I could tell he was interested in this soap opera of my life. Probably thought I was a real doofus. "You see," I continued, "Nick was in love with Sandy, an old girlfriend, and it would have been simpler if I had just . . ."

"Died?" Sonny mouthed.

"Yes, and I didn't. He wants to marry her. Class act, huh?"

Sonny wasn't laughing.

This monologue on my life made me nervous.

When is Cassie going to return? Who really cares what happened to me? God, I sound so self-absorbed. Look at him, lying there, unable to move.

"I shouldn't be talking about myself so much. I mean, look at you. Oh no, that doesn't sound right. But how awful it must be to have your body betray you that way. I get so angry when my mind refuses to function, but at least I can get up and move around."

Oh dear, I'm shoveling myself into an even deeper hole of embarrassment. Why does he bother me so? Is it his condition? Is it that I can't hear his response and I don't know what he's really feeling? Is it the way he looks at me, a mixture of sadness and longing?

"I'm an English teacher, or was. Would you like me to read to you?"

That produced an affirmative reaction.

I teased him, thinking up the dullest genres until I hit upon suspense novels with some sexual overtones. Mysteries, perhaps. Well, did I have a real mystery for him.

I told him about Cassie and Haven's Heaven, how it didn't all add up. People dying under mysterious circumstances. A chain of improbable inheritance. I got his attention with that, as he had already experienced Cassie's angelic side.

But the subject of angels always evokes the darker side in me.

"Nick wants a divorce. And with my traumatic brain injury, I can't work. I'd be homeless if it weren't for Cassie. Oh heavens, I sound so pitiful, don't I?"

Sonny, of course, didn't say anything.

I couldn't read his thoughts or expression.

Maybe all my troubles are burdening him down. Don't I need to lift him up?

"Well, they say that everything happens for a reason. It's how you deal with it."

Why am I offering him such inane platitudes?

He seemed to disappear behind his eyes. No movement of his lips. I think he realized that I had been ungenuinely kind to him.

Sometimes in the start of a relationship, it's like walking through a brand new house with corridors leading past closed rooms. In conversation, you sometimes stumble into passageways that lead simply to a broom closet, so you try to clean up the mess you are currently making. Or you arrive at a room that is bare and stale, with nothing fresh to offer. Do you back out or keep sweeping ahead with the sound of your own voice, scattering the dirt as you go? Or do you simply shut the door and say goodbye?

I panicked. As I was about to use the excuse of finding a bathroom, Cassie sailed back into the room to save Sonny from my incoherencies.

"Well, how are you young people getting along?"

Like I said, the whole experience was mortifying.

Sonny

Chapter 12

· ◆ ·

THE TELEVISION NEWS STATION that night reported on yet another Catholic diocese under lawsuit by child sex-abuse victims. Being sheltered in an all male school, I had frequently fantasized about expert sexual instruction by a female teacher, but nobody abused me in The Most Precious Blood Academy. Maybe that was because the Catholic brothers had to regularly report to the Chicago Social Services who maintained guardianship over me. If I'd been molested, the social workers probably would have known about it.

I could write an extensive book, however, on emotional abuse, beginning with the severing of the bond between Mama Dora and myself. But Mama always told me to look on the positive side, and I did get a first-rate education at the boarding school.

But I forget. I can't write anything now, can I?

When I inform people that I spent many years in a Catholic boarding school, their reaction is always about the problem of

sexual abuse. In the history books, there is so much made of
the scandals about the selling of indulgences in the Middle Ages
by the priests and how that led to the Reformation.

*Man, that scandal doesn't hold a candle to what's
happening now. One thing to have a pedophile in your midst,
but quite another when the bureaucracy of the Catholic Church
in the United States, Latin America, and Europe seems more
committed to shielding the priestly wolves than safeguarding
the innocent lambs.*

When that became clear to me, I stopped being a Catholic.

When your whole belief system crumbles, doubt is the
only thing left.

I eventually decided that all religious institutions eventually
ossify into rules, hierarchies, dogma, and the lure of power
over others.

Better to play it safe and take the agnostic position.
Is anyone at all out there?

Jane Smith showed up late in the afternoon.

I was eager to know if there was any news of Mama Dora.

She shook her head. "You were right. She did work at Sara
Lee. They said she took sick and had to quit. I went to the old
address they had on her, but the landlord there said she left a
couple of years ago. I asked if anyone knew what kind of illness
she had, but nobody remembered her that well. My guess is
that she either moved on or . . ."

I nodded. I didn't want to hear that she had possibly died.
But if she had, I knew what had killed her.

A broken heart.

Jane Smith promised she wouldn't give up. "I'll see if the people at the Social Security office can track her down for us. And . . ." she looked away from me, "I'll check the local death records."

Tess Outerbridge wasn't the only one having to deal with mysteries.

It made me feel sick.

Have I traveled so far and come so low only to find a grave waiting for me?

Tess

Chapter 13

• ◆ •

CASSIE PICKED ME UP after lunch at the rehab program and drove toward the hospital. "Sonny will be glad to see you today."

I frowned, having planned instead to walk around town window-shopping until Cassie was finished with her volunteer gig. "It didn't go so well yesterday." An opening gambit.

Cassie turned to look at me, a stern look, that made me turn my head away. "I won't presume to tell you what to do, Tess, but he needs all the friends he can get."

It's always that BUT that hooks the guilt. You can do what you want BUT if you do, it means you're a selfish, unloving ingrate, a miserable human being. Following every BUT comes that ugly word SHOULD. Well, I "should" on myself most of my life, until Nick came along. He was the one to teach me that unless you truly violate your own ethics, guilt is a pretty useless emotion. Now here I am, dependent on the generosity of Cassie McDermott and falling under the lash of old BUTS and scolding SHOULDS.

I chuckled.

"What's so funny?" she asked.

I looked at her. "How I wish I could make Nick feel at least a smidgen of guilt for leaving me. Instead, he pities me."

Cassie pulled the car over to a curb.

I waited for her to speak shaming words of anger for my reluctance to see Sonny, for the meanness in my soul when it came to Nick's emotional welfare.

"Tess, you think I suggested that you become Sonny's friend because he's alone in a strange city, unable to move his body, and that I feel sorry for him."

I nodded.

"Well, you're wrong about that."

I waited for her to explain, but instead she shifted into drive and eased the car back into traffic.

What don't I understand? It seems obvious to me. If I'm not there to help Sonny, then why does she want me to get to know him in the first place?

I rubbed my eyes, but my vision didn't clear up any. I looked at Cassie, at the fuzzy edges around her. A woman of mysteries.

Needless to say, I dutifully accompanied her into the hospital and headed up to the ICU.

Sonny gave me a wan smile when I entered the room, this time without Cassie's introduction. I sat down on the chair and pulled it close to the bed.

Sonny didn't look so good. His eyes were watery, his face flushed.

I reached over and put my hand on his forehead; it was hot. My hand must have felt cool, because he gave me the sweetest smile.

"You've got a fever?"

Sonny nodded. He listlessly tried to lip talk but I couldn't understand him.

A young nurse came in with some liquid medicine that she injected into the line, telling me, "The infection on his neck is causing his temperature to spike." She shook a thermometer and placed it under his tongue. When she pulled it out, she said, "102.5. That's better than it was this morning." After charting the numbers, she left the room, all efficiency and purpose.

"Do you want me to go too?" I asked.

"Noooo," he lipped, his eyes watching my every move.

"I forgot to bring a book," I said. Actually, I hadn't forgotten. I had no intention of visiting him.

So, what's there to talk about?

Then it hit me again. Sonny really couldn't share what I said with others. I could tell him anything.

"Is it okay if tell you about what happened when I was in a coma?"

Sonny smiled. I guess anything would be okay with him as long as he didn't have to try to make himself understood by my feeble brain.

I thought he might not like what I had to say, but I felt a need to tell someone about my experiences, someone who couldn't force me into a mental hospital.

"I was at the bottom of a dark sea," I began, "and there were people there. Dead people with untamed hair, floating but upright with pale arms and hands that kept opening and closing. There was a man with a long seaweed robe swaying in the current. Without words, he kept asking a single question."

Sonny mouthed "What?" He seemed to understand that it was easier for me to read single words from his lips than a full sentence.

I shrugged my shoulders. "I'm not sure, but I think he was giving me a choice—whether to stay there with him or to come back here."

I elaborated, "To stay meant to do nothing, to just float off into the currents, perhaps to dissolve into fish food."

Sonny smiled.

"But to return meant to enter back into suffering. You know what happens to divers who've been down real deep, where the pressure is so much greater? When they come back up, if they don't decompress, they'll explode when they hit the surface. I didn't know what to expect upon surfacing, so how could I properly decompress?"

Tears started gathering at my eyes. "The explosion didn't really happen until after I awoke." I took a deep breath. "Since then, it's been like an earthquake on the surface with a lot of continuing aftershocks."

Sonny's eyes were intense, studying me, noting the whirlpool of my emotions, the fine muscles of his face shifting with each nuance of feeling.

I kept talking. "The man with the robe, he wanted me to stay, to give up being human and become . . . maybe his lover, I don't know. I was tired and I was tempted."

Sonny grinned and spoke, but I didn't couldn't make out what he was saying. Again and again, he tried to articulate with larger and more exaggerated lip movements.

I felt like I was failing both of us.

His face grew brighter, more feverish, with his efforts, a halo effect that only accentuated the Jesus look. His lips scrunched up in frustration at the canyon between us, the words that couldn't bridge the gap.

Luckily, Cassie returned at that point. She took one look at his tense face.

I nodded toward Sonny, repeating myself like a dummy. "I don't understand what you're trying to say."

Cassie proceeded to Sonny's side, took his limp hand, and stroked it. "Jesus, you look awful, Sonny. Okay, tell me what you want her to hear."

Sonny smiled, relief easing across his contorted face. He lip-spoke only two words, neither of which I could decipher.

Cassie kissed him on the cheek and said we would return again soon and hustled me out the door.

"Well," said I, "What did he say?"

Cassie laughed. "What in the heck were you two talking about?"

"Cassie, what did he say?"

"He said, 'Like Persephone.'"

Sonny

Chapter 14

⚬ ◈ ⚬

GOD, I'M TIRED. I'm doing my best to stay calm and wait, but what am I waiting for? I'm clinging to that branch, not daring to look down into the abyss. Is that what the future holds for me?

To let go, to fall, to fail, to feel the wind on my cheek, to fly with no buoyancy.

A dead weight hurtling down.

What scares me is that I fully understand the temptations of Tess and the seduction of the sea lord.

To live is to struggle.

I exist now as a reminder to people to take each day more intently, to love intensely, to live interesting lives because tomorrow life can suddenly pivot on you.

A young female physician with short hair and a trim waist, checked in on me. "How's my favorite patient?"

I gave her the prerequisite smile.

She listened to my heartbeat and felt my forehead. From the consternation on her face, I knew I was burning up.

"We're going to give you something to bring down the fever. We're having trouble with that infection, but we're hoping to find the right combination of antibiotics."

I had read something a few months ago about the drug-resistant infections one can find in hospitals. Too many antibiotics in our food, too often taken for medicine, and we human beings have enabled a whole host of bacteria to adapt and flourish.

Mercy? Isn't that one of those drug resistant infections?

Such were the ruminations of my overheated brain.

She could see the puzzled look on my face. "My guess is that it's a strain of MRSA." She touched my shoulder. "Try to get some sleep."

What other alternative do I have?

If I stay awake, I will obsess in riptides of helplessness.

If I go to sleep, I'll skip right on past modern civilization back to the time of the pagan gods and goddesses. While Tess may be like Persephone, learning how to emerge from her own underworld, I'm like Icarus, confined to the prison in Crete and desperately wanting to fly home to my Mama.

The next person to appear in my sterile prison cell was Jane Smith, the scrawny social worker. As she dragged the chair closer to the bed, I found myself praying that she had good news for me. I even promised God I would believe in Him if only Mama could be found. I know those are the wanting, begging prayers of a child, the kind of magical prayers the Catholic brothers told me were like wishing on a star.

But I could do with a sprinkle of magic potion or a spell to restore enchantment to my world.

Jane Smith had no such divination skills.

"I've really tried to find her," she said. "There was a D. August who was buried at the Grand Traverse Memorial Gardens about a year and a half ago. Maybe they simply forgot to put an A on the end of the name."

Maybe the gravestone was too small to encompass the whole of big Mama. Please God, make it a Dan, David, Dawn, Debbie but not a Doreen or a Dora. Please God, please.

"I made an appointment to go out there and check at the end of the week." She reached out and briefly touched my still, unfeeling hand, then drew back as if burned by such contact. "Is there anyone else?" she asked.

"Out there?" I mouthed, but Jane could not understand what my lips were saying.

"No," I exhaled. "No."

I wanted Tess to come back and see me again, to find out how she planned to leave Hades behind.

I should warn her about what the pomegranate seeds did to Persephone. A little yes to temptation flings open the dark passage.

But as for me, even wings of wax won't help. I cannot fly into the sun, like Icarus.

The sun will have to find me instead.

Not even a moonbeam can find its way into this prison.

Tess

Chapter 15

• ◆ •

I THOUGHT ABOUT WHAT SONNY SAID. Persephone, the Greek maiden who was kidnapped by the great Lord of Death, Hades, and dragged down into the underworld.

So why did I say no to the minister of Death, the man in the murky seaweed robe? Why did the painful bubbles of air return me to the miracle of life, when what waited for me above was another kind of death?

I sat glum in my thoughts as Cassie drove me to the lawyer's office to discuss the impending case of divorce. She insisted that I had to hire an attorney.

Bespectacled, with impressively thick, speckled hair, the middle-aged lawyer reviewed the document I had received in the hospital. Without looking at me, he said, "Michigan is not a community property state. It looks as if your husband, Nicholas Outerbridge, inherited the house and the land from his parents, so that would not be considered marital property."

I nodded.

"Well, does she get anything?" asked Cassie. "That two-timer lured her to Michigan under false pretenses, had an extra-marital affair, and then dumped her while she was in a coma! On top of everything else, she's suffering from a severe head trauma."

He looked up at me over his reading glasses, his eyes softening in pity. "I could perhaps delay the proceedings."

I shook my head. "He doesn't love me anymore."

He nodded. "First off, the court has to determine what is marital property, then what is the value of that property. After that, the court can order a monetary award that one spouse must pay the other based on several factors."

"Like what?" asked Cassie. She turned to me. "You ought to sue that bastard for every penny he owns."

I shrugged my shoulders. I was too tired to wrangle for pennies. We had spent most of our savings on the move and settling into the house. For the past few months in Michigan, Nick had been the wage earner and I was the freeloader. We'd talked about this being a good time for me to get pregnant and to write poetry, only he never seemed to be much in the mood for lovemaking.

Gee, I wonder why?

The lawyer, having assessed my passivity, addressed his remarks to Cassie. "Well, the court looks at the economic circumstances of each party."

"She has nothing." Cassie remarked, "Just her clothes and an old dog."

"Imp is a jewel," I protested.

"The court does take into account the circumstances that led to the estrangement," he continued.

"Such a gross betrayal," added Cassie.

"And the length of the marriage . . ."

"Thirteen years," I said. "Imp was only six months old, when we got married."

"Was she yours before you lived together?" he asked.

"No, we were living together when we brought her home as a puppy."

The lawyer scribbled a note on his legal pad. "Other factors are the age of the parties involved and their physical and mental condition."

"Tsk, tsk," Cassie clucked, shaking her head about the state of my well-being.

"I'm thirty-seven, and I used to have an I.Q. of 132." I smiled brightly.

"Very superior intelligence," added Cassie, lest he not know what that meant.

The lawyer caught the past tense. "And now?"

I clammed up. This was getting too personal, too embarrassing.

But nothing would shut up Cassie if she thought it would work to my advantage. "Preliminary testing at the hospital suggests she is now functioning in the I.Q. range of 87. Dull normal."

"But they tell me that as the brain heals, it'll improve," I said in my own defense.

Cassie slit her eyes at me, warning me that I needed to keep quiet and let her do all the talking.

"I guess the first step is to determine what you want of the marital property," the lawyer said.

"Imp," I answered.

"Money, alimony, health insurance, and one of the two cars," said Cassie.

I shook my head. "No alimony. When we divorce, that'll be the end of it. I need my books, photographs, personal items, one car."

Flustered, Cassie's face turned red. "Look, Tess, I can understand your wish to be done with him, but at the very least you need the health insurance to pay for all your treatments. And if he can't carry you on his insurance after the divorce, then he has to compensate you until you're better."

"Employable," clarified the lawyer.

Cassie nodded. The two of them were now on the same page.

"Does he hold any mortgage on the house and land?" he asked.

"No, it was given to him free of any debt."

Cassie smiled at the lawyer, who smiled back at her. "Pot of gold," she announced.

"The monetary award," he answered.

After this torturous visit to the attorney, Cassie drove me to Moomer's Ice Cream shop on the outskirts of Traverse City. Despite her plump figure, Cassie had no hesitation in ordering a large chocolate chunk, coffee ice cream in a waffle cone, while I indulged in a small, fat-free frozen cappuccino yogurt cone. We sat outside on the picnic bench and watched the cows wandering back toward the barn from an outlying field.

In between bites, Cassie muttered, "You know, this is considered the best ice cream place in the whole country. It was on one of those morning shows." Some of the ice cream dripped onto her blouse.

There was something so endearing about her. Maybe it was the battle between her smart intellect and her essential klutziness, an observation I was making with increased frequency.

She laughed as she looked down at the smear of ice cream on the front of her blouse. "I'm always dropping food on my boobs. Devin used to call them the Great Barrier Reef." She licked her finger and tried to rub off the blob, only making the mess wider.

"This ice cream place was started by teachers such as yourself," she added.

"Great," I said. "If I can't manage to go back to teaching, I can always scoop ice cream." I looked out at the shuffling cows. "Or shovel manure in the barn."

Cassie rolled her eyes. "That's not what I meant."

"I was a good teacher, an excellent teacher." I looked back at her intently.

"I'm sure you were, Tess."

"And I can be again," I asserted.

Cassie said nothing, and that scared me more than anything.

Ever since I'd gotten out of the hospital, I had been completely dependent on Cassie. One morning, she decided it would be a good experiment in independence for me to wander around downtown Traverse City on my own while she went shopping.

I knew this was my chance to follow through on a plan I'd devised. I suspected Cassie wouldn't approve, but sometimes you do ill-advised things because your heart demands satisfaction.

I wanted to meet Sandy on her own turf. She probably wouldn't even recognize me, as the only time we'd seen each other was when I was in the car at the house.

I knew she did her psychic work at the small New Age bookstore downtown, so after Cassie dropped me off with a promise to meet two hours later at a coffee shop, I headed up Front Street. I made sure to keep my head level so I wouldn't get dizzy.

As I opened the door and walked into the bookstore, the sweet aroma of incense enveloped me. A young woman in a light cotton, gypsy-type dress with sandals greeted me. "Is there anything I can do to help you?"

"Does a Sandy Hufnagle work here?"

"Yes, she's reading the cards for someone in the back. Would you like to wait for an appointment? She should be free in about ten minutes."

I nodded.

The young woman got out the appointment book, ready to inscribe my name on the ledger. "Name?" she asked.

I thought a minute, then answered, "Jane Smith."

I perused the titles on the shelves, books of divination, goddess worship, Native American spirituality, herbal healing, crystal power, Tantric sex, wiccan wisdom. Nothing about traumatic brain injury and everything about healing yourself from within.

If it were only that easy.

The door opened in the back and out emerged two women, one in her early forties, the other younger and presumably

Sandy. They shook hands. Sandy smiled at me, the prospective customer. I was relieved that she didn't recognize me.

She ushered me into a small darkened room, lit only by candles, and sat opposite me, smiling a beneficent smile, waiting for me to say something.

I cleared my throat. "What exactly do you do here? Crystals? Cards? Fortune telling?"

She laughed, not at me, but at herself. "No, I work with Spirits. Sometimes customers like the structure of a card layout, and I can do that for you if you would like."

"Or?"

"Or you can put your hands on my hands for about ten seconds."

"And then?"

"Well, then, the Spirits tell me what is happening to you and around you. Who knows?" She shrugged her shoulders. Her eyes had a way of smiling with her face.

I strained to pick up a trace of guile in her presentation and was surprised that I could find none. Perhaps my powers of perception had also been dulled in the accident.

"Okay," I said, bravely thrusting my hands forward, palms down, noting that they were damp with nervousness.

"Just relax," she said.

Her hands were warm and steady as mine trembled ever so lightly. After a brief moment, she dropped her hands.

"The Spirits say that you used to be, how shall I say it, closed off, in your head a lot of the time. That recently something happened, I don't know what, but that it was something really big, and everything in you is changing. That this change is painful for you and that, at times you fight it, but it's happening in you no matter what you do."

She shook her head. "Wow, they're banging on my head and it hurts. Does any of this make sense to you?"

I nodded, unwilling to give away too much information.

She continued, "They say that this fracturing event is the catalyst of transformation for you. I see doors opening up into other dimensions, doors you had kept locked due to doubts and . . ." She paused, as if listening to the air.

"And stubbornness. That's their word, not mine. The Spirits say that as this all plays out, you are discovering a spiritual dimension and a sense of compassion for others who are very different from you. They say that this event will ultimately prove to be one that . . ." She searched for the right word, "that makes you see the difference between intelligence and wisdom and that you are now paying more attention to your heart than just your head. There's love in all this, but not what you expected." She blew out air, as if she had been holding her breath while deciphering the language of these invisible Spirits. Then she stopped and looked straight at me.

"My head is killing me," she said. "I don't get headaches like this, ever. I think we are going to have to quit this session. Sometimes it can get too powerful for me. I'll have them give you back your money or else have you credited for a future session. I'm sorry." She got up out of her chair, one hand massaging her right temple.

"Try Nortriptyline, " I said.

Her brow wrinkled in puzzlement.

"For the headache," I said. "It really helps."

I wanted to but I couldn't discount what she had said, nor could I doubt that she believed in what she was doing. I didn't have to like her, but I could no longer hate her.

Nick had always been the touchy-feely one of the two of us. I used to console myself as the brains of the operation. A lot of good that did me now. In this brief encounter, I caught a glimpse of what he found so attractive in Sandy. She was warm, a bit fuzzy on the cognitive side, and far more open than I had ever been.

But I still didn't have to like her.

Meeting Sandy didn't solve anything. I was still confused. The world had become too complex, too multifaceted for my battered brain.

I stopped at Horizon Bookstore in Traverse City and turned toward the young adult section. An English teacher, I could no longer follow the plots in adult novels, because I kept forgetting what had happened and who were the main characters.

I needed a world that was simple, pastoral, easy to understand. Where the child and animal characters were clearly good and some of the adults were clearly bad, and where the stories were short enough for me to finish in one reading.

From experience, I knew life wasn't really like that at all. The adult world is full of grey ambiguities, and one often has to compromise with moral choices. But when your brain is on the fritz, you gotta go with simplicity.

Still, I thought it better to keep quiet about my visit to Sandy. Cassie had a way of zeroing in on troubling issues that I simply did not want to face.

Sonny

Chapter 16

●◆●

I AWOKE TO THE SOUND of soft chanting and a rattle. A man in his mid-to-late forties with dark hair and Native American features was shaking a horn rattle over my still body in time with the sighing of the ventilator. I blinked a couple of times, unsure whether I might still be dreaming

Noting that my eyes had opened, he smiled and continued his singing, giving a little dip of the head for a welcome. When he finished, he put the rattle away in a paper bag. "My name is Hawk," he said. "You told the staff to check Native American as your religious preference, so here I am."

It was a joke! I don't cotton to any religion now. Mama Dora was the one with the Cherokee blood in her.

I mouthed "Hello."

He continued to stand, his hands hovering, circling over my body as if searching for something. Then he placed his hands upon my head, hands that radiated warmth and something else.

Peacefulness.

After a few moments he spoke. "I am smoothing out the energy in you."

He next placed his hands over my heart but I couldn't feel his touch there. Then one hand moved to my chest and one to my forehead. Hawk's face tensed in deep concentration. His lips moved as if in silent conversation.

I waited, wondering if by some ancient magic, he would bring life back into my limbs, but I felt nothing. I watched him in deep prayer. I also prayed.

Please, please, let my body return to me.

He nodded, as if hearing some message from beyond, and removed his hands from my head and chest. "I work with Spirits," he explained, "and They tell me that our time together is short. There are things I need to teach you."

No magic here. And why is time short? It rather seems to me that time stretches like a rubber band into infinite boredom and helplessness.

"And," he added, "there are things you need to teach others."

Well, that snagged my interest.

What do I have to offer, tethered by a useless body to a hospital bed?

"Spirits say that you have a gift, one earned by a lot of suffering and by what people place on you because of your face."

Oh, so now he's going to tell me I look like a black Jesus. Well, I would sure appreciate it if Jesus would come and perform a miracle here on his avatar.

"Spirits say that your gift is of the heart, that you have a strong heart, a good heart, and it will heal you."

I smiled at that and said with my lips, "Walk again?"

Unlike others, he didn't seem to have trouble understanding what I was saying.

"There are all kinds of healing. Even death is a form of healing, something which most people do not understand. There is a lot of hurt in there." He nodded toward my heart.

He sat down on the chair and began to talk, not looking at me but rather at his hands and his feet. He told me stories, mythical stories about his Lakota people, about how his people lost the knowledge of community and what was important. How the White Buffalo Calf Woman came nineteen generations ago and gave them the Sacred Pipe and ceremonies in order to bring the sacred consciousness back into their lives. "Human beings have to learn to live in balance with all of Creation," he said.

It was quite a different world view than the one I had gotten from the Brothers at The Most Precious Blood Academy. To them, man was created in the image of God and held stewardship, dominion over the rest of the animal and plant kingdom. Man was at the top of the soul food chain.

But not so with Hawk. He said human beings were simply two-leggeds in a world of fins, winged ones, crawling things, and four-leggeds. The "web of Creation," he called it, the interconnectedness of all the species living on Grandmother Earth.

I listened with a split consciousness.

The world around Hawk is personal, animistic, full of Spirits and a sense of wonder—what the Catholic Brothers would have called "the dark and primitive world of paganism," a world of spells and witchcraft.

Yet Hawk treated me with respect, neither trying to convert me nor argue theological points. He was just telling stories.

I didn't have to say yes. I didn't have to say no.

But before he left my room, he looked at me, smiled, and said, "Stories are medicine."

I knew he would return.

My next visitor, besides the medical and nursing staff, was the beleaguered Jane Smith with the shapely legs.

I found myself hoping she would bring me closer to my own story, but her efficient demeanor had lost its edges. She was softer, almost tiptoeing as she approached my bed. Her eyes and face oozed compassion. That meant bad news.

"I found your mother," she said. "I went to the Grand Traverse Memorial Gardens and asked to see the headstone of D. August. Written in stone was *Doreen Augusta*. I'm so sorry, Sonny. I know how much you wanted to see her again."

Then Jane Smith sat there in silence for about twenty minutes, holding and stroking my hand.

It was for her benefit, as I couldn't feel a thing. I practiced holding a stiff upper lip until she got up and left. When she had disappeared from view, leaving me alone, I broke down and cried baby tears, little boy tears, tears that I couldn't even wipe from my cheeks.

That empty space in me that had been walled off for years, that empty space that was Mama collapsed in on itself, leaving only a rubble of despair.

What had been a space of hope had been converted into a grave.

"You're going to be okay," said the pretty young nurse, wiping the trail of tears off my face. "Your fever is down and your friend, that auto accident woman, will be here soon."

She called for an orderly who moved my body around, while she sponge-bathed me. "You'll feel a lot better after you've had this bath. I hate to feel dirty." She chattered on and on, but I was so far down deep in my sorrows that her voice floated above me, all noise and nothing to acknowledge.

Modesty had long since disappeared along with the ownership of my body. I was all face, brain, and fluids now. Something else did the breathing for me. Food came into my stomach through a tube so that I wouldn't choke and suffocate. Piss and shit no longer concerned me but rather flowed into containers to be whisked away. And while I still entertained sexual fantasies, my penis had become irrelevant.

The only thing human that was left of me was my mind. What I thought. What I felt.

I had become an alien life form.

Mama, come for me. I'm already halfway there.

Tess

Chapter 17

• ◆ •

AS DEEP SUMMER FULLY ARRIVED, visiting crowds of tourists flooded Traverse City, and my chaotic life began to assume a predictable rhythm. A van for the disabled picked me up in the morning and drove me to the rehabilitation program in Traverse City. Then, after lunch there, I'd walk the mile to the hospital to see my friend Sonny. I had gotten a lot better at reading his lips.

One afternoon, I picked purple and yellow wild-flowers along the edges of the sidewalk and brought them with me into the hospital. If Sonny couldn't get out of his sterile grey prison, at least I could bring some of Nature's extravagant palette into his room.

Before he could rearrange his face upon my entrance, I could see that despair had set in behind his eyes, a kind of haunted look as if death had already claimed a part of him.

I held up the rainbow bouquet.

"Bring them to my nose," he mouthed. He inhaled the earthy

aromas of life and decay. Then his nose twitched with the tickle of pointed leaves, and I scratched it for him.

"Tell me . . . about your . . . rehab program," he whispered through the sigh of the ventilator.

I groaned. "Right now, I have to connect the dots from one to twenty. That's not so bad, but then they ask me to alternate numbers and letters, to draw a line from 1 to A then to 2, then B."

"Sounds . . . easy enough."

"You try it. They tell me it has to do with sequencing ability, and frankly, Sonny, I've a hard time doing it. I can't deal with multiple choices anymore. I can't figure out what happens next, you know."

"Become . . . a Buddhist," he said.

"Huh?"

"Live in . . . the moment." He grinned at his own joke.

The English teacher in me prevailed. "It's like that poem by Robert Frost that goes: 'Two roads diverged in a yellow wood and sorry I could not travel both.' I can't remember the rest of the poem, and I don't know which way to go anymore. I'm like Hansel and Gretel, lost in that yellow wood without even a trail of bread crusts to guide me."

Sonny, the-black-Jesus-Christ-turned-Buddha, lipped, "How can . . . you be . . . in two places . . . when you are . . . nowhere at all?"

I repeated aloud this mysterious riddle: "How can you be in two places at the same time when you are nowhere at all?"

"That's easy," answered a smartly dressed, middle-aged woman who appeared in Sonny's hospital room. "It's called dissociation. You can learn to leave your body and go someplace else. A very handy skill when the body is paralyzed and uncooperative."

She moved over to Sonny's bedside and touched his cheek. "My name is Dr. Meggie O'Connor. I'm a clinical psychologist affiliated with this hospital. Sometimes they ask me to come in and see how a patient is doing."

Before I could excuse myself, she turned to me and offered a handshake. "And you are . . . ?"

I snorted. "Sonny can't move, so I'm his legs and hands. But since I've had a brain injury, Sonny helps me with my thinking."

Sonny smiled.

"Tess Outerbridge," I said.

She shook a finger in the air. "You wouldn't be the one who lives with Cassie McDermott?"

I nodded.

"Well, then, I'll have the pleasure of seeing you soon."

Is this the therapist Cassie picked for me? She seems nice enough.

I leaned over Sonny's bed and gave him a quick peck on the cheek. "See ya tomorrow."

He mouth-lipped something and I laughed.

"What did he say?" the psychologist asked, not yet skilled in reading lips.

"Oh," I answered, "he said that choice was simply a matter of connecting the dots."

The next morning, I flew into a rage at the rehab staff. They had promised me they would give me enough time between each session to get myself together, but that was a lie. Each therapist needed to produce results in their individual sessions.

Their pressure to perform was frying my brain. By the third session of the morning, I felt overwhelmed, unable to think, mind on the fritz. Why couldn't they see I needed a break?

It made me wonder if I'd done that to my students back in Massachusetts. Wedded to my own rigid standards of performance, had I ever recognized that someone couldn't do the work? I'd used the grading system like a cattle prod, and if an essay was poorly written, I'd assume that the student was lazy and unmotivated.

One young man had referred to me as "Dr. Tough Tits" because I'd expected so much from these sons and daughters of Harvard and MIT professors. In truth, most of them had risen to the challenge. At the beginning of each school year, I'd explain that I'd give a C to anyone who had memorized the material, a B to anyone who had really learned something, and an A to anyone who could inspire me or teach me something new.

Now it no longer mattered that I had a Ph.D.; so much had gotten wiped out in a matter of seconds. There is no such thing as a mind/body split. If the brain is severely injured, the mind cannot function.

When a couple of the rehab staff dismissed my rage as simply a quirk of my brain injury and "emotional lability" (and thus without any validity), I went numb. I hid in the bathroom for forty minutes, until the morning sessions were over.

Prickly as a pissed-off porcupine, I headed down the sidewalk path toward the hospital. The trees fluttered in the gentle breeze, flickering dark and light forms on the pavement. A child-like glee edged out my mood of sour darkness. I started to skip in and out of the frolicking shadows. No A to B or logical lines to follow.

I arrived at Sonny's cloistered room with pink cheeks glowing and a renewed smile on my face. I gave him a quick kiss on his cheeks, asked him how he was doing, then said, "Enough about me these days. You don't want to know. Tell me about you, instead."

Slowly, the story of his short life unfolded in the afternoon hours. Sometimes he had to spell out the words I could not read on his lips. He chose his sparse words carefully. He told me about Jane Smith's discovery and how his trip north had not only been in vain but that it also ended in tragedy.

Sonny didn't linger in self-pity. The discipline of the Catholic boarding school hadn't allowed for such indulgences.

I asked him about his faith, whether he believed there was a God who watched over us.

Instead, he told me about the Lakota medicine man who'd come to visit him. "Married . . . to that . . . psychologist."

I had already forgotten about her. How was it that Sonny didn't seem to feel cheated by what life had offered him? Or get angry like me?

"You forget," he mouthed. "Mama Dora loved me."

The inability to move even his body, however, was a different matter. In an instant, a blink of an eye in time, he had gone from an able-bodied young man to a head on a stick, a body that wouldn't move. This reality he could not accept.

"There must . . . be something . . . that can . . . be done. Stem cell . . . therapy . . . nerve . . . reconnections . . . physical . . . therapy." He was adamant about it. He wanted me to give him hope, to tell him that miracles happen.

What can I say?

The truth was too harsh.

I looked away from his face, from his question and prayed that Cassie would soon arrive to take me home. I was too chickenshit to be honest with him.

On the way back to Hagen's Heaven, I started crying. It seemed so hopeless for Sonny. He didn't even have his Mama Dora to comfort him.

"He has you," said Cassie.

"A lot of good that does."

Cassie's face appeared troubled. "He needs you, Tess, because it's going to get worse for him."

"But how could it get worse?"

Cassie sighed. "Insurance. The time will come when the insurance company will say that the hospital is no longer treating him but simply maintaining him. When that happens, the company will insist that he be moved from the expensive hospital setting to a nursing home setting."

"Why is that worse?"

"Because the level of care will drop. He's young, without money, without family to advocate for him, so they'll warehouse him. That's what our *compassionate* society does these days. The bottom dollar rules," said Cassie.

"Could we, perhaps, bring him back home to live with us?" I knew it sounded like a crazy idea.

"I wish we could, but he needs more physical care than we can give him. And, unfortunately, I have yet to discover a secret chest in the attic loaded with diamonds, emeralds, and rubies. But you're his friend, Tess, and that means a lot to him."

Sonny

Chapter 18

• ◆ •

PSH, PSH, PSH—the sound of the ventilator breathing for me.

The rise and fall of my chest, blown up like a balloon, then deflating, the in/out robotic rhythms.

The soft squeak of the nurses' shoes as they traipsed in to check on me and the equipment that defines my existence.

They bombarded me with chatter, questions that acknowledged me as a human being: "Do you want the television on? How about some music? Would you like me to put a cool washcloth on your forehead?"

To which I answered in a polite negative, because if I said yes, I'd be stuck. I couldn't change the channels, so the television would continue to fill up the spaces with noise. I couldn't turn off the radio, so I'd be forced to listen to whatever was playing. I couldn't get rid of a washcloth as it morphed from cool to clammy.

I can only control my world with the response "No."

Then it occurred to me:

No is the beginning of Will.
Will is about choices.
And choices express who I am.

Hawk arrived. He greeted me with respect, one man to another. He circled his hands over and above my body, perhaps looking for some signs of movement.

"Your heart is strong," he said.

Great, the dummy will live!

In his native tongue, he prayed for the Grandfathers to watch over me and help me on my journey.

Where am I going? I wanted to ask him. I waited for the answer to his prayers and found none.

Then he sat down, smiled, and said, "I have a story to tell you."

I was all ears.

"There once was a man who was a great hunter. He had a fine wife and three healthy children who had survived yet another harsh winter on the Plains. His children loved him because he played with them a lot, chasing them around the campfires, not caring whether or not the other men thought him silly. His wife loved him because for every hardship they endured, he was able to laugh at himself and at the absurdity of what life offers each of us. He loved her and was not afraid to let her know what he felt deep inside of him.

"The other natives respected him for his skills. He made them laugh as well. At first they didn't know whether he was making fun of them or of himself, but eventually they learned to let down their guard and enjoy his foolish brand of humor. Although they never would have chosen him as their war chief, he was the one they sought for companionship. He had the ability to make them accept that they were simply two-leggeds in a world of other creatures. He would jest with anyone who took himself too seriously.

"But then one day a terrible thing happened to his tribe. The U.S. cavalry gave his people the gift of blankets, most welcomed during the time of great cold. What they didn't know was that these blankets came from people who had died of smallpox. The U.S. Army had decided this was an easy way to get rid of the 'Indian problem.'

"Not only did this man see his chief and friends die of smallpox but the disease also took his cherished wife and three children. Brought in with those blankets, this terrible disease destroyed his people's way of life. His grief was so great that he cut off his long hair and left. He wondered what his people had done to deserve such treatment."

"The story . . . of Job," I said on the exhale.

God tested Job with great trials, and Job failed the test by questioning God.

Hawk continued, "The only way this man knew how to heal the hole in his heart was to take himself to Grandmother Earth. Over the next few months, he watched how She chased winter away with the first buds of spring, how the ice melted into rivulets that merged into creeks and then rivers. How the trees began to fill the barren spaces with the lightest touch of green and migrating birds built nests and sang songs of love. How the sun lingered longingly upon Her skin, and life forced itself up from the buried roots."

Pretty much the same argument that God gave to Job: 'Look at me, you puny man.' So, am I to fear God and say it's okay to be a quadriplegic? Baloney!

Hawk must have noticed a grimace, a tightness to my lips. He leaned forward. "A man cannot give up his grief. To do so would be to deny the loss."

Hot tears fell, unbidden, upon my cheeks. I could not contain them, as much as I wanted to. It was embarrassing to be crying like a baby before another man.

Hawk did not brush them away. Instead he went on with his story. "The man would never forget how things had been. His deep love for his wife, children, and friends would be with him always. But something else began to move in him, something as he watched the death of winter yield to the hope of spring."

The tears stopped. I wanted to hear what came next.

"Death sat on his left shoulder, neither friend nor enemy, but rather a teacher. The man became aware of all those who came before him and all those who would come after him. That time was a sweep as well as a speck, and he realized that what he did with his life was up to him. He could drown in the angers, the what-ifs, the pity that can swamp a life. Or he could take what he had learned, squeeze whatever wisdom he could from it, and then live in the way of the Grandmother who brings the dead back to life."

"How?" I whispered.

Hawk sat with that question for a long while. "Well, that man's talent was humor. He could make people laugh when they became too self-important. Every one of us has some sort

of gift that brings life to others. So, the question becomes—
what is your gift?"

So many things came rushing into my mind:

*How can I help others if I can't even get out of bed? How
can I find humor in having lost both my body and my mother?
He tells me a story about spring when instead we are heading
from the end of summer into fall and then winter.*

No, I don't have any gifts.

But I didn't say anything because I no longer knew what
was true.

He sat for the longest time in the room without uttering
another word. It was oddly comforting, a silence that let itself
be heard, a way of holding us both together in the same spool
of time.

He only got up to leave when Tess arrived.

They nodded to each other in passing.

"How you doing, Sport?" she said, reaching over to feel
my forehead. "No fever today. That's good. I brought a book
to read to you if you'd like. A little bit of sex, a lot of adventure.
Should I go ahead?"

She pulled out a dog-eared novel from her canvas bag.

Truth was, I wanted to linger in the silence, but her sparkly
words tumbled out, a waterfall of good wishes. So of course I
smiled and let her know it was okay.

She made herself comfortable in the chair and cracked open
the book, but before she began to read, she looked up at me
and said, "Now I'm an English teacher and I want you to know
that what I'm going to read to you is absolutely the most perfect
beginning of any novel."

That caught my interest.

Tess licked her lips and began to read.

"It was the best of times, it was the worst of times, it was the age of wisdom, it was the age of foolishness, it was the epoch of belief, it was the epoch of incredulity, it was the season of Light, it was the season of Darkness, it was the spring of hope, it was the winter of despair, we had everything before us, we had nothing before us, we were all going direct to Heaven, we were all going direct the other way . . ."

Tess

Chapter 19

＊◆＊

IT SEEMED LIKE I read Charles Dickens' *The Tale of Two Cities* forever before Cassie arrived to drive me home. I couldn't be sure whether Sonny was listening with rapt attention or whether he was drifting in and out of sleep. He kept his eyes closed for much of the time.

When Cassie and I got back to Hagen's Heaven, it was still light outside. Cassie handed me the German walking sticks. "Time for you to do your mile."

Sensing that she was going to get exercise, Imp began circling in excitement. I noticed that she seemed to be getting thinner, bonier. When I ran my hands down her back, I could feel the sharp outline of her vertebrae. I hated the idea of her getting older.

Cassie plunked herself down into a kitchen chair.

"Aren't you coming?" I asked.

"No, gotta pay bills," she said. "It's good for you to be able to do things for yourself, builds self-confidence. Besides, if you fall, you can call me on the cell phone."

That was Cassie, a woman of a big heart inside but tough as worn leather on the outside.

Imp and I set off in the dying fall afternoon. Days were shortening, scrunching the light. I noticed that some birds had already begun peeling off Cassie's feeding station, heading to warmer places. Above in flight formation, a flock of Canada geese honked out raucous farewells.

On the walk by the open field, the bright reds and yellow leaves on the trees had begun to spot more muted colors of rust and burnt amber. Too soon the deciduous trees would be naked gray silhouettes in the surrounding woods. How quickly the seasons turn, letting us know that the only thing constant in Nature is change.

Imp ran ahead of me. She stumbled over the gravel and righted herself. I looked closer. As she trotted ahead, her right hind paw awkwardly angled toward the left paw.

"Imp," I called.

She came running, ears flattened, her mouth in a smile.

I knelt down and massaged her hind quarters. She showed no flinching or evidence of pain, but why hadn't I noticed before this odd gait of hers? Something wasn't right.

I stood up, about to turn back, when her ears shot up and twitched. She loped around the corner. I listened. There were a couple of adult voices ahead, but I couldn't see them or they me.

A man's voice said, "And over there is the old maple tree I used to climb as a boy."

"It's a beautiful place, incredible," said a woman. "And who is this little furry creature?"

I turned the corner. Imp was wagging her tail and getting acquainted with a woman about my age.

The man eyed me with suspicion. "Who are you?"

"Tess," I answered, wondering at his rudeness.

In his early sixties, he was portly, balding, and dressed in clothes too natty for hiking in the woods.

"That's Imp," I said to the slender woman who was bent over, rubbing Imp's ears.

"I'm Sally McGovern and the grump is Spenser." She nodded, winking at the man. A natural grace inhabited her movements, a woman at ease with her body.

"Spenser Mudge," he said. "You with that McDermott woman?" No trace of kindness in his voice.

"Mrs. McDermott is a friend of mine," I answered, a bit defensively.

Who in the hell does this man think he is?

Sally stood up and brushed off the dog hair. "Beautiful animal. It's so peaceful here, isn't it?" She ignored Mr. Mudge.

"Cassie describes it as a sanctuary for humans and animals."

"Harrumph," said Mr. Mudge, who then pretended to clear his throat.

Sally shot him a disparaging glance. "Pay him no mind. He didn't get enough bran cereal this morning. It's a lovely place. I hope she doesn't mind our walking up her driveway."

"I don't think that she would."

"Better not," Mr. Mudge growled. "I've more of a right to be here than her."

"Tsk, tsk, tsk. You're sounding a bit bitter, my darling," scoffed Sally. She scooped up his arm with hers and turned him around in the opposite direction, saying, "It was nice meeting you, Tess."

Off they retreated down the driveway.

Imp tilted her head at me, as if asking a nonverbal question.

"Well, *she* seemed nice enough." I was trying real hard these days to mute my irritability and put on a pleasant face.

When I reported the encounter to Cassie, still sitting at the kitchen table surrounded by unpaid bills, she arched her eyebrows and sighed. "Spenser Mudge is the only living relative of Natalie Hagen. Perhaps he thought this place was someday going to belong to him. Who knows?"

She flipped back a bang of wispy white hair to dismiss Mr. Mudge from her thoughts, as if he were a pestering gnat flying about the room. She returned to writing checks.

"Cassie, I hate to bother you, but could we take Imp to see the Suttons Bay veterinarian? I don't like the way she's moving her right hind paw."

"Oh?" Cassie looked at Imp, who was peering up at her with endearing eyes while perched on the offending hind end. Cassie bent over to rub Imp's ears. "Does our little doggie woggie need to see the big, bad doctor?"

Imp's tail swept the floor.

"Okey dokey," said Cassie. "Tomorrow afternoon we'll take her to the vet, right after you see the psychologist and I get a chiropractic adjustment from Dr. Russ. That way, we get done with all the appointments at the same time."

I hated to miss my daily visit with Sonny, but I was worried about Imp.

At the first session, Dr. O'Connor mistook my expression as fear of psychotherapy.

"What you say is . . ."

"Confidential," I interjected. "I've been in therapy before so I know the rules. Cassie thinks I need help."

I looked around the room, small but cozy. A bookcase of toys for children sat in one corner, a brown couch in the middle and two stuffed chairs, enough for a family or a couple in marital counseling.

Dr. Meggie O'Connor's shoulder length, curly hair could have used some styling, as it looked like she had slept on it wrong, the curls at odd angles. She wore little makeup, but her face was kind and thoughtful. I liked her eyes; they crinkled with warmth. I judged her to be at least ten years older than myself. Today, her clothes were stylishly casual, country doctor, and her figure was a bit plump. I didn't pick up any pretentiousness in her presentation.

She'll do.

"I'm sure Cassie told you about the accident."

She nodded, her silence an opening for me to tell my version of the events.

I folded my hands in my lap and studied my cuticles for a minute, then dug my nails into the palms of my hands. "Truth is, I'm depressed as hell."

"You've every right to be," she said.

It was not what I'd expected her to say. I looked up.

"A traumatic brain injury is exactly that—traumatic. Not just to the brain but to your whole sense of yourself, your feelings, your body. If you weren't depressed, I'd be worried about you."

I didn't know whether to be relieved or to become even more depressed. For a get-up-and-go person for whom work had provided a significant measure of self-worth, I hated this whole miserable state of hurt. Why couldn't I simply jar my brain back into place, reattach all those dangling neurons?

Tears began forming at the corner of my eyes. I looked away from her, embarrassed.

"Cassie told me that you have a Ph.D. in American Literature and that you taught English at a very prestigious private school out East."

I nodded and smiled inwardly.

She knew I was once competent, smart, and productive.

"I need to ask you some questions if that's all right with you?"

Good. I don't want to deal with feelings anyway.

Dr. O'Connor ascertained that every day I had horrible headaches, worse than any migraine, and that I was taking medication for them. "They will become less frequent over time," she said, "but we need to let the neurologist know about them in case he wants to readjust the medication."

We reviewed my progress in physical therapy, substantial except for my still needing a chair in the bathtub shower as my balance wasn't yet stable. She asked about the morning rehabilitation program, and I gave rather disgruntled answers. "All these card games, the memorization of numbers forward and backward, the maze work on the computers—what does that have to do with returning to my work as an English teacher?

Besides, they don't give me enough time between sessions to let my brain rest and reset!"

"You sound angry," Dr. O'Connor said. "And your face looks like you've been sucking on lemons."

I pretended to massage my face with my hands, while really trying to rearrange my expression from sour to sweet.

"I think," she continued, "that you're feeling very frustrated with your progress."

"I can't do those stupid tasks!" I shouted from behind the mask of my hands.

She leaned toward me. "Think of all those years you put into graduate education to get that doctorate. It wasn't easy. Well, this period of recovery from traumatic brain injury isn't going to be easy either. In fact, it will prove to be a lot harder than your dissertation process. But the ability to persevere is obviously one of your strong personality traits. And persevere, you will."

"And then what?" I dropped my hands. "Will I be able to teach again? Will I be able to read adult books again? Will I stop seeing double and getting dizzy? Will I recover what I lost?" The anger reverberated with each question.

She sat back and did not answer, waiting for me to come to my own conclusions.

"So what's next? Will you have them give me mood-regulating pills so I don't go around feeling all pissed off and angry at the world that doesn't seem to give a damn about brain trauma? What can you do to help me, Dr. O'Connor?"

"Call me Meggie. I'll tell you what's going to happen next. You're going to see me on a weekly basis. We'll talk about your feelings and strategies for coping."

"Don't you see that I'm tired of being angry and depressed?"

"The anger will last only so long. It's a protection, a shield to your battered sense of self-esteem."

"So then what happens? Do I go from anger at others to self-loathing?"

She shook her head. "No, the next stage will be grief. You will mourn what you have lost."

"Oh, I think I like the anger better."

Things went from bad to worse, when the orthopedic specialist visiting Suttons Bay Veterinary Hospital examined Imp. After looking at the X-rays, he spent the better part of his time palpitating the tissue around her hind legs, while she stood there, stoic and calm. She knew that as long as I was there, she could trust him.

"Is it just old age?" I asked. "She doesn't seem to be in any pain."

"No," he answered. "It's a weird, rare condition she has, not yet written about in the literature. I've only seen it a couple of times before and only in Shelties."

My heart started beating faster, fearing the worst.

Imp lowered her head and pushed into my side while he poked and articulated movement of her left and then right knee as well as her ankle joints and paws. She even licked his hand in passing.

"Such a sweet baby," said Cassie, her face crinkled with worry.

The veterinarian straightened up his back and moved away from the examining table.

Imp wagged her tail to show there were no hard feelings, despite his turning and twisting her legs.

"The X-rays show severe arthritis in both ankles, but what's causing it is that she's losing tone in the ligaments and tendons, making for instability in the ankles. We haven't the slightest clue why this is happening. Not an infection or a disease process that we can tell. If it gets really bad, we can fashion braces for her and then later fuse the ankle bones, but I don't think that will be necessary, given her age. I'd be a lot more worried if she were only a five-year-old dog."

"But what can we do for her now?" asked Cassie.

"Physical therapy. Anti-inflammatory medications. That's about it. Exercise is good for her as long as she can tolerate it."

Along with the bill that Cassie paid, he gave us a referral number for a veterinarian in Traverse City who specialized in physical therapy for animals.

On the trip home with Imp contentedly sitting in my lap looking out the window, Cassie said, "You're really quiet. A penny for your thoughts."

"Look at her, staring out the window. She doesn't even know what's happening to her. She's my pal, my best friend. And we've both become crippled in our own way."

Imp must have noted the sad tone of my voice because she snuggled closer against my chest and licked the lobe of my ear.

Cassie briefly took her eyes off the road. "At least you're both still alive," she said in an ironic tone of voice.

Of course. She's thinking of Devin. Some losses never come back.

I bit my tongue and hugged Imp all that much closer.

Sonny

Chapter 20

•◆•

THE FEVER RETURNED, jacking all the way up 104 degrees. The nurse later told me that I was hallucinating and mumbling in the exhales of the ventilator. I wanted to answer her back that my whole life now seemed like a bad hallucinatory trip.

Tess had described her vivid dreams during the coma. Well, one such vision came to me.

In the inky night, I arrived at a river as wide as the Mississippi but deep in a slurry black. A large pier extended out into the water. I waited for the appearance of a paddle wheel boat, the kind that old-time gamblers used to frequent. A boat finally arrived and nestled to the iron pilings on the pier. Passengers in old-style dress disembarked down the white plank stairs. I approached the mutton-chopped, mustached ticket master but he refused to sell me a ticket. Either the boat was not making a return trip or else he found me unworthy of passage. I slunk back off the pier.

Desperate, I searched for another means of passage. A grizzled old man sat hunched over in a rowboat, hands perched on the oars. He nodded at me in sly greeting. I scrambled down the riverbank, ready to make a deal with him. Suddenly a mastiff rose up in the front of the rowboat, a dog with three heads and jaws drooling, deep brown eyes unsettled in expression. The oarsman smiled, shrugged his shoulders.

There was no way to jump into that rowboat without first maneuvering past the damn dog. As much as I wanted to start the journey onto the black river, I was too frightened of the beast. I retreated to the riverbank and sat down, feeling lost and alone with nowhere to go.

Such is the murky stuff of fever and dreams.

Tess didn't come that afternoon so I slept, waking up only when the nurses arrived to adjust the antibiotic drip or wipe my forehead with a cool washcloth.

When finally the fever diminished and I could stay awake, I thought about Hawk's stories. Like the humorous man in his tale, I too had lost everything of meaning to me. How I would have liked to be able to resort to some sort of faith, a belief that a beneficent God was watching over me.

But truly I am the man clinging on the side of the cliff in the moonlight and nobody answers. The sad part is, even if I call out, my despair and my loss of faith tells me that no one is there.

Nobody but Tess knew that I was once a devoted Catholic, an altar boy trying to figure out how to be good enough in order for the Brothers and the social worker to allow Mama Dora to come visit. While some of the Brothers were kind and some of the priests were gentle, it was the Princes of the Church who corrupted what was once so beautiful to me. They were the ones who threw the rocks into the stained glass images of the child-loving Jesus.

I will never forgive them, not only for what they did in terms of transferring the pedophiles from one church to another but for their original sin of denying me the only real love I had ever experienced in my life. They dragged me away from her and, in so doing, broke both our hearts.

I will also never forgive God for hiding behind the Pope's shadow.

What good is all that Father, Son, and Holy Ghost stuff if the church can't recognize a mother's love?

I hate the Catholic Church.

I hate God.

I next awoke to the sound of the curtains being pulled aside. It was nighttime.

"See there," Hawk said at the window, pointing up, "Hanhepi wi. The moon. She's coming on full now. When all is dark, she lights the way."

I didn't say anything.

He moved closer to the bed. "She's also called 'the dark sun.' A reflected light. She takes what she knows and passes it on to us so that we don't need to be scared of the darkness."

"She disappears," I lipped.

He laughed. "That's part of a woman's mystery, but she always returns. You have to grant her leave because you can't lash time to your desires."

A moon is a moon . . . is a mystery.

"Some don't . . . ever return," I whispered. He wasn't going to banish my cynicism with his animistic symbolism. My doubt was the only certainty I possessed.

"Isn't she beautiful?" He nodded toward the window, indicating that I should take a look too.

Indeed, it was a golden harvest moon, full and plump and probably radiant. I imagined that if I had been able to get out of the bed and walk outside, bathed in moon rays and tree shadows, I would have been struck by the brilliant silence. Here in the sterile prison of the hospital, the ventilator wheezed and sighed. The ever present lights over me denied the night of its depth.

How can this man know of my utter and complete despair? I am neither dead nor alive. I am caught in the in-betweens. A facsimile of a human being.

Then he did a most curious thing. He opened the hospital door and peered into the corridor, then quietly shut the door and flicked off the lights.

"Look now," he said. "Quick."

For the briefest of moments, I saw what he saw: the velvety pitch of the night, the magical mystery of the moon. An exquisite, fleeting experience of awe.

Then an officious nurse entered, switched on the lights, and calmly inquired, "What's going on here?"

Hawk looked at me and answered, "He's learning how to escape from prison."

What crime did I commit to end up like this?
Did I abandon God before He abandoned me?

Or is this some nasty fluke of fate, some karma from a previous life? Am I supposed to find meaning in this paralysis?

I am literally stopped in my tracks. I am going nowhere.

I'd scream if it would accomplish anything. I'd yell out all kinds of profanity just to get a reaction if I thought God would hear my cries.

I'd will my own death if I could, but what I can't even do is will my own life.

So I lie here, immobile, a head upon a pillow, a machine to breathe for me, tubes to feed me and take away my piss and shit.

God, how much longer do You expect me to hold onto that slim branch of life?

God, God, God, have pity on me.

Chapter 21

• ◆ •

BEING A NIGHT OF THE FULL MOON, I didn't need to turn on the light when I found Cassie in her dimly lit bedroom, sitting on the side of the bed, holding a framed photo of her husband.

"I'm sorry," I said, standing within the doorway.

Surprised, she looked up and settled the photograph back on the side table. "What about?"

"You've been good to me, Cassie. I get so frustrated with my limitations, wrapped up in myself. I'm not the only one who has felt losses this year." I nodded my head toward the photograph, then sat down on the bed next to her.

I expected her to say something wise, profound, or at least pragmatic, but she remained disturbingly silent.

"You miss him, don't you?" I said.

"Well, you don't live with a man that long, organize your daily routines around him, share all those old memories and then . . . boom!"

"He's no longer there," I finished her sentence. I hadn't totally lost my capacity for empathy.

"Nature abhors a vacuum," she said, sweeping invisible lint off her knees as if ready to get up and resume a chore, yet she didn't move.

I put my arm around her. As night darkened the windows, we remained there for the longest time, neither one of us speaking, Cassie lost in her thoughts, and me?

Simply lost.

That night, the man in the seaweed robe entered my dreams again and I awoke to the sound of my heart beating. Fearful, my eyes raked the room to make sure he wasn't swimming on the ceiling or sidling up the wallpaper. The tidal sounds of waves peeling onto the shore disseminated into the gentle rock of Imp's breathing. Her little paws twitched to some dream of running.

I shook my head but could not clear the memory of the robed minister of death coming to me during my coma, when the promise of seeing my dead parents had not sufficiently tempted me to stay in the watery graveyard.

"We all have dreams," he'd said. "In the hereafter, you can do, you can be, whatever you would like. You can shed your mortal skin, become a playful seal, a river otter, a leaping dolphin, a huge whale singing across the ocean bed. No limitations. When one form bores you, you simply slip into another. Time is irrelevant. Forever is your friend."

"But . . ." I had answered, knowing there was more to it than that.

"But what?" he had persisted. "The only requirement is that you say 'Yes' and you only have to say that once. No more fighting to breathe. No more struggle. Peace."

"But . . ."

"A simple yes will do."

"But I want to live."

He had looked puzzled. It made no sense to him. He'd offered me a peaceful passing, and I had stubbornly refused. His limbs stirred up a furious whirlpool, sucking me under, swirling me about. My lungs had fought to keep breathing.

Looking at the ceiling, I wondered if that had been when I'd developed pneumonia, when the medical staff had thought I wouldn't live to the next day.

I turned on the bedroom lamp and read until the morning light.

"Where . . . have you . . . been?" Sonny asked that next afternoon, letting me know that he had felt neglected.

I told him about Imp and her problems. I told him about sweet Sally McGovern and sour Spenser Mudge. I told him about catching Cassie in her moments of sadness. But I didn't tell him why there were bags under my eyes.

"Where have you been?" he persisted.

I guess when you have a lot of time and no ability to move, it sharpens your focus and intuition.

"Flashback cinema," I said.

"The seaweed . . . guy?"

I nodded.

"So there . . . really . . . is a . . . choice." Sonny's eyes narrowed.

"I guess it's lucky that I didn't know about my husband and Sandy then. I might have taken up his offer of a peaceful end."

"Or beginning," lipped Sonny. "You seen . . . that . . . psychologist?"

I nodded. "She wants me to call her Meggie. The illusion of friendship, I guess. She's okay. Pills would be faster. She tells me that the next stage of recovery is grief, but I think I'll stick with the anger. It feels stronger."

"Her husband . . . Hawk. Lakota . . . Indian . . . Long black . . . hair . . . bandanna. Came . . . last night." Sonny paused, as the ventilator sighed. Sometimes he whispered his words between the beats of the machine; other times, I had to read his lips.

"Do you like him?"

"He can . . . travel . . . outside . . . his body."

"You believe that?"

Sonny frowned as if he didn't welcome my question. "I want . . . I want . . . so many . . . things, Tess."

I could have kicked myself for even suggesting doubt. Sonny needed all the help he could get.

When Cassie and I got back home, there was a telephone message from Nick. He suggested we meet "to sort things out."

"I don't understand. What does he mean, 'sort things out'? Does he or doesn't he want a divorce?" I asked Cassie. It was hard on me to understand the subtleties of communication. The brain injury had made a literal beast of me.

Cassie snorted. "He's hoping you'll take pity on him and not ask him for any financial support. Believe me, you don't want to make any promises to him. Okay? That's what you have a lawyer for."

From somewhere deep inside me, a little voice, the vestige of hope, I guess, spoke up. "I'd like to meet with him."

Cassie shrugged her shoulders. "Your funeral," she said.

"Pick a quiet place where you won't get so distracted," said Dr. Meggie O'Connor. "Did you get the noise cancellation headphones I recommended?"

I nodded and pulled them out of my purse. I affixed them to my head, batted my eyes, and said, "Fashion's newest accessory."

She laughed. "Humor is good."

"So, do you think I'll ever be able to go back to teaching high school English?"

"It depends."

"On what? On how long it takes my brain to heal? What I'm asking is whether I'll ever get back to the old me."

"You told me earlier that you're now reading young adult books because you can follow their simpler plots. Even so, you have trouble remembering the characters and who they are. You find yourself overwhelmed by the noise of crowds, and what is noisier than a high school class? You're retaining a lot of old knowledge, but it's really difficult for you to learn something new." She was summarizing but not answering my question.

"My friends and colleagues back East keep telling me not to give up hope, that I will soon be back with them."

Meggie O'Connor shook her head. "There's a difference between the well-meaning platitudes of friends and relatives and the reality of traumatic brain injury. The fastest recovery is in this first year, but the brain continues to heal in the second, third, and fourth years, making new connections. These connections are not the same as the former ones and neither are you. The 'old me' is gone, Tess. It's the 'new me' that you're in the process of creating."

"But I like the old me!" Much to my embarrassment, I began to weep. The old me was stoic; the new me cried at every opportunity.

The old me knew where she was going and loved her work as a teacher. The new me was a babbling idiot, unable to read adult books.

The old me could distinguish what was important from what was not. The new me couldn't even follow the sequence of a simple cookie recipe.

The old me was pretty happy, content with life. The new me felt like a failure, a nincompoop, a sappy, dependent, homeless wretch of a human being. Educated with a Ph.D., but nowhere to go.

Dr. Dodo, Dumbbell, Do-Nothing.

Meggie handed me a tissue. "Be gentle with the new you, Tess. She needs support and protection right now, as she is learning to walk."

"Crawl is more like it," I interjected. "I can't stop this damn crying."

"It's okay," she said. "Your tears are washing away the old path you were following. You're starting out on a new journey in your life."

"No, I'm like Hansel and Gretel, their trail of breadcrumbs being eaten up by the crows."

Dr. O'Connor's eyebrows raised at this reference to the Brothers Grimm. "'Tis true that they ended up at the witch's house, but in the original German version, it was their mother who put them in peril. She couldn't take care of them. You have to learn, Tess, to be a loving mother to the new you. You can't keep measuring yourself up to the old standards. It's not fair."

"What am I supposed to do? In the morning rehab program, we play stupid games that I can't do well. I keep coming up against blocks, dead end streets, confusion. When I'm tired, my brain goes on the fritz. I stare off into space, unable to do anything. If it weren't for Cassie and my need for her approval, I'd probably stay in bed most mornings."

Saying so much to the psychologist tired me out. I simply wanted to curl up on her sofa, bury my head into the couch pillow, and close my eyes.

"Be gentle with yourself, Tess. Be a good mother," she said in a soft voice.

Cassie grumbled about picking me up at the rehab program and dropping me off at L'Amical restaurant downtown. "I'll be back in an hour. I think this is a damn stupid thing, meeting with him before the divorce hearing."

I nodded to her as if she were right, but inside I felt excited to see Nick again. I held my breath as I opened the door and entered the restaurant.

With a boyish grin, Nick waved to me from the back, near the gas fireplace. He was wearing a familiar, turquoise blue shirt I'd given him on his thirty-fifth birthday. It looked really good on him. He stood up as I approached and wrapped me in a big hug. He seemed genuinely glad to see me. For a few seconds, I was able to inhale the scent of this handsome man that I'd known so well for such a long time.

He had ordered coffee for us both, making sure that mine had cream and sugar. I was pleased by this reference to our old routines.

Others in the restaurant were talking, so as he helped me take off my jacket, I retrieved my noise cancellation ear phones and placed them on my head.

"Oh ho, what are those? Are you communicating with aliens these days?" he asked.

"Nick, you've been the only alien in my landscape."

"Ouch." He made an exaggerated face of being wounded.

Silently, I cursed myself. I didn't want to be so blunt. Words had a way of tumbling out of my mouth before I could catch them and weigh their meanings.

"How are you doing these days? I mean it. I'm concerned about you, Tess. So much has happened to you in these past few months."

I could feel the tidal surge behind my eyes.

Damn it, I do not want to cry in front of him!

I bit down on my lower lip, causing external pain to divert my attention from what was happening inside. I gulped my coffee.

He reached out and took my hand in his. Touch had always been an important way for him to establish connection, whereas words used to be my friends. Now they too often betrayed me.

I kept silent.

"I want to be fair to you. I realize that you probably feel I brought you out here to the Midwest under false pretensions."

I nodded in agreement.

"But that's not the whole truth. I honestly did not know whether I wanted to stay with you or make a new life with Sandy. This move was the only way I could find out."

"The new you," I said, echoing Dr. O'Connor.

Nick looked puzzled and then said, "Well, yes. Living with Sandy does add new dimensions to my life that I didn't have with you, Tess." He pulled back his hand, so that now there was a gap, a separation between us. No touch.

I turned my hand over and studied the deep lines in the palm, trying to decipher the destiny of my life.

Shouldn't there be a strong line cut short, with a new branch above or below the cut?

"You will need one of the cars, and I'm willing to give you the newest one, the Prius. Plus, I won't contest the dog."

I looked up. "Imp. You now call her 'the dog'? You used to call her 'my baby.'"

"Tess, that's not what we're talking about. It's not important what I call her. She belongs with you. See, here's the scar where she bit me. That's about as clear a communication as you can get."

He flashed the back of his hand, briefly revealing two faint scars. "Besides, Sandy prefers cats."

Oh, Nick, how can you be talking about another woman? I loved you. I still love you, brain injury or not. Why do you sound like a stranger to me now? Where did you go?

I kept quiet.

"What else do you need from me, Tess?" Nick's face reflected utter concentration, compassion written in the wrinkles but underscored with a little tinge of anxiety.

I want, I need for you to hold me, Nick. To lie down on the bed beside you and snuggle into your strength, my nose against your chest. I want to tell you about my dreams, about the seaweed man, about my struggles with the brain injury. I want you to tell me that it will be okay, that you will love me, be there for me, that you will support whomever, whatever I'm becoming.

I looked at him and knew words would never express all that I felt. I smiled and said, "I could never be a cat, Nick. I don't like cats. They rub against you. Their love is conditional. I like dogs. I love Imp. She makes me laugh. She loves me, Nick."

I could see that Nick was really puzzled, frustrated by the new me. I was headed down a path, leaving behind a stunted trail of words. The psychologist part of him thought he should have been able to follow me, but I could clearly see that he was simply one of those fairy tale crows pecking away at my past.

Sonny

Chapter 22

• ◆ •

As I BECAME BETTER at reading faces, it was clear that the physicians were unhappy about the infection and the inability of the antibiotics to clear it from my body. They conferred over the X-rays that showed the infection slowly eating away at my bones, although I was experiencing no pain.

One benefit of being a quadriplegic. What goes on down below my neck is of no immediate sensate concern.

But no one would really spell out the implications of all this. I had to know because knowledge and the ability to say no was the only power left to me.

"Tell me the truth," I demanded of the most pliable member of the medical team: Jane Smith.

She held the medical reports in her lap, uncomfortable with being the messenger. "There's good news and bad news," she finally answered.

"Bad news first," I lipped.

"The infection is resistant to the antibiotic cocktails they've been giving you. All it does is buy you some time while it continues to do damage to your system. Your body is trying its best to fight the infection, and that's why you get the intermittent fevers. So, it's not a good prognosis."

So is my death the good news?

"Time. How much?"

"No one knows. Maybe months." She looked away, unwilling to look Death in the face. She waited while I digested this piece of information.

"Good news?" I tried to smile.

"Oh," she said. "The infection prevents them from shifting you out of the hospital to a nursing home. They have to control the fevers."

Good news, indeed. Is the hospital a better tomb than a nursing home?

"Would you like hospice to come visit you?"

End of the line treatment.

"No," I answered, then added, "Not yet."

What I really wanted to say was, *I'm nineteen years old. I've been accepted at Harvard with a full scholarship. I have a life ahead of me, something to show for all those lonely years in a Catholic boarding school. I've tried my best. I really have. I've been a good person, a worthy person. I'm too young to die.*

But I said none of this to Jane Smith.

"That's horrible," said Tess when I told her the news of the infection. "Surely there's something they can do to stop it!"

It pleased me to see her all riled up, but I held out no hope for any medical miracle.

Tess charged out of the room trying to find someone to talk to about my prognosis. She didn't return for a full half hour, but when she did, she couldn't hide the sense of defeat written on her face.

"They said we shouldn't give up hope, that maybe the antibiotics will finally do the trick."

But I could see that was not the whole truth. She was trying her best to cheer me up with a little dash of hope.

So, what's the big deal? I want to die, don't I?

It's just . . . that I'm not ready.

Yet.

Tess

Chapter 23

A COLD WIND AND SPACKLING RAIN blew across the Lake, presaging the chill of winter. Cassie turned on the windshield wipers as we pulled away from the hospital. My time with Sonny had been cut short due to my feeble attempts to find out what was really happening to him. In essence, the medical staff informed me that the infection would soon take Sonny's life. But I couldn't tell him that.

Burnt yellow leaves swirled in the wind. *How I wish that Sonny could hear the sound and witness the descending dance of maple leaves, instead of all the tubes running in and out of him, instead of the stillness in his body, instead of the bland walls of a hospital room.*

"I wish . . ." I said but stopped mid-sentence.

"I know," Cassie answered as if she could read my thoughts.

"I'm so goddamn helpless! I don't want him to die." The emotions in me were spiraling up. My breathing became shallow. Sad and stupid, that's how I felt.

"I know," Cassie said.

I looked at her, driving with ease, as if she had not a care in the world. Her brain worked normally, tackling problems, working out the steps 1, 2, 3, giving her the confidence that she would survive with grace. Not this herky-jerky world of mine where continents clashed and threw up mountains, where people you loved careened toward dangerous cliffs.

We stopped at the post office to collect mail—a few bills, a large, legal-looking manila folder for Cassie, an insurance check for me, and a postcard from a friend back East. Upon our arrival home, while I let out Imp, Cassie turned on her computer.

"Should I have told him the truth?" I poked my head into her study.

Cassie's shoulders slumped. "Oh, Tess, you ask such hard questions."

"I'm not sure I can do it," I said to the psychologist the next day. "Isn't it better for him to have hope? His world is grim enough."

Meggie O'Connor's expression reflected such sadness that it surprised me. I had thought therapists had to mask their emotions, lest they get in the way of the session.

"Sonny's become a really good friend, you know. He doesn't mind that it takes me a lot of time to figure things out. He's patient when I can't understand his lip movements. Here I am, with over sixteen years on him, and yet sometimes he seems wiser and older than I. How can I do this to him?"

"I know the situation. Hawk's been there every day."

"He really likes your husband."

"The two of you are the most important people in Sonny's life right now. You're letting Sonny know that even if he can't move his body at all, he's still himself; he's still important; he still has the ability to inspire others. You've given him the gift of friendship, and he has returned that to you. Simple but profound."

I grimaced in a self-mocking way. "You mean the blind helping the lame to walk."

"But the physicians may be right."

I didn't like the sound of this.

She explained, "Hawk tells me that when he prays for Sonny at night, the owl always answers."

I waited, trying not to breathe, trying to hold time at a standstill for what I didn't want to hear.

"In the Native American world, the owl is often the harbinger of death," she continued. "As a psychologist, I know that there are many kinds of deaths. There's that passage that we all eventually make when we cross over into the next dimension. But there is also the death of the old self."

"The old me."

Meggie smiled. "The truth is that without death, there cannot be life. The point is to live now, to live fully within your capacity, to help Sonny live as full a life as possible within his limitations."

"The new me. The new him."

"So what does the new you want to do with what the doctors told you about him?"

I hadn't the foggiest idea.

A telephone call from Sally McGovern awaited me upon my return back to Hagen's Heaven, asking if I would like to join her for dinner. One look at Cassie's glum face as she pored over the accounts and bills made me eager to spread my wings.

"Do you mind if I go?" I asked Cassie.

She didn't even look up from her desk but waved her hand, a gesture of yes and goodbye and don't bother me now.

I returned the call and Sally agreed to pick me up. Strange, how this simple act of going out to dinner with a new friend meant so much to me, a slice of normality.

I tied a reddish orange silk scarf around my neck, a dash of color on a blue turtleneck blouse and black pants. What a relief to be done with the walker. On my ear lobes, I hung deep blue, glass earrings that reflected the light around me. Yes, I could look in the mirror, and except for the fuzziness of my peripheral vision, I looked like the old me. Not beautiful, but pretty.

I didn't even know whether Sally McGovern was aware of my brain injury. The mischievous thought crossed my mind that perhaps I wouldn't tell her, or at least I wouldn't tell her until the evening was almost over. I knew there was something I was forgetting, but I couldn't think of what it was.

Imp, meanwhile, was pressing her nose against my leg, letting me know it was time for her to be fed. Cassie had decided that maybe Imp's wasting problem was due to the dry food we were giving her, so she insisted we cook up layered casseroles for her full of rice, vegetables, and chopped chicken or beef. Imp was living the high life. Where before she had approached her bowl with disdain, Imp now became insistent at mealtime.

I got out the casserole and spooned a cup of it into her bowl. Imp began whining in anticipation. She couldn't resist inching toward the bowl, led by a nose sniffing all the delicious contents, but she knew better than to start eating until I gave her the signal.

"Okay!" I said.

That's all it took for her to begin wolfing down the food. It didn't take long to eat, but Imp lingered, licking the bowl again and again, trying to conjure up any hidden morsel.

A knock upon the door, and there stood Sally, dressed smartly in a brown skirt, sweater, and calf-high boots.

"I made reservations for the two of us at the Riverside Inn," she said.

What a relief that she didn't bring that Mr. Mudge with her.

She knelt down to ruffle Imp's ears. "I wish we could take you too, but they don't allow cute little dogs like you in restaurants." She frowned and Imp simply wagged her tail in response.

I shrugged on my coat, yelled goodbye to Cassie who was upstairs, and left with Sally. Something was nagging at my attention, but again nothing popped into my fragmented brain.

"Thank you for accepting my invitation," she said, navigating the twists and turns of the driveway in her car. "It can get really claustrophobic up here on the peninsula when all the summer people have gone. It's nice not to have to fight the crowds, but I miss certain people." Then she turned and gave me a full smile. "So, when I met you, I said to myself, 'Here is a new friend.'"

She couldn't see the light glowing inside of me. *A new friend.*

"Well, I'm glad too."

"Are you a relative of Mrs. McDermott?"

"You mean Cassie?" I shook my head.

How was I going to explain my relationship with Cassie without giving away my rather desperate circumstances?

"Smudge is rather harsh in his judgment of her."

Smudge? Is that what she calls Spenser Mudge?

"Cassie's a wonderful person. She saved my life. I'll never be able to repay her for that." I knew I sounded a bit defensive.

But Sally didn't seem to take offense. "Oh, don't pay any attention to Smudge. He growls a lot because he lives in the land of what ifs. Life to him is always a missed opportunity to become whatever his latest fantasy is of himself."

"Are you two married?"

That resulted in a big laugh. "Heavens no! We don't even live together. Look, if you stay in this area, you're going to find out that sex in the sticks is not the same as sex in the city. Smudge's a good looking guy, a bit on the stodgy side, but he knows how to have a good time. So, you take what you can get up here, if you know what I mean."

I looked out the window at the encroaching darkness. As we whizzed by a field, three does picked up their heads, made nervous by the car headlights. How precious was the sight of them, as they leaned into the darkness of the surrounding tree line; how quickly gone was the vision.

"We are here but a moment," I said.

"What?" asked Sally.

Cassie was used to my speaking out of context, unable at times to follow the normal flow of a conversation. I think she rather enjoyed that quirk of my brain's short-circuits.

When I didn't answer, Sally smoothed over the gap, the hole I had made in the conversation.

"So, are you married, Tess?"

"Yes, but not for long." I then told her the sad tale of Nick's pursuit of an old high school girlfriend.

"I think I've met Sandy Hufnagle at a party," Sally said. "She didn't seem like the kind of person who would do that. But, like I said, there isn't a lot of choice up here for a woman."

Sally pulled the car into a parking space. She linked arms with me as we walked toward the restaurant. "C'mon, let's go have a drink or two or three and put the problem of men into a more proper perspective."

I had a light beer, not wanting to bring on one of those horrible headaches, while Sally drank a single malt whiskey. "Part of my Irish heritage," she said. "They say that the only difference between an Irish funeral and an Irish wedding is one less drunk."

She regaled me with stories of her various jobs in a glass factory, a chocolate production line and a used car lot, before she returned to college and graduate school. "That's how I ended up as a high school teacher in Suttons Bay teaching American history."

"No."

"Yes."

"But I'm a high school teacher too. English."

That's when Sally jumped up and gave me a big hug. "See, I knew you were going to be a good friend. Imagine that. Where are you assigned?"

Whoosh, I could feel the elation slipping away from me.

"I taught at a private school in Cambridge, Massachusetts, before coming up here with Nick. I've not explored teacher requirements up here."

"Oh." A look of disappointment washed over Sally's face. "Well, I can help you with that."

"I'm not sure that's what I want to do anymore."

A puzzled frown replaced the disappointment.

"Maybe it's time for me to think of a second career," I stammered. "I'd like to write and . . ."

It's taking too much energy to cover up the truth. I can feel fatigue settling over me.

The waitress rescued me from this moment of shame by serving our appetizers.

Sally wisely dropped the whole subject of my future career and instead concentrated on my marital problems. The food was elegant, a visual as well as a gustatory delight. I ordered the white fish, gulping a bit at the expense of the entree, but I was determined to show Sally that I could afford such an expense.

"And how about you?" I asked. "Did you ever get married?"

She laughed. "Four times."

"Four times?"

"First there was the high school sweetheart, Smitty. Nice guy but not much up here." She tapped the side of her head. "At that age, you think looks are the most important asset to a man. He was on the football team. You know, the muscular type. He decided not to go to college but to sell used cars. It didn't last but two years before the boredom drove me crazy."

I could see Sally as a high school cheerleader.

"Then I fell for Roger, one of my college professors. He was the one who got me interested in American history. He wore rumpled corduroy suits, sported bushy hair, smoked a pipe, and spouted all kinds of interesting but trivial facts. I thought he was the smartest man I'd ever met. I was totally in awe of him and didn't think that the age difference of twenty-six years made the slightest bit of difference. I felt elevated in his presence. But once married and living day by day with him, I discovered he was not only brilliant but moody, childish in his demands to be pampered, and he drank too much. That marriage lasted five years and probably would have gone on longer, but he began to take up with yet another bright-eyed student."

"I'm sorry," I said, having so recently experienced that kind of abandonment.

"No, really. Although I didn't realize it at the time, it was for the best. I'd have probably ended up with a hypochondriacal old geezer by now."

Sally started in on her third glass of wine.

I made a note to myself to offer to drive home, even though I hadn't driven since the accident.

"It was the third marriage that broke my heart. Todd was good looking, bright, and going somewhere in his life. He didn't seem to mind that I had been married twice before, whereas he had only one divorce to his name. We had lots of fun together, lots of late night talks. In our early thirties, we agreed to start a family, and I got pregnant soon after we got married."

"So you have children then?"

Sally shook her head. "No. Todd died in an automobile accident. A drunk guy shot through a stop sign and slammed into the driver's door. Todd didn't have a chance. I thought I'd at least have his child, but then I had a miscarriage."

Even now, the memory of those events flushed her face with sadness. She looked away.

I reached out and touched her hand with mine.

She let herself linger in the moment, then pulled her hand away. "You'd think that after Todd, I'd have been able to make better choices, but I fell for the first sympathetic widower who came along. We tried our best to merge our separate griefs, but both of us fell far short of the dead spouses. That marriage lasted only four months before we had the sense to call it quits. His name was Mark. I've heard, via the grapevine, that he has since remarried and it appears to be a good one for him. I wish him no ill. So there you have it. I've been single now for over eight years. I think I've given up on the institution of marriage. It's a bit like golf. You can only hit so many mulligans before you have to accept your lot."

Sally finished her glass of wine. "You know how when a wind storm comes up and tree limbs fall and your power goes out in the house? Then you take your car and you drive up and down the road, hoping that everybody else is without power too, because that means the power company will be under more pressure to get you back up on the grid."

I nodded.

Sally reached over and touched my hand this time. "It feels good to share my marital history with someone who is going through some of the same issues."

"A massive power failure," I quipped.

"Exactly."

After dessert, we lingered a bit. Sally wanted to know more about Cambridge. I asked her about the Leelanau Peninsula and whether she thought it was a good place to live year-round.

"Beautiful and isolating," she answered, letting me draw my own conclusions.

Time to go. I reached into my pocketbook to pull out a credit card, but my wallet wasn't there.

That's what I had forgotten. I had left it on my bed, after extracting my medical card to give to Cassie. She needed it to communicate with the hospital about all the expenses of my forty-day coma, as the figures and numbers were too much for my confused brain.

"I forgot my wallet," I mumbled, embarrassed and ashamed.

"My treat," said Sally.

"But it's so expensive," I protested.

"Yes, but I hope that we will have more restaurant adventures. So you can pay next time." Sally smiled at me.

I thought, *Now I have three friends: Cassie, Sonny, and Sally.*

No, make that four friends.

I can't forget the loyalty of my sweet little Imp.

Sonny

Chapter 24

•◆•

NOT MANY PEOPLE KNOW *how they are going to die. I'm going to be eaten away by bacteria, bones first, then the major organs. It will be a cascading shut-down. The extremities will probably turn blue as the circulation shrinks back to the core. What will go first—the liver, the kidneys, the heart?*

Nobody is going to spell this all out to me. Too gruesome. Instead, they will give me gentle lies, reassure me that time is still on my side, but I will be able to tell from their faces the state of the body's corruption, dissolution, putrefaction. At least the hospital environment will prevent the black flies and maggots from heralding my imminent departure.

I wonder if Jesus, forewarned of his death, thought about the process of dying? At least he had an audience of worshipers, marking his every groan. At least, he felt the pain of a body in its last throes.

Me? I feel nothing but the heat of a recurrent fever.

Depression curled around my psyche like a warm blanket. I wanted grief, sadness, a touch of anger, maybe a healthy dose of denial, but what I got instead was a slowing down, a shrinking inward, a need to fall asleep. If only the sleep could have remained constant, but it was fitful and full of dreams.

I thought that this time I might be allowed on the paddle steamer, given admission by the bewhiskered ticket master, but I could not find the black river, the Styx, anywhere in my imagination. Nor was the seaweed king of Tess' dreams making any kind of appearance. The approaching wreck of my life was not finding any symbolic sea stage in dreamland.

Instead I found myself dreaming of Tess.

In bare feet, she approaches my bed in a white willowy dress, translucent enough to show the outline of her naked body. She laughs and strokes my cheek, as if in a ballet, all grace and goodness. She winks merrily, then kisses me on the mouth, a sweet taste of summer melon. With great purpose, she blows into my ear, grasps my hands, and pulls me upright. My feet find purchase on the floor.

She curtseys, an invitation to dance. I am dressed in a ruffled shirt and white satin pants with buckled, heeled shoes. Tess looks country western in a twentieth century outfit whilst I look like a French courtesan from the eighteenth century, without the powdered wig. Time has escaped me.

We start with a bow and curtsy, then graduate to complicated footwork, twists, and turns. The heat is rising between us. We are alone in this dance, she and I. Not another person around us. I am flattered by her flirtations and her beauty, which I had not really noticed before. I am hungry for her touch and want to embrace her, to slow down the dance, which seems to be getting more frantic in tempo. I want to hold her and stop time from moving forward.

I think I am falling in love with her.

I woke up with a sigh and tried my best to go back into that pleasurable dream, but the sound of the ventilator wheezing and breezing for me tethered me to the hospital room. I laughed at the absurdity of it all—me as the fop, Tess as the virgin. If the truth were known, I was the virgin and sorry for it. While fantasies flourished in a Catholic boarding school, reality was another matter.

How can I love Tess when I barely know her? Yes, we have both been in a dance around our separate disabilities. Yes, we both have our secrets and our unimpaired imaginations. But there the similarities end. I am young, untried, about to enter college, my future profession unknown, my future wife not yet encountered. She is married, soon to be divorced, with a Ph.D. in English, years of teaching, and certainly no virgin.

Our lives have been thrown into a swirling limbo, mine with a definite ending, hers with a long period of recovery and uncertainty. Both of us unable to go home again.

Love her?

Get a grip!

She's too old for me.

I'm too crippled for her.

It's weird that when you try so hard to face death with a sense of courage and integrity, your imagination throws life back at you in unforeseen ways.

Hawk interrupted one of my sleeping/dream cycles. I awoke to find him scanning my body with his hands, eyes closed, lips moving in silent prayer. When he opened his eyes to see me watching him, he smiled, then touched my head and cheeks in a manner like a priest, making the blessing of a cross.

"For old times' sake," he said.

"I'm not a Catholic," I lipped.

"The Bible says we see through a glass darkly. I like that. If any of us had a clear image of the Creator, we'd probably melt. Too bright, too big for the human mind. The darkness shades us. We only see specks, true of every religion. The moon, Sonny, is always safer than the sun. Reflected light."

I waited for the exhale of the ventilator, because what I had to say was important. I wanted to hear my own voice, my own words. "I am . . . going . . . to die," I sputtered.

"Yes," he answered with no rebuttal, bullshit, or platitudes.

"Soon," I added for dramatic effect.

"Yes, soon," he answered.

I waited for him to say more but he kept quiet, not out of any awkwardness, but out of respect, an acknowledgment of my statement.

Silence ensued.

"Help me?" I didn't know whether I was asking a question or begging for an answer.

Hawk cupped his hands around my head. "Yes."

A surge of energy flowed from his electric hands into my head, followed by a release into serenity and surrender: a sense of safety because this man was going to lead me into death's embrace.

Love arrives in many disguises.

Tess

Chapter 25

MY ATTORNEY CALLED ME early in the morning to notify us that a date had been set by the court for the pre-divorce hearing. He reassured me that he had sent in the information from the neurologist, the neuro-ophthalmologist, and the psychologist, all testifying to my inability to work at the present time. Having a strongly documented disability would make the court much more inclined to grant me a financially favorable settlement.

"Besides medical coverage, the car, and money to live on for several years, is there anything else you need?" the attorney asked.

"An apology would be nice."

We both laughed.

"One other thing," I added.

"What's that?"

"I'd like my maiden name back, Tess Thornhill. The old me," I explained.

At the rehab center, they assigned me to plan, grocery shop, and make a meal for the other patients. With staff assistance, I worked out a shopping list for beans, ground turkey, tomato sauce, chili seasoning. They helped me figure out the amounts needed but then asked whether I thought of any additional elements to the meal. I added lettuce, carrots, celery, and salad dressing to the list. They gently suggested a loaf of bread, butter, and dessert. One of the therapists accompanied me to Oleson's grocery store where I picked up the items. Then I threw the chili ingredients together in a big pot and set it to simmering. I cut up the carrots and celery, washed the lettuce, and emptied it all into a salad bowl. I put out the butter and sliced the bread. Everything was ready for lunchtime.

When one brain-damaged adolescent client served himself and started to gobble down the food, I confronted him and told him to watch his manners and wait for the others. He glared at me, but the old schoolmarm voice still carried power. He stopped and propped his elbows defiantly on the table. The staff heaped praise upon me, little knowing that I used to be seen by my friends as a gourmet chef. Now the brain injury had reduced me to the simplest of cooks.

Still, it felt nice to accomplish even that one small step toward independent living.

With renewed self-confidence, I left the program and headed to the hospital. The wind gust shifted from wintry nips to pockets of sunlit warmth. Nick had once warned me that fall on the outer rim of Michigan was moody, unable to decide between summer and winter, one day cold, one day hot. The native population used to camp on the Leelanau Peninsula from late spring to the onset of winter, as the mighty Lake Michigan, heated by the summer sun, kept the area warmer for a much longer time than the state's interior. Conversely, the cooling of the water during winter prevented spring from arriving at the coastal areas until long after the interior had already sprouted trillium, columbine, jack in the pulpits, tulips, and daffodils.

Being a New Englander, fall was always my favorite time of the year due to its display of startling colors before the barren introspection of winter. The sun was in retreat, and the days were getting shorter. The trees in Michigan had already shed much of their foliage, leaving the cedar and pine woods to stand out in their dark green robes. I was grateful for the annual cycle of life, death, and rebirth. Unlike Sonny, I did not come from a religious background, but still I felt there was a Presence behind this great drama of nature.

I wondered what Sonny truly believed, as he thought about the value of life and the meaning of death. At some level he knew the truth of his circumstances, despite my cowardice and empty words of hope. Dr. O'Connor had gently shown me that I had withheld the truth not so much from Sonny but from myself. I did not, I could not, look death in the eye.

When I entered his hospital room, Sonny broke into a smile as wide as I had ever seen. His eyes were clear and his look intense.

"Tess, come here," he lipped.

I thought perhaps he had an itch to be scratched and situated myself by the bed.

"Closer," he whispered.

I leaned over to catch what he was about to say. His lips brushed my cheek, then gave my lips a peck. I jerked back in surprise. "Sonny!"

He grinned at his trick.

This is a joke, isn't it?

I pretended to scold him but kept my distance.

"What's that about?" I asked.

He began to lip talk quickly, but I couldn't understand what he was saying.

"Slow down," I said.

I had to lean in closer but not so close as to encounter those wandering lips.

What's he trying to tell me?

"Tess," he was saying. "Come lie with me."

I looked at him and realized he was serious.

His eyes, while merry, were also pleading.

Two things happened at once inside of me. First the thought: *Desperate times call for desperate measures.*

Then tears sprang up, unbidden, because something in Sonny's demeanor touched me at the core. I turned away, lest he see the tears and think I was crying out of pity for him.

Oh Sonny, why does life do this to us?

I was crying for myself as much as for him.

I did not want to be chickenshit, so I turned around and gathered the tears from my cheek and traced them down his cheek, then reached over and kissed him on the mouth.

"You are such a naughty boy," I scolded him in a mocking voice.

He kept a steady gaze on me, neither smiling nor frowning, a pensive look as if he knew that was the most that was going to happen. Then he struggled to speak in the exhales of the ventilator, knowing I would pay close attention to what he had to say.

"Thank you."

On the way home, Cassie noted my silence. "Did anything happen at the rehab program?"

"I cooked a meal for everyone."

"Well, that's a sign of progress, isn't it?"

I shrugged my shoulders.

"What's bothering you? Is it the hearing that's coming up?"

I shook my head. How was I going to put into words the jumble of emotions I felt?

"Something changed between Sonny and me today." It was the best I could do.

"Oh?"

"Why can't men be more like women? Uncomplicated relationships."

Cassie threw a sharp look at me. "Women are uncompli-cated? What planet do you live on?" she sputtered. "Do you think Natalie Hagen and I could have had an uncomplicated relationship? It would have been like one bone between two terriers."

Then she stopped, realizing she had let me off the hook. "So," she said, "he's sweet on you."

I nodded.

"What's the harm in that, Tess? It's not like he's going anywhere or can do anything about it."

Little does she know.

I remembered what Dr. O'Connor said about the healing

effect of facing the truth, not being ashamed of one's own feelings. I forced myself to be honest.

"It's not him that worries me, Cassie. It's me."

"You're just lonely. It's a reaction to losing Nick," she said.

No, it's not. Something has changed between Sonny and me.

But the old me decided not to risk any more dismissal of what the new me was feeling.

We stopped by the post office where we both retrieved official-looking letters. Mine was a letter from the court setting the date of the pre-divorce hearing. Cassie tossed her unopened letter into a small box on the backseat to be read later. Only after arriving at the house did she pick up the envelope. The darkening look on her face as she read the letter spelled big trouble. When she finished it, she slammed the document down on the kitchen table.

"What's the matter?"

Cassie's eyes were slitted in pure malice. "If they think they can blackmail me into giving up this place . . ." She didn't finish the sentence before storming out of the kitchen, heading for the telephone.

I probably had no business doing so, but I was curious. I picked up the document. It was from the legal firm of Jason and Carr, stating that Natalie Hagen's nephew, Spenser Mudge, was instituting a suit against one Cassidy McDermott with regard to the ownership of "Hagen's Heaven." In the suit, Mr. Mudge asserted that (1) Natalie Hagen was not of sound mind and body when she left everything to Devin McDermott and that (2) circumstances and the possible involvement of Mrs. Cassidy McDermott with regard to the deaths of both Natalie

Hagen and Devin McDermott raised suspicions as to the actions of Mrs. Cassidy McDermott. The firm of Jason and Carr, however, stated that Mrs. McDermott could spare herself the public examination of these issues by restoring the rightful ownership of "Hagen's Heaven" to the aforementioned party of Mrs. Natalie Hagen's nephew, Mr. Spenser Mudge, and all such other claims would then be dismissed.

I could hear Cassie in the other room leaving a long and agitated message on the telephone for her lawyer to call her as soon as possible. I quickly put down the letter.

This was too much for my tired mind. Already a headache was taking possession. Off I went to find my medication and get it down before my head exploded. One quick look at Cassie's face and I kept on going with a lot of unanswered questions in my brain.

Why are there any suspicions about Devin McDermott's death? Cassie told me he accidentally fell off a bridge and drowned.

I can't trust that man on the driveway, despite what Sally McGovern says. It's all about greed and throwing manure up in the air, hoping it'll land and fertilize something.

There's got to be something I can do to help Cassie!

Jonny

Chapter 26

"REVENGE, REVENGE is what I desire" were the first words out of Tess when she came into my hospital room. At first, I was afraid she was referring to me.

Was I too forward with her yesterday? Who knows how a woman's mind works?

But no, I was irrelevant to her current passion. She detailed the threat of legal action against Cassie, saying she needed to do something to help, something to derail Spenser Mudge. Then she looked at me and said, "You've got the brains. I've got the willpower and the means to carry out a plan. What should we do about this?"

I savored the "we."

"It has . . . to be . . . legal," I lipped. I didn't want Tess to end up in jail.

"His girlfriend, Sally, is becoming a friend of mine. She could be a good source of information to us but . . ." Tess paused. "I don't want to hurt our friendship."

"Anonymous revenge," I said.

She nodded.

What Tess didn't know was that I was a master at this kind of plotting, honed by years at an all-male boarding school where revenge is a practiced art, where I had presented the sweet face of Jesus to the adults but the demonic face of Beelzebub to my peers.

"Discover . . . his strengths," I said in the exhale of the breathing machine.

"His strengths?" she said. "I'd rather know his weaknesses, his liabilities."

What I had to say could not be said in two words. "Come . . . closer," I whispered.

"Ha! I know that trick." Still she edged closer, watching me closely. It pleased me to see the shadows of ambivalence ripple across her face, a smile edged by the creases of nervousness.

I spoke very slowly with my lips. "His strengths . . . are his . . . weakness. Over-reliance."

That was a secret I had discovered a long time ago. People will automatically go towards what they do best, leaving other skills undeveloped in their pursuit of perfection. Know their strengths and you will know their weaknesses.

Our eyes locked as she waited for me to say more.

I have a million and one things I want to tell you, Tess. I want to tell you of my dreams cut short, where I was going in my life. I want you to know of my potential. I want you to see me, neither as a bodiless mind nor a black Jesus. I am teetering on the edge, Tess, and still I want to taste life in all its fullness.

"My name . . . is Sonny."

"Of course, and mine is Tess, soon to be Tess Thornhill." She was replying on automatic, her eyes uncertain as to the meaning of our exchange.

She doesn't get it.

"Cogito . . . ergo sum." *I think, therefore I am.*

"I disagree," she answered. "You are more than your mind, Sonny. You are more than your feelings. You are more than your body. I think I would call it 'a soul,' and a deep one at that. You confuse me. Am I being too honest here? Dr. O'Connor has been telling me to get real. I'm trying, Sonny. I really am."

Tess sometimes had a way of letting words rear up and fall around her like a wild team of horses, their reins suddenly cut, moving quickly in different directions.

"Like right now, I thought you wanted to kiss me. Should I let you? Should I reach over and kiss you first? What do I want? Where is all this going? Why am I so confused? I mean, we're friends, really good friends, but we're at different stages of our lives. Oh hell, I don't mean it like that, Sonny. I really don't. It's just that . . ." she stopped, mid-sentence.

I waited, curious to see where all this was going.

Then she reached down and carefully cradled the back of my neck with her hands and raised my head to her lips. She kissed me.

Oh where are the hands, the arms to rise up and embrace her? All I have are my lips, my thoughts, my eyes, and the taste of her in my mouth.

She lowered my head, smiling and grimacing in alternate manner. "See? That's what I'm trying to tell you. It's wrong, so wrong."

"No," I lipped, smiling and amused at her discomfort.

Blushing, Tess backed away. She grabbed her pocketbook from the chair. "I gotta go now. Be thinking about Spenser Mudge and help me come up with a plan."

But I had no intention of giving my thoughts over to Mr. Mudge while still relishing the sweet imprint of Tess' mouth upon mine.

When Hawk arrived, he found me indulging in delightful daydreams, all having to do with Tess.

"You're looking better today."

I lipped, "The lunacy of love."

"Ah, the tidal urges that have drowned many a man on his spiritual passage." Hawk laughed. "Been there, done that."

I thought of Tess' seaweed king and all the dead people in his underwater principality.

Were they also on a spiritual passage and doomed by heeding the sirens' call?

"Tess," I explained.

I waited for him to tell me that she was too old and struggling with brain trauma, that I was too young and about to die.

Instead, he replied, "The moon is a harsh mistress."

I frowned.

"It's an old song," he explained.

Tess

Chapter 27

· ◆ ·

ON THE WAY HOME, Cassie was uncharacteristically silent, lost in thought, with tension and anxiety coursing through her. Her fingers tapped on the steering wheel. She honked at an older person whose car was moving at a snail's pace. She took the corners too fast and crested fifteen miles over the speed limit, until I yelled out, "Slow down! There's a doe there, wanting to cross the road."

She slammed on the brakes, then pulled over to the side of the road, stopping the car entirely. "I'm sorry, Tess." She lowered her head to the steering wheel, as the doe jumped back into the safety of the woods.

"Are you all right? I could try driving. Nobody's taken away my license."

Cassie raised her head in weary fashion. "And get us both killed?" She wiped away emerging tears, saying "Damn allergy."

"It's hardly pollen season," I said.

"It's that letter that came from the lawyers," she explained.

"But it has no merit, so why worry?"

"Because you need a lawyer to fight such a suit, and I don't have the money."

I could have kicked myself for being so insensitive. The brain injury sometimes made me ignore the obvious.

"I could sell my car, Cassie. You could use that money. Smudge, I mean Mr. Mudge, is the one who has to prove that Natalie Hagen was incompetent at the time she wrote her will."

She smiled and patted my knee. "Sweet of you, but it's more complicated than that."

"How so? I mean he could say she was overwhelmed by grief over the loss of her husband, but she'd have to show signs of dementia or mental illness to be seen as incompetent."

"Mr. Mudge sent me a box containing a Xeroxed copy of Natalie's diary."

"Any evidence of insanity?"

Cassie shook her head.

"Well, there you have it. He stupidly gave you the ammo to fight this suit." I was pleased at how smart I sounded.

Cassie looked over at me. "I read the whole damn document last night . . ." She grimaced. "Detailing the love affair between Natalie and my husband. It had been going on for years. All those business trips he took to Chicago."

"Oh, Cassie, I'm sorry." I reached out and touched her arm.

In the dying light of the afternoon, the sun was not kind to Cassie's face. The pale rays wrinkled across her face, making her look older than seventy-three.

How awful to read the words of her husband's mistress. It would be like my invading Sandy Hufnagle's e-mail account of the past year; no, it's much worse. Cassie was married for a very long time to Devin and this affair was not a one-night stand by any stretch of the imagination.

I didn't know the right words of comfort.

Should I show anger at Devin or Natalie? Should I tell Cassie everything will work out okay, that it just takes time?

Meanwhile the doe, sensing no movement on the road, ventured out from the dark woods, sniffed the air for predators, and then strode cautiously across the pavement, making it to the other side, her ears twitching to catch any suspicious sound.

She knows the world is dangerous. What makes us human beings think otherwise?

Cassie started up the car and pulled out onto the road. Her face sagged with fatigue. "It's not like I didn't have any suspicions, but I adored him. I didn't want to know."

She wiped her brow with one hand while steering with the other. "Like me, Natalie's husband was in the dark for a very long time. Apparently a colleague of his spotted Devin and Natalie at a Chicago hotel. Her cover had been that she was on the board of an art museum in Chicago and had to attend frequent board meetings. Suspicious, he checked with the art museum and discovered that the board rarely met."

"Ouch."

"The diary, of course, records only one person's point of view. When her husband first confronted her, she initially lied about it but then acknowledged the affair. He vacillated between threats of divorce and bouts of violence. She promised not to see Devin again, because in her own way, she did love her husband. There's a lot of suffering in the diary about the hurt she caused him by the affair. She didn't see Devin for seven months."

Cassie absentmindedly fingered her gold wedding band. "I thought back to that period, how depressed Devin appeared. I suspected his business investments weren't doing well. Little did I know that his depression was due to being deprived of Natalie's company."

She laughed. "Ironic, isn't it? When she picked back up with him, his mood improved dramatically. In turn, that made me happy. Life is very confusing, Tess."

"But why did Mr. Mudge send you the diary?"

"It lends motive to both the suspicious deaths of Natalie and Devin, as I became the only one to inherit the two estates. I suppose one could also try to make the case of emotional instability on her part, that she couldn't keep the promise she'd made her husband. I don't know. Maybe he simply sent it to hurt me. In that, he succeeded. I want to hate her. Does that sound strange?"

I thought of my encounter with Sandy. "No. But Natalie's change of mind is not a sign of instability. It was simply a woman's prerogative."

Cassie laughed, then gripped my hand. "You're a good girl, Tess."

"Yeah, that's what they all say. I think the car accident dented my halo, though."

Once we got back to Hagen's Heaven, I immediately called Sally McGovern and suggested we go out to dinner.

"Sure. When?" she asked.

"How about tonight? Can you pick me up?"

Sally mentioned all the papers she had to grade and her fatigue from the day of teaching.

"My treat," I said.

"I'll see you in about forty-five minutes."

Sally was kind. She drove us to Martha's Leelanau Table in Suttons Bay, known for its excellent cuisine and moderate prices.

"How was your day?" I asked as we settled napkins upon our laps and perused the varied menu.

"I need a drink," she answered. "And yours?"

"Interesting."

She looked up at me with a questioning expression on her face. "Yes?"

"How well do you really know Spenser Mudge?"

"Smudge? Well enough that he's now on my shit list."

"Why? I thought you enjoyed him."

"He broke up with me. I deserve a pomegranate martini."

"Make that two, please," I told the waiter. "What happened?"

There was an amused glint in her eye. "I'm not sure. It could have been my calling him 'stuffy' but I rather think it's because of you."

"Me? What have I done to him?"

"It's the company you keep."

"You mean Cassie? What's his problem? Tell me about him. What does he do for a living? What does he enjoy doing for fun? What are his particular strengths?"

The waiter returned with our drinks, and Sally took a long sip. "Why all these questions of a sudden? Are you developing an interest in him? If so, good luck." She took a much longer sip.

"He's on my shit list too."

Sally raised her eyebrows and grinned.

"But I can't go into why right now," I said, not wanting to compromise Cassie's position.

"Okay," said Sally. She raised her martini glass in a toast. "To shit lists and men who make our lives miserable. I'll tell you everything I know about him."

Sonny

Chapter 28

I WANTED TO STAY awake for Tess' afternoon visit, but I could feel the fever taking over and dragging me into an equatorial abyss. The newest combination of antibiotics was ceding ground before the onslaught of the bacterial troops. The worried look on the nurses' faces didn't offer me much comfort. They sponged my forehead with wet compresses.

Oh Tess, come quick before I fade away from this life.

Across the stage of my imagination slid the image of Sleeping Beauty lying in a glass coffin, all white and Disneyfied, waiting for her prince to awaken her with a magic kiss.

A black man doesn't get a glass coffin or the option of royal intervention.

Oh Tess, come kiss me awake.

But the clock hands barely budged, except for moments I fell into feverish naps.

I struggled to emerge from my fitful nap to the sound of the privacy curtain being brushed aside, but it wasn't Princess Charming or Tess. Rather it was Hawk surveying the battlefield of my body with his hands.

"Who's . . . winning?" I whispered on the ventilator's exhale.

He paid me no mind but continued in quiet concentration, his hands moving in ever smaller circles above my body.

I fell asleep.

When I next awoke, he was standing by the bed in such a way that he was able to place one hand behind my neck, one hand on my forehead. His eyes were closed but his lips were moving. Again, I felt a surge of energy flowing into my head.

And promptly fell back to sleep again.

When I awoke, he was gone and the fever had broken. I was a sweaty mess, but I knew I was going to survive the day.

A very pretty young nurse's aide came into the room and said, "You're looking a lot better. Is it okay if I give you a sponge bath?"

Only if I can continue to look at your loveliness while you do it.

But, of course, I said no such thing. I gave her a big smile of consent.

Tess arrived in the afternoon, unaware of the morning crisis. She was bubbling over with news she wanted to share with me.

"Sally and I had dinner last night. I remembered what you said about discovering Mr. Mudge's strengths. Spenser is the business manager of a new winery on the peninsula. He dresses the part and roams the tasting room as if he's some big wine connoisseur. He was hired due to old-time connections in the area, thus bringing in not only the locals but also the summer people. He does have an MBA and some managerial background. His strength is his self-presentation."

"His persona," I lipped.

"The vintner doesn't think much of him, but as long as they stay out of each other's hair, they co-exist. The owner from downstate is another matter. He demanded that they produce an award-winning wine for the publicity and keep costs to a minimum. But it's a new winery and the vineyard is still young. Much to everyone's surprise, their Entre-Nous Chardonnay won Best of Class in the Michigan Wine Competition this past August and that brought in a lot of good publicity and customers."

"Did you . . . bring me . . . some?"

"Hush. I'm about to get to the good part here. The white wines are all labeled as from the Leelanau Peninsula. Legally, that means eighty percent of the grapes have to be grown on the peninsula. Mr. Mudge confessed one night to Sally that their award-winning chardonnay actually only contains thirty percent of grapes from this area; the other seventy percent come from a vineyard in the downstate Paw Paw area of Southwest Michigan. The owner doesn't want to know the details so as to appear that his hands are clean, so Spenser Mudge and the new vintner would be the obvious scapegoats if the secret ever got out."

Tess stroked his cheek. "You really are a genius, Sonny. Mr. Mudge's need to look good has propelled him to perform unethical business practices. The funny thing is that he likes to throw around all these terms like 'a bit oaky' or 'with a hint of grapefruit' or 'dry but with an aftertaste of almonds' to describe the wines, when he really doesn't like wine at all. He makes it all up but does it with great flourish. At home, he only drinks beer or single malt whiskey."

"A ham," I lipped.

"A stuffed pig I'd say, wanting what doesn't belong to him. Imagine accusing Cassie of . . ." Tess sputtered.

"Murder?"

There, I've said it. Put it out in the open.

"She didn't do it," Tess insisted, her voice a tad louder and defensive to the core.

"You sure?"

"Sonny, how can you even suggest such a thing? You've met Cassie. She saved my life."

She brought you to me. I'm grateful. But I want to protect you, Tess.

"Ask her," I croaked in the exhale of the ventilator.

Tess stepped back and looked at me as if I were a cobra about to strike.

"Ask her," I said.

It was a sacrifice and a risk to push Tess, because she stormed out of my room and left me with no kiss. I was a little afraid she might not come back tomorrow. I never even had the chance to tell her about the fever this morning.

Much to my surprise, Hawk returned in the early evening. "I'm waiting for my wife to finish her work, so I thought I'd drop in and see how you are doing."

"Better," I whispered.

"Yes."

"Thank you."

He nodded. "It's time you start learning how to get out of this bed, this room."

I frowned.

What's he talking about? He knows I'm paralyzed from the neck down.

"People are simply bodies of energy, and energy moves in many ways. Up here in the northern woods, there are a lot of stories about the medicine people and shape-shifting, moving that energy into different kinds of bodies besides the human form."

"Vampires?" I lipped.

He laughed. "There is also the practice among many Native American tribes of being able to transmit energy across great distances or of people being able to see something that is hundreds of miles away."

"New Age . . . psychics."

He knows I'm skeptical but I can't help liking him, and he did bring healing to me this morning.

"Not New Age but Old Age wisdom," he countered. "Your mind tells you that you are trapped in a useless body."

"Yes."

"That you are stuck and can't do anything about it."

"Yes."

"But your mind isn't stuck."

Where's he going with this argument?

"Your mind is free to wander, and wander it does. Probably right to that woman you like."

But it's all the imaginary stuff of daydreams. Big deal.

"It is a big deal," he said, looking straight at me.

Wait a minute! He just responded to an unvoiced thought! How did he do that?

My jaw fell open in astonishment.

"There's a door in your mind. Call it the imagination. Call it a portal, whatever you want, but it allows you to move in and out. It allows me to listen in. I don't often do that, but you're chickenshit, hiding behind a wall of fear dressed up as reason. Now you can stay behind that wall and pretend to feel safe, or you can start moving out of this room. You don't have to be a vampire to enjoy the moon."

"How?"

This is crazy stuff. Mumbo-jumbo. I'm tethered to this bed. An infection is eating me up, and you tell me to go dance in the moonlight?

"Sonny," he said, "there isn't that much time. Practice opening that door and letting yourself move on out."

Tell me how. I want instruction. I want a manual of steps 1, 2, and 3. I want certainty. Tell me how.

But he didn't. He picked up his felt hat with the eagle feather stuck in the brim and placed it on his head. He stopped just shy of the doorway and said, "It doesn't matter if you dance in the moonlight or dance in the sunlight. You do what you have to do. You go where you have to go. The wall or the door, it's your choice, Sonny."

Tess

Chapter 29

• ◆ •

WHY DID SONNY PUSH ME to ask Cassie about the death of Devin? Didn't she say it was a simple accident, a fall from a bridge?

That night after dinner, Cassie sat at a table in the living room working on her finances. A bright fire crackled in the fireplace, the flames flicking shadows across the room.

I approached her with some trepidation. I sat down and tried to figure out how to frame my question without it appearing to be a suspicion.

She scratched her head, looked up, put down the bank statements, and smiled. "How you doing, Tess? I've been so preoccupied that I didn't have a chance to ask about your morning at the program or your conversations with Sonny."

"I told Sonny about the legal stuff. He said to ask you about your husband's accident."

Blame it on Sonny; that's the way.

Cassie grimaced. "See, that's how it starts, Tess. The facts don't matter. As soon as your name is trotted out in public for everyone to see as a potential murderer, people start looking at you differently. Mr. Mudge is a longtime resident of this county, and he could do me a lot of damage. He knows that and is hoping I'll slink away in the middle of the night, leaving everything to him."

"But you won't, will you?"

Cassie looked back at her bank statements. "Even if I mortgaged this place up the kazoo to get a lawyer, I don't have an income sufficient to pay the interest." She sighed a big sigh.

"You didn't kill your husband. You didn't kill Natalie. You're innocent, Cassie. Anyone can see that."

Elbows on the table, Cassie framed her face with her hands as if her thoughts had become too heavy for her head to bear. "It'd be different if I had lived here for several years, had become part of the community, but . . ."

It really bothered me to see her in such a state of despair, so unlike the tough pragmatist I had come to know and respect. This defeatist mood scared me.

"You aren't going to simply hand this place over to him?"

"To that sonuvabitch? Over my dead body, but he's sure going to make me bleed."

What a relief. For a minute there, I thought she'd gone soft.

"What about threatening him with a countersuit? If Natalie's death was suspicious, wouldn't he be the more obvious suspect? He could have pushed her off the top step after an argument."

Cassie looked at me as if I were out of my mind.

"And give them the opportunity to go poking their noses into what is none of their business? I don't want anyone bringing Natalie or Devin back from the land of the dead. Let them rest in peace. Besides, they'll want access to the diary."

I had to admit that I was curious. I too wanted to read Natalie's diary.

There's a voyeur in all of us.

Cassie shook her head and nodded at the fireplace. "I burned the diary," she said. "I cast all her adulterous longings into the fire. Devin was my husband and that's the way I want to remember him."

But she has to know that Spenser Mudge would have kept a copy of the diary. Nor do I dare point out that it takes two to have an affair.

"If I were a rich woman," she continued, "I'd toss out everything that belonged to that woman. In fact . . ." Cassie stood up and went over to an oil painting of Natalie Hagen, unhooked it, and leaned it up against the wall. She then proceeded around the room, taking down all the photographs, paintings, and images of Natalie, her husband, and their ancestors, leaving rectangular patches of lighter paint on the walls.

"This is what I will offer Mr. Mudge in trade." She gestured toward the stack of paintings she'd compiled. "Drop the lawsuit and he can have all the pictures of his late aunt and other relatives. That should be worth something to him. Otherwise, I'll threaten to build a big bonfire, burn them in the field, and invite him to the event."

She cackled and rubbed her hands together.

My guess was that the threat would have little impact on the pretentious Mr. Mudge. If only there was a way to get evidence of wrongdoing on his part in his business dealings. All that Sally had given me was hearsay. I decided to wait and tell Cassie what I'd learned about Mr. Mudge at a later time, when I had something substantial to back up the gossip. I didn't want to get her hopes raised only to have them quashed by some fancy legal maneuver.

It didn't occur to me until I went to bed that Cassie never did answer any of my questions about Devin's death.

"Are you ready for the big day?" Dr. Meggie O'Connor brought my distracted mind back to session the next day. I had been conjuring up rescue fantasies of saving Cassie and Hagen's Heaven from the evil Mr. Mudge. Instead, she wanted me to focus on Nick and our upcoming motion hearing on spousal support and other such information relating to the divorce.

I shrugged my shoulders and blew out my cheeks. It made me anxious to think about the hearing.

The psychologist tapped a document on the table before her. "I have the neurologist's report here. He says that you can't go back to work for some time, that your ability to multi-task and sequence is impaired, that you can only remember two out of a series of six words so your short-term memory is affected, that you still get significant headaches, and that you're more impulsive than before, more emotionally labile."

"The new me!" I tried to make a joke of it.

"Yes, the new you with a brain that is still trying to heal from all the shearing of neurons. I understand that your lawyer also has a copy of this report."

"I guess Nick will be glad to get rid of a wife in this condition. I can't help but hope that either I win the Michigan lottery or else make tons of money writing a best-selling novel in the near future."

"So that he would regret this divorce?" Meggie smiled.

My legs started jiggling as I knotted my fingers together. "Do I have to go to this hearing? Can't I simply have my lawyer do everything?"

"What's the problem here, Tess? Is it embarrassment about the traumatic brain injury?"

I shook my head, bit my lower lip.

She waited for me to answer, but I didn't want to summon up all that hurt and grief. I bent my head and looked away, ashamed of my feelings.

Suddenly Meggie O'Connor got it. "You still love Nick, don't you?"

Yes, god-damn it. Yes, I still love him.

Cassie pulled the Subaru into the hospital parking lot. We both were quiet on the drive over, except for a brief mention of the freakishly early snow storm working its way across Minnesota, heading our way. My thoughts were on both Nick and Sonny.

How can I love two men at the same time? Neither is available for any future. Tomorrow will be the day the cord is cut between Nick and me. Finis. It's over. But why doesn't my heart get the message? He loves Sandy.

Why couldn't he keep living a double life, like Devin with Cassie and Natalie? If I can love two men, why couldn't Nick possess a heart big enough to love two women?

I know, I know. He'd say something about it not being fair to either one of us, that he can't live in secrecy.

No, I've got that wrong.

He loves Sandy, not me.

And what about Sonny? Does he really love me or am I simply the last stop on his foreshortened life? And really, what does it matter? He's going to die and we all know it. So what if we are of different ages, races, motivations?

Love is love.

Sonny

Chapter 30

·◆·

COME TO ME, TESS. Lie down on the bed beside me and put your head against my cheek. Let me taste the strands of your hair and smell the soap upon your skin. Come to me, Tess.

But it's morning, and Tess is in her rehabilitation program. She won't arrive until late afternoon, after her appointment with the therapist.

Does she talk about us? Does she even know of the burst of gladness in my heart when she enters my room?

Tomorrow is her big day. The motion before the judge, the last step to divorce. I want to be there, to put my arms around her and say to that stupid husband, "See what you have given up? Well, you can't have her. She's mine now."

"Well, you're looking bright-eyed this morning," chirped the pretty nurse. She had come into the room to check the bags and ventilator. She placed a cool hand on my forehead and smiled. "No fever today."

She switched out the catheter bag and busied herself with cleaning the bandage on my neck while humming a cheerful tune. She smelled of lilacs but spoke of winter. "It's only October, but we're going to get a real snowstorm later tonight. Everything will be covered in white and the land will go to sleep. I love the coziness of a storm. Everything slows down. The world closes in. A time when the moon is often brighter than the sun. Gosh, I'm gabbing on so. I'll be back to check on you in a little while." With that, she disappeared from the room, her words and the smell of lilacs lingering in the air.

A time of year when the moon is often brighter than the sun.

A time of year when love blooms beyond the garden's frozen boundaries.

Tess, come to me. Bring your light into this room, into my heart.

It is the best of times. It is the worst of times.

Tess, I need you.

While waiting for her, I closed my eyes and tried to summon up the image of swinging my legs out of the bed, fitting my feet into shoes, my hands like that of a conductor orchestrating the whole dressing procedure, pulling on the briefs and pants, slipping on a shirt, buttoning it. But it was all forced imagery, nothing but hollow representations, translucent, fake.

The priests would laugh at me, saying that this is the magic of paganism—sincere hope matched by false promises. Better to trust in Jesus who died for my sins.

Only I'm not old enough to have done much sinning.

I gritted my teeth, trying to shut out the Catholic criticisms in my head and get on with the ability to imagine myself into another reality.

Hawk never told me HOW to do it. He said, 'Find the door.'

Eyes closed, I concentrated first on my breathing. Then slowly I constructed a doorway.

Can I slip out of this body and move forward through it?

A hand touched my cheek. For just a brief second, I imagined it was my hand that I had been able to summon with the power of my mind. But reality asserted itself through my nose— the sweet smell of Tess.

My lips parted into a smile. I kept my eyes closed, enjoying the sensation.

She kissed me.

"There," she said, "You can now open your eyes. I am no one's fantasy."

"But . . . you are."

She stepped back, pulled up the chair near the bed, and stroked my cheek. "I told Dr. O'Connor about you."

I raised my eyebrows.

"We discussed the upcoming meeting with the divorce judge and Nick. I said life gets pretty confusing. I still love him."

I didn't want to hear that.

"As for you . . ." but Tess didn't finish her sentence.

I understand. It's hard to know the end of this love story. But you love me, Tess.

"You may be sixteen years younger than I am, but you're an old soul, Sonny. A wise, old soul."

Oh, but I'm young, Tess, and full of love. I'm not the personification of wisdom. I am simply a man unable to talk much and forced to listen.

"Tomorrow, big day," I lipped.

She twisted the gold wedding ring and held it up for me to see. "Soon to quit being Mrs. Tess Outerbridge and back to old Tess Thornhill."

"Doctor . . . Thornhill," I said on the ventilator's exhale.

That brought a smile to her face, then a shrug of acknowledgment. "Probably best not to use that address. People will begin to expect too much of me. Cassie keeps telling me that my problem is that I look and sound normal but that my brain is still missing lots of connections."

Kiss me again, Tess.

But she was in too much of a nervous buzz of anxiety about the pre-divorce hearing, about saying goodbye to Nick and to marriage to open herself up to love in the present.

Patience was my only option. I remembered how I used to dwell in the comforts of the past and rushed about preparing for the future while ignoring what was happening around me in the moment.

Well, NOW is all I have, Tess.

Tess

Chapter 31

MUCH TO MY SURPRISE, the judge for our pre-divorce hearing and spousal support turned out to be a middle-aged woman with blowsy hair, shell-rimmed glasses, and an impatient expression of let's-get-this-over-with-quickly on her face.

This is not good news for Nick, I thought.

Stacked before the judge sat a ream of briefs filed by both my attorney and by Nick's attorney, detailing the length of our marriage, our respective ages, the value of the two cars, the assessed value of Nick's house, our previous standard of living in Massachusetts when we were both working, our current economic circumstances, our physical and mental health, and profuse medical documents relating to the car accident and my traumatic brain injury. My attorney had also insisted upon a document detailing the facts concerning Nick's extramarital affair as the precipitating cause of our marital split.

The judge removed her glasses and rubbed the bridge of her nose. She addressed Nick. "It says here that you're only earning about a third of what you made in Massachusetts as a clinical psychologist and that you have very little in terms of investments or savings."

Nick's attorney jumped to answer that question. "My client hasn't had the time to establish a full private practice."

Although Cassie suspected that to be a simple ruse on Nick's part to appear penniless, I believed it to be the truth. Several months earlier, he had told me that since it cost less for him to live in Suttons Bay, Michigan, than Cambridge, Massachusetts, he planned to work fewer hours and give more time to fishing and kayaking.

"Am I right to assume that most of your assets are tied up in the house?" asked the judge.

"Yes," he answered.

His attorney interrupted, "It takes a lot of money to set up a private therapy practice."

Annoyance crossed the judge's face. "As I look at your proposal, Dr. Outerbridge, it appears that you would like to give your wife a set amount of money over the next three years at which time she will return to work as a teacher."

Nick nodded.

"But," the judge continued, "that is under the presumption that Mrs. Outerbridge, I'm sorry, Dr. Tess Outerbridge would be able to return to her former type of employment."

"Three years is a reasonable time, Judge," argued Nick's attorney.

The judge rifled through the papers and reinserted her glasses upon her nose, looking straight at Nick, while ignoring his attorney. "I also see that your wife not only paid off her student loans but also contributed significantly to the payment of your student loans, almost to the amount that you are proposing to pay her over the next three years."

"Don't forget, your Honor," interjected Nick's attorney, "that Dr. Nicholas Outerbridge was the sole support of the couple since last September upon their move to Michigan."

My attorney spoke up. "Dr. Tess Outerbridge loved her teaching position at Buckingham, Browne, and Nichols in Cambridge, Massachusetts and had little desire to give up that position and her friends to move to Michigan. It was solely due to her husband's insistence that she agreed to relocate to Michigan. We are likewise here today, against the wishes of my client. She did not want this divorce."

I sat up straight and stared self-righteously at Nick. He refused to look at me, the aggrieved party. He kept a poker face, rolling a number two pencil back and forth across the table he shared with his attorney. I turned around to see Cassie also glaring at him.

Why won't he look at me? Does he regret this action? Does he ever think of me with fondness in his heart?

The judge began to tap her fingers on the stack of papers. She then turned toward me. "Now you both have agreed on the division of cars, the dog, and personal items. But I am disturbed by the medical reports that give no assurance of when you will be employable again. The neurologist is quite clear that currently you are not able to work."

Nick's attorney then blundered. "My client thinks that the accident may have been self-inflicted, as his wife was depressed about the move from Massachusetts to Michigan."

Cassie let out an audible whisper, "For shame!"

With a sharp and angry retort, the judge let her displeasure be known to Nick's attorney. "There is nothing in the accident report to substantiate that supposition. Pure conjecture. If I need to hear from you again, I will address you, Counselor. Otherwise, if you continue to interrupt the proceedings I will cite you with contempt."

My attorney struggled to keep a smile from emerging on his craggy face.

The judge continued to address our table. "As I understand it, Dr. Outerbridge, you are requesting health insurance and spousal support until the time you are cleared to reenter the work force. Is that correct?"

My attorney nudged me.

"Yes, your Honor," I dutifully said.

"It appears to me that Dr. Nicholas Outerbridge owes you insurance coverage due to your continued medical bills. The court will order him to pay such insurance coverage until such time that you are able to secure such coverage through employment or through remarriage. In addition, this Court will grant you the amount of annual spousal support that your husband proposed for the next three years, at which time you will either be receiving Social Service Disability payments or be able to return to work."

"But your Honor . . ." sputtered Nick's attorney.

The judge didn't let him have the last word. "Your client is the owner of a valuable piece of property by which he will be able to secure a mortgage in order to make such payments."

"Yes," Cassie mouthed silently.

Nick sighed, knowing that he would have to work longer hours to afford the mortgage and the insurance payments to me.

"Your Honor," said my attorney. "My client would also like to relinquish the surname of Outerbridge and return to her maiden name of Thornhill upon the final judgment of divorce. Due to the impoverished circumstances in which my client finds herself due to the move to Michigan and the relinquishment of her cherished teaching position in Massachusetts, I would also request that all attorney fees be paid by Dr. Nicholas Outerbridge."

Nick's attorney held a brief conference with Nick about whether to contest the demands for spousal support and payment of attorney fees, but I could see by his troubled expression that Nick felt a smidgen of responsibility toward me. His attorney agreed to the conditions set forth by the court.

The judge then assented to both my request of a name change and payment to my attorney. She directed that Nick's attorney draw up the final Judgment of Divorce, setting forth the court's rulings.

"Sixty days," said my attorney, "then it will all be over."

Thirteen years of marriage.

I did not experience the congratulatory glee of Cassie or the satisfaction of my attorney.

All I felt was immeasurable sadness.

Sonny

Chapter 32

· ◆ ·

I EXPECTED TESS to arrive relieved and jubilant. I was hopeful the pre-divorce decree would open her up to the joy of what was beginning to happen between us.

Instead, her shoulders slumped and she averted her eyes by cleaning the trash around the bed table.

"Uh," I said on the ventilator's exhale, trying to catch her attention.

She turned toward me and burst into tears. "Why did all this happen? You, me, Sandy, Nick, Cassie?" She dabbed at her eyes with a corner of my sheet. "Why did life have to get so complicated?"

I adopted my most Jesus-like expression, hoping to say something wise to her, to give her comfort, but nothing came to me.

"I didn't ask to come here to Michigan. I was happy in Massachusetts. I had wonderful friends. I was a good teacher, Sonny."

I smiled in agreement. All I could do was be a patient listener. She had to get it out of her system.

"I thought Nick and I had a good marriage. Friends used to hold us up as the ideal couple. He was the one who knew how to cook and talk about feelings. They say every woman needs a good wife, and Nick was kind of like that. I was the intellectual, the one who kept encouraging him to think beyond the boundaries. I was happy, Sonny."

But he wasn't, Tess. He kept a part of his heart to himself. I won't do that to you.

How I wished I could communicate all this to her, but the damn ventilator kept me on a perpetual stammer.

Tess sat down and buried her head in her hands. The free-flowing tears that had burst out of her now slowed to a trickle.

"God, I sound so pathetic, don't I? I don't hear you complaining about being paralyzed and overwhelmed with infection. At least I can walk and talk, moan and groan. You know what?"

I arched my eyebrows in a questioning way.

"Depression is boring. Words just rattling against bitter walls, and all you hear are the echoes."

I smiled at her metaphor.

"How was *your* day?" she asked. She wiped away the last evidence of her sorrows.

"I'm . . . waiting," I answered.

"For what? For God to come down and speak to you?"

The image of the man hanging on the cliff face popped across the screen of my imagination.

Yes, it would be nice if God would speak to me.

"For you," I answered.

For you to lower a rope, each link knotted in love, down to where I am clinging to a spindly branch of existence.

Tess touched my cheek with her hand. "Sometimes you say the loveliest things. I feel cherished by you, Sonny."

It's the truth. I do cherish you.

Then typical of Tess, she zoomed off to another topic of discussion. "Have you been practicing what Hawk taught you?"

"Yes," I answered, silently cursing her scattered ability to attend to what was important.

"Any success?" She meant, was I able to use my imagination to get out of bed and go walking outside.

"I love you," I said.

One good diversion deserves another.

"I love you too," she replied, but she said it too quickly, too complacently, not measuring the meaning of her words. She loved her dog. She loved Cassie. She loved books. She loved Nick.

Love ME, Tess.

Only I didn't voice my feeling.

I can wait a little bit longer. I am learning how to take my measure of time.

Just when resignation had slipped its mantle of protection over my impatient heart, Tess broke through her disparate thoughts to say, "I'd never have asked for the accident or wished that you had ended up here in the hospital, but you're really important to me, Sonny. We might never have known each other otherwise. We might never have met. What a loss that would have been for me."

She placed both hands around my face, cradling it, staring into my eyes so that I could not mistake her sentiment. "If circumstances had been different, you'd have said, 'Oh, she's just another middle-aged white woman' and I'd have dismissed you as a cheeky kid. It doesn't matter, does it? You love and accept me, damaged as I am. I love you, even if you can't hold my hand or walk with me in the moonlight."

She tapped her left breast. "Here, where my heart speaks the truth, your heart answers."

Then she kissed me, and tears came to my eyes.

Before she left, she had one last thing to say. "I've been thinking, Sonny. You know, if Hawk is right, if your mind can help you leave your body and move out of this bed, if my mind can choose to come back from the land of the dead, well then maybe, just maybe as you travel around, you'll finally be able to meet your mother's spirit."

Could that really happen? Meet Mama?

Hope surged like a wave inside of me, only to have doubt break and froth over such expectations.

I should be content with what I have now.

She loves me. This unexpected joy ripples across a large, dark ocean of unknown depths.

Hawk arrived in the early evening, snow dusting his black cowboy hat. "Seems winter has come early." He peered out the hospital window. "Still, there is muffled moonlight out there to guide your way."

I take note of his word "your."

"How?" I asked him.

He knew what I meant, but he pretended to be stupid, shrugging his shoulders, then flapping his arm wings as if to take off and fly.

"Dodo . . . bird," I said, laughing inside.

He pulled the chair toward the bed, took off his hat, looked around as if to impart a sacred secret. "First, there must be desire. Without that, nothing can happen."

"I wish . . ." but the ventilator struck off the rest.

"I know," he said, "but it has to be stronger than a wish."

"Commitment," I lipped.

"Belief," he added, "in the possibility. Desire and openness."

"But . . ." I whispered.

He shook his head. "*Buts* are for those who are too scared to leave what is comfortable."

"If I . . . leave . . . can I . . . come back?" The ventilator punctuated my speech.

"Good question. The answer is yes, but . . ." He raised his eyebrows. "Will you want to?"

Tess

Chapter 33

·◆·

THE EARLY DARKNESS and the snow were beginning to gain on us as we hurried home to Hagen's Heaven. As we pulled into the garage and I got out of the car, I listened for the familiar bark of greeting from Imp.

All was quiet.

I hurried up the porch steps, thinking that maybe she was sound asleep and getting a little deaf, but she wasn't in her cozy den on the porch. I checked outside the house. There weren't any paw prints on the new snow.

"Imp," I yelled. "Come!"

My voice echoed across the field and woods. No bark returned my call.

Cassie came up behind me. "What's the matter? Where's Imp?"

"I don't know. She's disappeared. She's never done this before. What if the coyotes get her? Or she gets out on the street and is hit by a car?" My voice was ramping up with anxiety.

"Imp! Imp!" I yelled repeatedly.

Cassie retreated inside, then returned with a hat, boots, gloves, and big flashlight. "Here, put these on and walk down the driveway and see if you can find her. She probably caught scent of a deer and wandered off."

I scrambled into the boots. "No, she wouldn't do that. Oh Cassie, it's going to be cold tonight. She may freeze to death."

"With that heavy coat she has? Shelties are made for cold weather, but we'll find her. I'll go make calls to the county animal catcher and nearby kennels to see if she's been spotted."

I made my way quickly down the driveway, calling frantically for Imp. "Please Imp, please, come to me!"

I begged. I pleaded. Then I prayed.

"God, will you find my little dog and bring her home to me? I need her. She's my best friend. She's family to me."

With a heavy heart, I turned around when I came to the end of the driveway. A quick look up and down the quiet road showed no evidence of my little Sheltie. The cars were off the street due to the storm; only the wind and snow blew past me.

I hurried back up to the house, hoping Cassie had gotten word of her. Imp had tons of identification on her as well as being micro-chipped, but no one had reported seeing her.

Cassie had been busy during my brief absence. She had found an internet company that made robo-calls to neighbors within a one-to-five mile radius of where the pet had last been seen. Already she had pledged a hundred and fifty dollars to pay for it.

"Don't worry," she said. "Imp will turn up."

That night we made posters featuring Imp's photograph and our telephone number. We wrapped the posters in plastic wrap so the snow wouldn't blur the indelible ink.

I was up before the sun, dressing for the cold. The snow had stopped, and it wasn't very deep, but it was heavy and wet. A dog's paw prints upon the surface would indicate Imp's signature. I grabbed a cereal bar and a cup of coffee and left a note to Cassie that I was skipping the rehab program that day to go search the property.

Outside, the trees, still laden with lingering fall leaves, hung low, stooped heavy with the wet snow. Several times, I heard what sounded like gunshots but were actually oak trees breaking under the heavy weight of the freakish storm. It would only be a matter of time before the community lost power.

I got back to an empty house and wondered where Cassie had gone. I'd covered the entire property. I'd seen raccoons and porcupines scratching for grub among fallen logs, black, grey, and brown squirrels jumping from one tree to the next, three startled does, and one trundling skunk but no Imp.

When Cassie returned, she told me that after reading my note, she called the rehab program, then loaded up her car with the posters, nails, and a hammer. She'd driven around Leland, Lake Leelanau, and Suttons Bay, tacking posters to telephone posts. She'd stopped off at Business Helper in Suttons Bay and ordered a batch of leaflets with our telephone number, the photo of Imp, and her description.

Cassie showed me the box of leaflets without mentioning that she'd spent another hundred dollars, money she didn't really have.

"Time to go to the hospital," she said, checking her watch.

"Oh Cassie, I can't. What if Imp returns and she's hurt? I need to be here for her. Besides, we can stuff people's mailboxes with the leaflets."

"Sonny also needs you."

"I know, but I can't. I have to stay here for her."

Cassie sighed. "It's against the law to stuff mailboxes. Tomorrow is Saturday. We can distribute the leaflets at the library. Kids have sharp eyes for wandering dogs. I have commitments to keep at the hospital. I'm going." She paused to give me one more chance to join her, but I wasn't going to abandon my little pal.

Imp needs me here.

She shrugged her shoulders at my intransigence, fished her house keys from her purse, and headed out the door.

"Cassie?" I ran to the porch door and stuck out my head. She turned around. "Yes."

"Will you tell Sonny why I'm not coming today?"

Cassie raised a hand in affirmation, then turned back towards the garage.

I shut the door, then had an idea. I picked up Imp's bowl, pulled out a bag of kibbles and the homemade casserole, and mixed it together in her dish. Along with a bowl of water, I placed the dish outside on the porch. Although Imp was not a food fanatic, she had dearly loved Cassie's casseroles.

Perhaps the smell of food will bring her back home.

But Imp didn't return that night or the next or the one thereafter. It was as if she'd disappeared into thin air.

"Perhaps she went off to die," said one sympathizer on the phone.

"No," I answered. "If she'd been sick or hurting, she would have come to me for help."

When I had gone three days without visiting Sonny, Cassie sat me down at the kitchen table. "We have done everything we can to find her."

"Maybe someone kidnapped her?"

Cassie sighed. "That's always possible, but it's not likely. Who would want an old dog with an arthritic condition?"

I knew what was coming next, and I didn't want to hear it. "Maybe we should order more leaflets."

"You need to go to the program tomorrow. That's your job right now, to retrain your brain, to compensate for what has been jarred loose."

"But . . ." I couldn't say goodbye to Imp without seeing her again.

"Honey, this is life. Sometimes we lose those whom we love. Sometimes they simply disappear from us and we wonder why our love wasn't a strong enough glue to keep them near, keep them safe. If Imp is alive . . ."

"I know she is!" I couldn't tolerate the alternative.

"If she's alive, then someday she may come back to us. But until then you have to go on with your healing. Tomorrow we'll repeat our calls to kennels, dogcatchers, and veterinarian clinics, but today you need to go to the program and visit with Sonny."

"He of all people would understand. He knows how much Imp means to me," I said.

Frustration rippled across Cassie's face. "Tess, I have spent a lot of money trying to find Imp. I don't have anymore to spend. And Sonny doesn't have much . . ." Cassie stopped short of the truth, then added, "He's been sick again, real sick."

Sonny

Chapter 34

• ◆ •

A PRIEST CAME INTO MY ROOM and introduced himself. "Father Esperance" was older than I but still looked wet behind the ears. Clean-shaven, well-scrubbed, rosy-cheeked with a fine aquiline nose, cheery in disposition.

"I'm French Canadian," he said, with a slight trace of an accent.

"I'm not . . . Catholic," I said. I wasn't sure he understood my ventilator-exhaled words.

"The nurse said you had gone to a Catholic boarding school in Chicago, The Most Precious Blood Academy. It has a fine scholastic reputation."

"Yes."

"So I assume that at one time you were Catholic and that you've fallen away from the faith?"

"Fallen" is an interesting way of putting it. I'm over the cliff but not yet into the abyss.

I could detect no blame or criticism in his tone of voice, only curiosity.

How to condense what makes one lose his faith in five or fewer words?

I chose my sparse words carefully "God . . . doesn't talk . . . to me."

The priest pulled the chair closer to my bed. "Yes, I can understand that. God doesn't talk to me either, but I'm not sure that's God's problem. In seminary, I used to think that God might inhabit the body of an absent-minded professor who would invite us mortals into His chambers for a bit of espresso and illuminating conversation. Warn us when we were headed into dangerous pursuits, give us a bit of support when we addressed our bad habits, exhort us to better choices. A word or two when we prayed so diligently for wisdom."

I detected a bit of self-mockery in his confession. His eyes scanned my sheet-draped body, then returned to my face.

"It was a terrible thing that happened to you," he said.

"Random act . . . of God?" I lipped, but he obviously didn't understand my attempt at humor.

"It takes courage to live with the consequences of our well-meaning decisions," he continued.

He must know about the hitchhiker and the shooting.

"I'm not sure I'd have the ability to accept this as my fate," he continued. He shook his head in sorrow, not pity.

"What choice . . . do I . . . have?" It was so hard to get the words out of my throat with that damn ventilator heaving my chest up and down.

"Would you mind if I say the rosary? It might bring you some comfort," he said.

He's given up trying to understand my speech, so he resorts to ritual.

"Okay," I answered, thinking it would probably soothe his anxious soul.

If God refuses to communicate, we human beings will fill up the silence with our religious mantras.

He began, "Hail Mary, full of grace . . ."

My mind silently answered *Blessed art thou among women . . .*

Together, he with his voice, me with the words imprinted on my soul, we said the rosary.

Much to my surprise, it comforted me as much as it did him.

I slept the longest time after Father Esperance departed, and for once I remembered the dream that came to me. Hawk had told me that dream time is very important, sometimes a portal into the sacred mysteries.

I am walking up to a large Victorian mansion, one with a long outside open porch, four floors, turrets, and stained glass windows, a huge house with a large winding staircase. I find myself inside the familiar house. The chairs are stiff-backed and gilded, like Louis the XIV furniture, not offering comfort but rather demonstrating old wealth. Complex oriental rugs, of red, blue, and white swirls, cover dark wooden floors. Each floor contains multiple rooms with closed doors. It is up to me which rooms I choose to enter.

I am taking possession of this house.

Which way to go? Which passageway to take? Which room to enter?

On the fourth floor, I see a small doorway at the end of a long, dark hallway. I am tempted to bypass all the other rooms and go straight to that attic doorway. Relief is there waiting for me, as well as answers to my doubts and worries.

I am tempted.

"It's not time yet," a voice intrudes.

"It's not time yet."

My eyes opened to Hawk, standing there, one hand on my head, one hand on my heart. His eyes were closed. He didn't seem aware that I had leapt out of dream time back into reality. He was murmuring something in his own Lakota language.

It didn't matter to me what he was saying. I could feel his healing energy flow into my forehead, sending me back into a peaceful sleep.

The next time I awoke, it was to the touch of Cassie's cool hand upon my cheek.

I opened my eyes, hoping that Tess had come with her.

"You're starting to warm up again," she said. "Why can't they stop this infection?"

"Tess?" I lipped.

Cassie's lips scrunched together in disapproval. She shook her head. "Imp's disappeared, and Tess refuses to leave. She's hoping someone will call on the telephone to report having found the dog."

"Imp," I said.

"Frankly, I think the dog has gone into the woods to die or the coyotes have gotten her. It's stupid to love animals that way, isn't it?"

That was more of a rhetorical statement than a question because no sooner had she said it than Cassie's whole face crumbled and tears began to fall. She whipped out a tissue from her pocketbook and dabbed at her eyes. "I did so love that damn dog. I've tried not to show my sadness around Tess. She's having a hard enough time as it is. Anyway, she won't be coming in today. Perhaps tomorrow."

No, she won't be coming back to see me until she finds Imp.

And then a very strange thought came into my mind: *Maybe Imp will be the one to guide me through that attic door.*

Tess

Chapter 35

• ◆ •

"IMP, COME HOME NOW. I need you," I whispered, crying softly into my pillow. I was an emotional wreck, obsessing about all the dangers the cold world could visit upon her. I had retraced my steps over field and woods, until the calves of my legs burned with exhaustion.

The first of my installment payments from Nick had arrived by mail, no note attached. That was his way of saying he didn't appreciate having to spend his hard-earned money on me. I promptly turned it all over to Cassie.

She had protested. "No, I can't accept your money. You need it."

I knew she'd spent a lot of money on this search for Imp. She'd done it for my mental health, but I also think she'd grown quite fond of my little Sheltie, although she once told me that she wasn't "a dog person."

"I signed the check to you, so you've have got to accept it."

Cassie had sighed, pocketed the money, and muttered, "Thank you." I think it embarrassed her that I knew her income was barely sufficient to cover our living expenses.

"Imp, Imp, Imp," I whispered into the pillow, as if that mantra would let her know wherever she was, that I still loved her.

Lots of people called to express their concern, to let me know they, too, were searching the woods for my old pal. Sometimes, there would be a spotting of an unattached dog, but the size or the color let me know it wasn't Imp.

I would have stayed home on Monday had Cassie not insisted that I had responsibilities and an obligation to go to the rehab program and then to see Sonny. She reassured me that she would check the answering service several times to make sure no one called about Imp.

The program advisors were very sympathetic and kind. The vocational advisor said, "It happened to me with my cat. I searched for two months but he never returned. It would have been easier if I had known what had happened, even if he'd died."

The truth of that statement was dawning on me.

Over time, you can recover from the sting of death. It's a door that closes on you and you can't open it, but at least you know when and how and where. The disappearance of a loved one is different. The door is open but it's all dark and formless inside, and when you call out, all you hear are echoes of your own voice.

I cried for days.

I tried to cheer up, to cleanse my face of any trace of sorrow before entering Sonny's room, but upon seeing his concerned expression and the toll of the fever, I immediately broke down.

"Imp," he croaked in a whisper.

I put my hand on his forehead. He was burning up. I immediately snagged a washcloth from his hospital bathroom, ran it under cold water, and placed it on his head. The water trickled down into his eyes.

He smiled while blinking rapidly.

"Oh dear," I said, mopping up the water dripping down his cheeks. "I'm such a klutz."

"Imp," he said. There were tears in his eyes.

He's never met Imp. He's crying for me.

I regretted my absence. It hadn't been fair to him.

"We've tried everything to find her," I said. "Well, not everything. We haven't asked a psychic."

He lipped something, but I couldn't understand what he was saying.

I shook my head to let him know that I had missed it.

Slowly, he uttered, "Sandy."

"That unmitigated adulteress?"

It pleases me that I can retrieve literate words again. No more "eat poop" type statements.

Sonny gave me one of his enigmatic smiles as if he were simply going to wait out my little rant. He knew about my earlier encounter with Sandy at the New Age bookstore.

"You're giving me that Jesus look again," I sputtered while straightening out the sheets on his bed.

"Kiss . . . me," he said on the exhale.

I laughed. "My heart is broken by my dog's disappearancé.
You're being cooked by a fever. You tell me to go see my
husband's mistress, and all the while, your mind is on sex?"

He grinned. "Come . . . here."

I wrapped my arms around his shoulders and under his
neck and leaned forward. Our lips touched, soft and gentle, but
the taste of his mouth had changed. There was a sourness to
his breath.

Like something rotting inside.

I pulled back. "There," I said. "One kiss for proffering
advice."

A nurse entered the room and indicated that I needed to
leave "for reasons of modesty" as she had to wash Sonny and
change out his bags. "He needs his rest," she added, looking
as if she had caught us in some illicit activity.

"Okay," I said. "I'll see you tomorrow."

He gave me a feeble smile, reluctant to let me depart.

"I promise," I added.

When I joined Cassie in the volunteer office, I asked her if
she'd drop me off at the New Age Bookstore for a half hour
while she grocery shopped.

"Why do you want to go there?" she asked. "You aren't
planning to purchase a voodoo doll and do naughty things to
Nick?" Her eyebrows arched in mischief.

"No, I need to ask someone a question."

"Who?" she persisted.

"Busybody," I said.

"Me? Why Tess." She pretended to be astonished. "Okay,
point well taken." She gathered up her belongings, and we

headed out the door to the garage. "But," she added, "I do hope you'll share the answers to your questions."

I scowled and playfully elbowed her.

She drove to the store, but as I was getting out of the car, she said, "Do you think you might ask one itty bitty question for me?"

"What's that?"

"Would you ask the psychic where I can find some more money?"

That made me realize that things were a lot worse for Cassie than I had thought.

I straightened my hair in the store window before entering. "Is Sandy Hufnagle here?"

Before the clerk could answer, Sandy appeared from the back hallway, giving me a big smile.

"So, you've come back then? Very good. This time I don't have a headache." She grabbed my hand both to shake it and to lead me to the backroom.

"I haven't paid yet," I said, looking around to the clerk who watched the two of us disappear around the corner.

"You can do that when you leave," said Sandy, indicating a chair for me. She shut the door. The room was small and dark but lit by candles and smelling of incense. "Now, how can I help you? Oh, I remember, you wanted me to work with the Spirits, not with cards or a palm reading. Am I right about that?"

"You've got a good memory," I said.

She has no idea who in the hell I am.

"So what is your question?" She was all business and yet gentle.

"I have a little dog that has disappeared. I want to know where she has gone, what has happened to her."

"Okay," she said. "Here, rest your palms on my hands."

I did as she asked.

She closed her eyes, lifted her chin, slowed her breathing, and seemed to fall into a trance. "Such sadness is in your heart! I feel that heaviness go all the way through me. You have an animal that's gone. A little dog. Female. I am looking for her paws. No movement. She's still, but not asleep. I hate to tell you this, but I think she has passed on."

No, that can't be true. Imp must be alive!

I jerked my hands away.

Sandy let her hands fall to her lap but kept her eyes shut. "The Spirits say that something will come to you to help you with your grief."

No, it's not grief yet. It's anxiety. Is Imp going to be okay?

"The Spirits say you're fighting hard inside to accept her death. You feel guilty because you weren't able to prevent her going away. She wants you to know she was sick. She knew how hard it would be for you to see her die."

"No," I answered. "If she had been that sick, she would have come to me for help. That was her way."

What does this woman know anyway?

"She took off as animals do, to find a quiet place in which to go to sleep forever." Sandy opened her eyes to find me shaking my head.

"If she were dead, I'd know it."

Sandy picked up one of my hands and stroked it. "She loved you and wanted to spare you."

"No, she's alive. I would know if she were dead." I stood up to leave, not having gotten the answer I wanted.

Sandy pointed to my left side. "She's right here beside you. She won't leave you."

I looked to my left but saw nothing but the bare floor.

"I see her bending her head toward you, to get her ears scratched. She loved that."

I choked. It was an accurate description of Imp.

"I don't see her," I said. Frustrated, I opened the door to leave.

Sandy stood up and gave me an awkward hug, one to which I responded very stiffly.

I headed back down the hallway, ready to pay the clerk for the few disappointing moments I had spent with Sandy.

Sandy stood there in the doorway and called out, "No charge for today's session."

I turned around, surprised at her generosity.

Then she said something that shook me to the core. "It's in the nature of imps to disappear, but they always return in one form or another."

Sonny

Chapter 30

◦ ◆ ◦

I FELL INTO A RESTLESS SLEEP, hot with a fever and hurt with a headache. I awoke to see Hawk standing by my bed. I gave him a feeble smile.

"How?" I asked.

"Hau," he responded, more of a statement than a question. Then he clarified. "Hau is a way we have in the Lakota language of saying hello, okay, goodbye, whatever."

"I . . . can't do . . . it."

"Why not? You're already doing it in dream time."

The Victorian house. Does he know about the attic door?

"I'm . . . sick." I offered that up as an excuse. It had worked wonders with Mama, letting me off the hook.

Hawk reached over and felt my forehead. His brow wrinkled with consternation. "I'm going to work on you now, but you need to start practicing getting out of this bed and leaving this crippled body behind."

"Why?"

"White people, black people, yellow people—they have so many questions. How? Why? When? Where? Just do it before it's too late."

Well, that sounds ominous.

He rubbed his hands together, closed his eyes, steadied his breathing.

I had so many other questions to ask him but was loathe to interrupt his concentration before he began the energy work on me. I wanted to know how much longer I had before the infection crept up my body to the sensate area. Before the heart stopped or the lungs filled with pneumonia.

What happens when you die? Is it simply a passage through an attic portal, shutting the door behind you? Will a light, or a dog, be there to guide me? Is it the end? Or a beginning?

I can't buy into the image of sitting on a cloud, bedecked in a white robe, strumming a harp and singing God's praises— a 19th century Christian concoction. Booooring.

At least the Muslim vision of a bunch of nubile virgins or the Mormon concept of numerous heavenly wives carries a certain appeal, but those notions seem borne more out of earthly lust than heavenly sanctity. I can't imagine Tess going along with the idea of belonging to a polygamous angel.

I do feel sick. My head knows what my body can no longer feel.

Tess wonders why I don't complain more about my unjust fate, but words will drag me into the suck of bitterness. Mama always told me that negative thinking only leads to more negative thinking, that we all carry burdens of one sort or another. She believed that God had a plan for each one of us.

I'm dangling, God, and this time I'm holding on with only one hand to that branch. I'm trying to keep a smile on my face but I'm hurting more and more. What's the plan for me?

"Hush," said Hawk, his hands smoothing out the aura above my body. "You think too much. Go to sleep."

Instead, in a baritone voice, a slave spiritual reverberated through my mind:

Hush, little baby, now don't you cry.
You know your Mama was born to die.
All my trials, Lord, soon be over.

I could feel my brain start to shut down, but still the song persisted and repeated, this time now in a strong alto, female voice. Familiar, somehow.

There is a tree in Paradise
And the pilgrims call it the Tree of Life.
All my trials, Lord, soon . . .

Oh, yes, I can hear it now. My Mama's voice.

Tess

Chapter 37

．❖．

"ALL I HAVE ARE TROUBLES," I said to Meggie. "My dog's gone. Sonny is going to die. My friend, Cassie, can't pay her bills. I've got this brain trauma and can't keep things straight enough to go back to work. My husband is glad to get rid of me."

We sat opposite each other in her cozy therapist office. It felt good to complain. I wanted her to soothe me with words of sympathy, to feel as sorry for me as I felt for myself.

Instead, she asked me to prioritize. "What's the worst one?"

I started to say "Imp" but paused. "Sonny is more than just a friend."

There, I said it. Let her deal with it—the gap of our ages, the racial differences, his paralysis, the sheer impossibility of romance. The utter tragedy of it all. Now is the time to cry, but I have no more tears left.

"So Sonny is more than just a friend," she said.

I nodded. "We've kissed several times." Embarrassed, I turn my face away from her gaze, like a young adolescent caught in the act.

"Does he love you?"

"Yes, I think he loves me. No, I'm sure about it. He tells me he loves me. Is that so strange? Maybe it's the circumstance in which he finds himself, maybe . . ."

"All these *maybes*. You doubt that someone can love you?"

"I'm damaged goods." I looked down at the floor.

"Are these echoes from the old you or is this part of the new you?"

I started to give the old me a vigorous defense, blame it all on the traumatic brain injury, but I stopped. It wasn't true. Nick had often pointed out how I hid behind my intellect, afraid to let people see the real me inside. He'd once said, "Your students are probably terrified of you or else they think you don't like them."

At that time, that had made no sense to me. I loved teaching. I enjoyed the kids, at least the bright ones. True, I was a bit impatient with those who procrastinated on their homework or didn't study for the exams, thinking them lazy and unmotivated.

"I fell in love with Nick because emotions came so easy to him," I told Meggie. "He liked himself enough to be able to forgive himself the mistakes he made, whereas lurking inside of me was a harsh judge."

"What Freud called the superego." Meggie said.

"My inner judge has a nasty mouth that cuts me down to size whenever I start feeling really good about myself."

Meggie stood up and came over to sit closer to me, a curious move, one that forced me to pay special attention.

"When we're young," she said, "with very bright parents who had lots of expectations for our performance, it made sense to be able to predict what they wanted from us. The only way to do that was to internalize their voices, their probable reactions, what pleased them and what made them angry. We took our parents and put them inside of us."

I nodded to let her know that I was following her foray into child development.

She continued, "But the conditions in which this normal internalization happened were ones in which the child was small and the parents were very big, strong, and all-knowing. When we grew up and became adults, that all-powerful parental voice inside continued as if nothing had changed."

She looked at me.

I guffawed. "So Nick got the loving giant and I ended up with the faultfinder?"

"And both are equally unrealistic," she continued. "None of us are all good or all bad. We're simply human beings staggering about in a world of other species and trying to find our place in this Creation."

She took my hand and said, "It's time that you leave 'damaged goods' behind. You must now become the voice that says 'I'm doing the very best that I can do.' It means you have to give up being that little child trying to please the oversized parent."

Sometimes in therapy or in a conversation, someone says something that breaks through and changes everything. I didn't know it then, but I know it now. Meggie O'Connor, in her own quiet way, sent that mean old judge packing. A couple of times since, that cruel inner voice has tried to reenter my consciousness. No such luck. I simply refuse to respond.

But in one thing, Meggie O'Connor was wrong. She said that I must possess the voice that gives support to myself. It didn't happen that way. Instead, it was her voice that I internalized as the cheering section for the new me.

"Girls' night out?" The cheerful voice on the telephone belonged to Sally McGovern.

As Cassie was in a blue funk, I judged it would be a healthy diversion to get out of the house. Nobody had called about Imp.

"My treat," I insisted over the phone.

"I've got something for you too, a little present." That was all Sally would divulge.

Cassie said it would be good for me to spend some time with someone other than her. She pulled out her wallet and handed me all that she had.

When I started to protest, she answered, "It's your money, Tess. What's left of that check you gave me. Go have fun tonight."

It had already turned dark by the time Sally arrived. A grey manuscript box rode in the backseat of her Ford Escape, anchored by a paper bag with a wine bottle in it.

"Is that it?" I asked.

Sally smiled. "You betcha."

"Can I open it?" I had already pulled the box into my lap.

"Go ahead," she said, keeping her eyes on the road to the Leland Lodge.

I pulled off the top lid and nestled inside were Xeroxed copies of invoices and inventories from the winery managed by Spenser Mudge, none of which made all that much sense to me.

"I don't understand."

Sally looked straight ahead over the steering wheel onto the dark empty road. "It's the proof that they imported grapes from downstate and passed them off as Leelanau wines."

"How did you . . ."

A triumphant smile lit up her face. "Spenser hadn't let anyone at the winery know we had broken up. So-o-o I went there when I knew he was elsewhere and told them I needed to go into the back office to pick up something I'd left. They were very friendly and asked why they hadn't seen me for awhile. I made up some story about being too busy teaching. I couldn't believe how easy it was to find the material. You've got to give Spenser credit. His filing system is very well organized."

"Wow, you did this for me?" I was amazed at her bravado.

"No, I did it for me, Tess. No man drops me like a hot potato without getting a little burnt by the experience."

"Blistered is more like it," I said.

We both laughed at the English teacher in me.

The old me still has parts worth keeping.

Sally pulled into the restaurant parking lot and grabbed the bottle of wine. "I thought we should celebrate tonight, so I brought along a very special wine."

"Oh?"

She cracked a mischievous smile and showed me the unopened bottle with a medal hanging around its neck, reading "Best of Class."

"It isn't," I said.

"Oh yes," she answered, "Only the best. Chardonnay Entre-Nous."

Sonny

Chapter 38

⋅◦⋅

I OPENED MY EYES to find Father Esperance sitting quietly beside my bed, reading a leather-bound black missile.

Probably the Daily Devotions.

I did not begrudge his presence.

His lips moved as he silently read the prayers. He didn't know I had awakened.

It gave me time to study the man, to wonder what had brought him to the priesthood and what had kept him there. He had to be in his late twenties or early thirties. Irish perhaps, from one of those families that raised boys for the priesthood and girls for the nunnery.

Or maybe he was orphaned, found in the bulrushes and brought to the church as an offering.

I hated to admit it. I missed the Brothers who'd taught me at The Most Precious Blood Academy. They were Jesuits of liberal persuasion, having learned to fly under the radar of the more conservative branches of Catholicism. They valued the mind's ability to discern God in all things.

In the school, it was rumored that a couple of the Brothers had "a thing" going with the women who cooked and cleaned for them, leading to a lot of conjecture among my peers about sex and sin. What wasn't mentioned or discussed, due to our adolescent homophobia, was that clearly some of the Brothers were gay. The idea of celibacy, for those of us who had no yearning to become priests, was confusing. As an idea, it seemed noble, sacrificial, but on the personal level, it was abhorrent, an unnatural way to live.

I was curious about Father Esperance, how he put mind and body together, especially since mine had split apart at the neckline.

He looked up from his reading, his eyes a startling blue, a smile upon his lips. "So you have come back into this world."

"Do you . . . believe in . . . celibacy?" It was bold of me.

When life is so tenuous, it gives you all kinds of permission to ask intrusive, impolite questions.

"I pray about it," he said. "There is the temptation, of course, and I am glad of it, because it keeps putting me into the position of choice. Without choice, there is no free will."

"You're not . . . a eunuch."

"You get right to the point, don't you? I'm a man like yourself, which means I have lots of struggles inside and outside of me. What about you? Has the accident made you less a man?"

I think he expected me to say no.

"Yes," I answered. "My body . . . no longer . . . in my . . . control. . . . Can't even . . . masturbate."

"But what about your fantasies? Have you erased all

sensuality from your experience? Is love no longer possible?"

I thought of Tess, the lusciousness of her lips, the appreciation I had upon seeing her body move beneath her clothes, the wish to taste all parts of her, to nibble the salt off her skin.

"Being a priest does not mean you give up being a sexual human being. That's also true for a quadriplegic." Father Esperance smiled and reached out to touch my hand, forgetting that there was no sensation of contact.

"I enjoy my time with you, Sonny. Did anyone ever tell you that you look like . . ."

Jesus? Is that what he's going to utter?

But he didn't. He said, "Did anyone ever tell you that you look like someone trying to find his way home again?"

Mama, are you in that Victorian house? Are you sitting in one of those rooms, watching the soap operas, exclaiming over the stupidity of some of the white gals who should know that their men are cheating on them?

I closed my eyes and tried to visualize that house, see the detail of its exterior. I slowed down my breathing, then walked up the concrete path to the front door. I knocked on the opaque glass panes that did not allow me to see who or what was inside. I twisted the door knob and put my shoulder into the wooden frame, but nothing budged.

Perhaps my own mind is locking me out.

I walked around the house, jumping to see if I could look through a first floor window, but they were too high for me. I circled the house, past the long outdoor porch, and found myself at the back door. No ornate panes of glass in the back door. No welcome sign. But when I turned the door handle, the door began to open . . .

"Hello," she said.

It was Tess.

"Hey, wherever you are, I'm right here." She flicked her fingers in front of my opening eyes.

The Victorian house receded, everything flowing into reverse.

Meanwhile, Tess's cool hands traveled the length of my forehead to my cheeks. "Damn, this fever keeps hanging on!"

I stared at her, unable to talk, my mind all discombobulated, like I was somewhere else. It was hard to climb back into my body, my brain.

"I . . . love you," I squawked. It was the truth, and it bought me time.

"Yes, I know." She smiled and gave me a peck on the cheek. "Tomorrow I'm going to go see Mr. Mudge, give him a piece of my mind."

"Missing . . . few pieces . . . already."

"Yeah well, you don't look so hot yourself. Actually you do look hot." She meant the fever.

"You . . . too." I meant the sweater that stretched tightly across her breasts.

She ignored the flirtation and proceeded to fill me in on her rehab program of the morning, on her dinner with Sally McGovern, on her session with Hawk's wife. "I told her more about us, our feelings for each other."

A warm glow filled my mind. It could have been a sudden flush of fever, but I think not. More likely, it was love reminding me that I am a man first and a quadriplegic only a distant second.

Tess

Chapter 39

• ◆ •

CASSIE INSISTED I MAKE DINNER. "Here's the recipe. Follow every step. I made sure you have all the necessary ingredients."

An assortment of vegetables, some fresh, some frozen, greeted me.

"Oh my," I said, feeling a bit overwhelmed. "This is going to be a lot tougher than you think."

Cassie shrugged her shoulders. "You can't depend on me to do all your cooking."

"I'm sorry." I felt ashamed of my difficulties in following directions.

"No apology needed, Tess. But it's time you pick up some of your old skills."

Then with complete but foolish confidence in my abilities, she exited the kitchen, Scotch glass in hand.

I kicked myself for not being more sensitive to her needs. Here she was doing for me all the time, and what did I do for her?

I looked at the recipe for vegetable soup. *Slice the carrots thin.* I grabbed two carrots and pared them, then looked to Cassie's food processor, but I couldn't figure out how to lock it and get it going. No matter. With a long knife, I did my own slicing.

Chop the onions, mince the garlic, and simmer in butter.

Easy enough, so I did that. Then I thought, *Why not take the frozen corn, asparagus, and lima beans and throw them in with the cooking onions? It would be faster that way, instead of steaming them first.*

When they began to burn and stick to the bottom of the pan, I suddenly remembered that I was supposed to add vegetable broth.

I had to move quickly, because the vegetables were beginning to shrink and curl into themselves. I found the broth. Without measuring, I poured some into the pan. Burnt flecks of lima beans floated to the top of the bubbling soup. For good measure, I added a tablespoon of dried rosemary.

Then I remembered I was supposed to add canned evaporated milk at the end. I scanned the pantry shelves and found the canned milk. I very carefully measured out a cup of it and added it to the soup which immediately assumed a pale yellow color. I brought it back to a boil and then put it on to simmer, very proud that I had remembered to use all the ingredients. I found an extra can of evaporated skim milk on the kitchen table and put it away.

I toasted up a couple of English muffins, buttered them, and set the dining room table. I called Cassie to the table. She reminded me to make us some ice water, while she poured herself another class of Scotch.

We sat down to eat the soup. I watched her carefully as she took the first spoonful of it in her mouth. Her look was one of surprise.

"It's so very sweet," she said.

"Probably the corn or the carrots," I suggested and then took a sample of it myself. It tasted as if someone had poured a bag of sugar into the soup, then sprinkled a little burnt offering on top. I put my spoon down.

"This isn't edible, Cassie."

"The English muffins are great." She demolished one buttered muffin and then retrieved some jam from the pantry. She was gone for a couple of minutes and returned, not only with the jam but also the discarded can of milk.

"I found the culprit," she announced. "The recipe called for Evaporated Skim Milk. The empty can here says Sweetened Condensed Milk."

Elbows on the table, I dropped my head between my hands, a failure as a cook.

Cassie probably thinks I was trying to poison her.

"The muffins taste great with cherry jam. Here, try some," she said.

I looked up. Cassie was trying not to laugh, but it got to be too much for her. We both began giggling until the tears ran out of our eyes.

"I think you also forgot a couple of steps in the recipe," she said before going off into another spasm of laughter. "Maybe next time we'll try something a little easier, and . . ."

"And what?"

"I think I'll stand and supervise."

"I forgot something else."

"What?"

"At the rehab program, the occupational therapist suggested I use a ruler when trying to follow a recipe. That way I won't get distracted and skip a step."

"God Almighty, girl, whatever works."

Cassie insisted that on the days when my vision wasn't too squirrely that I also practice driving on small country roads. I mainly drove up and down the long driveway of Hagen's Heaven, peering into the woods on both sides for the sight of my beloved Imp, gone now too many days.

The weekend had come up and with it a break from the morning rehab program. I told Cassie a half truth, that I was going to practice my driving. She didn't need to know the real plan, as I suspected she would have tried to stop me. I owed Cassie a lot, and in this small way, I could make a down payment.

During the fall, the wineries offered limited weekend hours of wine tasting. I had made sure that Spenser Mudge would be present on Saturday morning.

My heart started beating fast as I drove onto the Leelanau Ridge to his winery. There were several cars already lined up in the parking lot, looking like horses tied to the hitch. I parked my car at some distance so as not to risk nicking another car.

When I walked into the tasting room, replete with a long bar and polished wood walls, I overheard an animated Spenser holding forth about the award-winning chardonnay.

"I don't mind telling you that we have the best vintner in all of Michigan, and this wine is just the first in what I anticipate will be a lot of prize-winning wines."

Spenser was dressed in a tweedy suit without the tie, looking more East Coast than Midwest. Despite being somewhat on the short and paunchy side, he stood with his shoulders set back and his chest forward, a man of substance. He held an unlit cigar in one hand, the bottle of Entre-Nous Chardonnay in another.

A young, pretty woman was pouring samples of wine, moving up and down the bar area, asking the customers what they would like to try next. It was below Spenser's station to man the bar. His job was to talk up the wines and interest the customers into buying more cases.

Unlike Spenser, I was dressed down in old jeans and a flannel shirt. I waited quietly in the background, until most of the crowd had finished the tasting, bought some wine, and gone out the door. When only two couples remained, I approached the bar and Spenser.

"I need to talk to you," I said.

"Has that friend of yours sent you to negotiate?" A tone of sarcastic skepticism underlined his question.

"Mrs. McDermott?"

"Mrs. in name only," he snorted. "Poor Mr. McDermott, so lately in the grave."

"As is true of your aunt."

Two can play this game of insinuation.

"Get to the point," he retorted. "I don't see what your presence accomplishes. She needs to talk to my lawyer and sign some papers."

"You're threatening her."

"Yes, I hired a private eye to do a little investigation into the activities of your so-called friend. What I discovered is not something she would like me to make public. You tell her that."

He turned his back on me and was about to walk away.

"I have a message for you. Drop the lawsuit or else."

He spun around on his heels. "What? You're threatening me? With what? You're way in over your head, Miss . . ."

He had forgotten my name.

No matter. As he stumbled about trying to recollect my name, I pushed my advantage.

I picked up the bottle of Entre-Nous Chardonnay and yanked off the Best of Class medal. I pointed to the phrase "Leelanau Peninsula" on the bottle and said, "Label fraud."

He grabbed the bottle out of my hand, his brow wrinkled in anxious confusion.

"What I know is not something you would like me to make public." I mocked his own words.

"I don't know what you're talking about," he said.

"First off is the Consumer Protection Division in the Michigan Attorney General's Office. Then there's the ATF and the FDA on a federal level. There's also the local police and, of course, I wouldn't want to forget the other wineries on the peninsula who play by the rules. Certainly they would be very interested in your award-winning chardonnay. Oh, what a field day the newspapers would have with all this publicity."

As I ticked off the list, Spenser Mudge's face turned grayer, but his jaw thrust out, defiant and belligerent. Then the facade crumbled.

"You know nothing!" he suddenly shrieked at me.

The pretty server and the two couples at the bar all stopped to look at Mr. Mudge losing his carefully cultivated composure.

"Knowing is nothing," I said. "Proof is everything. I think we have now come to an understanding. You drop the lawsuit and I will shrink back into my quiet, wine-sipping self. Otherwise I will do what I must to protect the integrity of the Leelanau wines."

I smiled at him.

His jaw trembled as he struggled for control.

I decided it was a good time to depart. "Please let Mrs. McDermott know of your decision by this time next week." I reached out my hand as if to conclude a deal, while the other people continued to look at us.

"Entre nous," I whispered.

His trembling hand barely grazed mine, but it was enough. After all, appearances were everything.

With my back to the bar, I smiled and gave him a "gotcha" wink, then walked out the door, mission accomplished.

It was late in the afternoon before Cassie drove to the hospital for her volunteer work. She seemed preoccupied. I was dying to tell her what I'd done, but I had to hold back, lest Spenser Mudge call my bluff.

"On the way home," she said, "we'll pick up the ingredients for an easy crab soup and salad. I'll give you the recipe."

I rolled my eyes. "Aren't you forgetting something?"

"Yes, yes I am," she replied.

I expected her to say something about my disastrous dinner the night before, and she didn't disappoint me.

"Let's not forget to pick up some English muffins," she said.

We exchanged amused looks.

"I'm serious, Tess. This week, I want you to cook every dinner."

"But what's the rush?" I asked.

"I want you to be ready."

"Okay," said the new me.

The old me would have stopped and asked, "Ready for what?"

Sonny looked kind of ragged. He was emerging from the latest bout of fever, but it was draining him. His body sagged into the bed, his face more gaunt.

Maybe it was my imagination, but the ventilator sounded louder, more dominant, pushing the breath into him and out of him. The whole machinery of life was wearing him down.

Yet his eyes seemed brighter, clearer, searching, as if everything were coming into focus.

I told him about my encounter with Spenser.

"Good work," he lipped.

I told him about my disastrous dinner and the burned lima beans.

Painfully slow, he spoke of the priest who visited him. Father Esperance, he said, had come to give him hope.

"I've . . . discovered," said Sonny, "that I . . . am still . . ." He paused, then continued, "a Catholic."

This confession of faith meant little to me, but I could tell it was very important to him. I guessed it meant he had forgiven the Church for depriving him of Mama Dora.

In truth, it scared me that he was coming full circle, that he was making peace with himself before it was too late.

Sonny, are you getting ready to die? God, I hope not, because I'm not ready to lose you.

I said nothing of my fears. If there was one thing the brain injury was teaching me, it was that we couldn't order time to bend to our own needs.

When Cassie and I left the hospital, it had already turned dark outside. I looked up into the blue-black sky and could see the moon rising over Grand Traverse Bay. Slowly but inevitably, the waning moon was slicing down the light.

Sonny

Chapter 40

. ◆ .

I'M PROUD OF TESS and what she has done. It took guts to confront Spenser Mudge. I would have loved to have been a fly on the wall and seen the whole thing.

You go, girl!

I know she is struggling to relearn old abilities, to make new connections within that rattled brain of hers, but she is moving ahead, taking chances, doing what seems right to her. Who cares if a few burnt lima beans float to the surface?

I wanted her to know that I, too, was moving ahead in my life. I told her about the priest, how by sharing his own humanity and struggles with me, I could begin to reconcile myself to my loss of faith.

Truth is, God never abandoned me, Tess. I was the one to walk out the church door, locking it behind me.

Truth is, Tess, that while chained to this bed in a lifeless body, I am rediscovering that God is in all things.

God is in the wind, Tess.

God is in the blue sky.

God is in the moon, in the night, and in the stars.

God is in Hawk's hands.

God is in your kiss, Tess, and in the love we have for each other.

And God is waiting for me, Tess, somewhere in that old Victorian house.

Tess

Chapter 41

· ◆ ·

ONE WEEK—that's what I gave Mr. Mudge. In the meantime, Cassie kept me to a schedule of cooking.

"Tonight," she said, "we're going to eat Moo Shu Chicken. It's a healthier takeoff from the Moo Shu Pork of Chinese restaurants." She handed me the recipe.

Moo Shu Chicken (4)

2 cups shredded cooked chicken
4 wheat tortillas
1 (8 oz.) coleslaw mix
2 Tbs. canola oil
1 Tb. soy sauce
2 Tbs. hoisin sauce

Heat oil in skillet.
Add slaw, cook 2-3 min., softened but crunchy.
Add chicken, cook 1-2 min.
Add soy and hoisin sauces.

Remove from heat.

Microwave tortillas on High 45-60 secs. with wax paper on top.

Place 1/4 chicken/slaw mix on tortilla, fold and roll.

"Okay," I said. "I think I can do that."

"If you like it hotter, we can add a more spicy Chinese stir fry sauce," Cassie added.

"No, let's keep it simple," I begged.

She watched me carefully as I pulled out the two-day-old, half-eaten roast chicken and started to cut it with a knife.

"That's not what I call shredding."

I rolled my eyes. "I don't know how to work your food processor."

We stopped while Cassie gave me a demonstration and then had me repeat the steps. She also presented me with a ruler to place under each succeeding line of instructions for the cooking process.

It worked. I actually made a tasty Moo Shu Chicken dish.

"Hurrah," said Cassie. "That calls for a drink."

She poured me a small glass of wine and a bigger glass of Scotch for herself. We both sat down at the table.

"Cassie, can I say something?" I was reluctant to broach the topic.

"What?" Her mouth was full of Moo Shu chicken.

"You've been drinking a lot of whiskey lately."

Her chin wrinkled upward as if she were thinking about what to say back to me. "Does it bother you?"

"It worries me."

She guffawed. "I'm not an alcoholic if that's what you mean." Then she paused. "Yet."

"Is there anything I can do to help you?" I was dying to tell her about my confrontation with Mr. Mudge, but I held back.

Her hand rubbed across her forehead. "I wish I had been an accountant, Tess. Or a banker or a stockbroker. I stupidly let Devin do all the bill paying and finances, so I had no idea of the debts we'd incurred. I guess he didn't want me to know. Anyway, I paid off those debts with the life insurance but it left me little to live on. You can imagine my surprise when I heard from the estate lawyer for Natalie Hagen. If only . . ."

"If only what?"

Cassie took a sip of her whiskey. "If only she'd left me a million dollars to maintain this place. The taxes alone will take most of my Social Security payments and now there's this legal matter."

"Surely this place is worth millions. You could sell it, Cassie, and go live elsewhere."

"Yes, that would be one solution. But where would I ever find a place like this again?"

I understood her dilemma, because there was no other place like Hagen's Heaven on the Leelanau Peninsula. This was Cassie's last chance at living in grandeur, before age began to force her into smaller and smaller spaces.

"Oh Cassie, I love you." I said. I got up from the table and put my arms around her.

"Oh now, now, now," she said, extricating herself from my exuberant affection. "I'll think of something. But in the meantime, you've got to do what you've got to do." She raised the glass of whiskey and polished it off, grinning at me.

It's hard for her to accept love and compliments. Maybe that's why Devin turned to Natalie. Maybe that's the same reason Nick fell in love with Sandy.

"What shall we have for dinner tomorrow?" Cassie asked, hoping to distract me from the topic of herself.

I tried to entertain Sonny with descriptions of cooking experiments and program complaints, but he was only half listening.

In the middle of my discourse on making a Caesar salad with smoked salmon, croutons, and Parmesan cheese, Sonny asked, "What do . . . you think . . . happens?"

"We eat it," I answered.

"At the . . . end."

"We burp." I knew what he was asking, but I didn't want to even consider such questions.

Sonny frowned at my evasions.

"Look Sonny, you've gone and gotten religious on me. I'm not a Catholic. I'm not an atheist or even an agnostic. I'm nothing. Now you want me to tell you what happens when we all die? I don't know." The irritation in my voice warned him to lay off the topic, but Sonny persisted.

"An end . . . or a . . . beginning?"

"I'll tell you what. If I die first, I'll come back and tell you."

Sonny stared at me, not finding what I had to say at all amusing.

I reached over to touch his forehead.

"No fever. Maybe the antibiotics have finally stopped the infection."

Sonny didn't look the least bit convinced.

The silence was killing me. It was the kind of silence you can fall into, like a crevasse as you try to climb a mountain. So, instead of going up, you hurtle down into areas you do not want to go.

"Sonny, I'm scared by what I don't know. I think you have other people who can talk to you about these things better than I. There's Hawk, the medicine man, or that priest. Surely they have some answers."

Sonny, talk to me. There's a gulf growing between us.

Wrinkles furrowed my brow. I put my hands against his cheek. We stayed there in the silence for a long time. Finally Sonny said, "I love . . . you, Tess."

"Me too," I answered, stroking down the side of his nose toward his mouth with my fingers.

He whispered, "Come. . . . Lie down . . . beside . . . me."

It was awkward, but I lowered his bed and climbed up on it, kicking my shoes off in the process. I kept my fingers touching his face, playing with his mouth.

Again and again, he kissed my fingers.

Words no longer mattered.

"I feel so helpless," I confessed to Meggie. "I was unable to answer his questions. I was scared by them as well. I can't bear the thought of losing him, especially after Imp."

"And Nick," she added. "And your job teaching," she continued. "And making gourmet meals."

"Stop! You're making me feel even worse," I said.

Sometimes, sympathy just gets you nowhere.

Meggie smiled. "He wants to talk about his death with you. If you continue to wallow in your fears, you cut him off from what he most needs to say. Words give shape to what scares us the most. While words can trap emotions into preset molds, the expression of feelings releases them and can even create something beautiful out of something overwhelming."

"You mean I've failed him."

"Temporarily."

"What should I do?"

She thought for a minute. "The task is threefold. You must first listen to what he has to say. You must reflect back to him your understanding of what he has said. Third, you must reassure him that whatever conclusion he has worked out for himself, it's going to be okay."

"But it's not okay if he dies!"

Why should I lie to him about that?

"We each come to our own understanding of what the end of our lives mean. Some see themselves as going into the arms of Jesus. Others to a place of fulfillment of all their earthly desires. For some, it's simply a period in the sentence of life. Then there are those who think we slip out of these bodies and enter new ones, returning back as babies."

"What do you think?" I was curious about how Dr. Meggie O'Connor had worked this out for herself.

Her eyes drifted over to a shelf on which rested a glass jar with a chrysalis, then shifted back to me. "I think death is a passage of transformation, that there is another life beyond this one."

I frowned with doubt. "It must be nice to have such faith."

"I once knew a Lakota woman by the name of Winona Pathfinder. She taught me many things but perhaps the most important lesson was to keep my eyes open to the world around me. I don't understand death through any profession of faith, Tess. Experience has been my teacher."

"I don't understand."

I could see that I was making her uncomfortable about sharing her personal life in my therapy hour, but I needed some guidance.

"Winona's been dead now for several years, but still she comes back to teach me from time to time."

"You mean you imagine her talking to you?'

Meggie shook her head. "No. Her reappearance is not a figment of my imagination. She comes and talks to me when I get out of balance."

"But she's a dead person."

"Yes," Meggie answered.

My mouth must have dropped open. I looked at Meggie and said, "But you seem like such a normal person."

"Yes," she said, and we both laughed.

God Almighty, what is my world coming to?

Sonny

Chapter 42

HAWK APPEARED in the morning hours, wearing his felt hat with a long black feather stuck in the beaded hat band. He touched my forehead and could feel that the fever had finally abated. His hands roamed in circles above my body. He then pulled the feather from his hatband and stroked it above my body, as if smoothing out surface wrinkles.

"It's an eagle feather," he explained.

When done, he seemed satisfied and tucked the feather securely back into the hatband.

"You been doing the homework?" he asked.

I smiled. "I've . . . gotten . . . through . . . the back . . . door."

"Most people like to go to the front door."

"Is she . . . there?"

"The Grandmother is always with you. You live on her skin. You eat her food. She grounds you."

My brow wrinkled.

No, I meant Mama. Is she there?

Hawk could see by my frustrated expression that I wasn't talking about Grandmother Earth.

"You talking about your girlfriend?"

"No. . . . Mama."

Hawk pulled up a chair. "This is going to take some time. I can only tell you what the Lakota think. Every tribe of human beings sees but a sliver of the truth. Even the Bible says we see through a glass darkly," he reminded me.

"What . . . happens?"

"When you die, your Spirit leaves your body. You cross over into the next dimension. Others have made that journey before you. Sometimes the Spirits of your loved ones come back to this dimension to help you make it across. When you arrive, it is new and confusing and there is a time of orientation. In the Lakota understanding, we say you then have to make a journey to the House of Grandfather of the West. There are things you have to learn there. When that is complete, then you travel to the House of the Grandfather of the North, then to the East, and then eventually to the South. We say new life comes from the South."

"Rein . . . carnation," I lipped. The word was too long to express on the ventilator's exhale.

Hawk shrugged his shoulders. He had told me as much as he thought I could digest.

But I had more questions.

"Does it . . . hurt?"

"The journey across is difficult, but if you're asking about physical pain, the answer is no. You shrug off the body. But emotional pain is something else."

He paused, then continued. "We're attached to those whom we love and have left behind. How can they let go of us when we're dead? How can we, the dead, let go of them? It's a problem. Love doesn't die at the point of death."

I thought of Tess.

It would be like a trade. I'd get Mama back but I'd have to give up Tess.

"Mama?"

Hawk remembered my initial question. "It depends on how attached she still is to you. If she has let go of you for some time now, then she will already be well on her way in the next dimension. She may leave you markers so you will know how to find her."

"Do I . . . have a . . . choice?"

Hawk's gaze turned inward, as if he had suddenly exited this conversation and entered into another. He grew very quiet.

I said nothing so as not to disturb him, and the silence continued for a very long time.

Then Hawk refocused back into the room, onto me. "Spirits say we all will die sometime, that you have a little time left but not much. They say, 'Use that time wisely.' They told me to tell you that when you're ready, I should sing you across with the old Lakota prayer songs. The choice is not *if*, but *when*."

The choice is not if, but when.

What he's saying is that the only control I have over events is the date.

After Hawk left, I was anxious for a visit with Father Esperance. Much to my relief, he came after the noon hour.

I had thought I would ask him about death and dying, but instead it was another question that emerged in hesitant fashion.

"Why . . . do you . . . come here?"

"To the hospital? No, I think you are asking why do I come to your room."

I smiled in agreement.

"If I told you that it was to give you comfort, that would only be partially true. If I told you it was part of my priestly vocation, that would only be partially true. I come for two main reasons. There is something about you, Sonny, something deep and searching that reminds me of myself when I was younger and not so tainted by the sins of the world. Maybe I am hoping to get some of that passion back from being around you."

I didn't expect such a personal statement.

He continued, "As for the second reason, not many of us know when we are going to die. We always postpone the date into some far and uncertain future, measuring our life-stick to those of our immediate ancestors. You don't have the leisure to do that. That's why you ask such direct questions. That's why I don't give you bullshit answers. I grow in admiration as you struggle to face your own mortality with so much courage."

He doesn't know how scared I am.

It was almost as if he could intuit my thoughts. "Courage doesn't mean being without fear, but it does mean asking good questions and trying to approach one's own death with a sense of integrity and purpose."

Purpose? That's a new thought: approaching death with a purpose.

Not being able to banter easily in a conversation requires that the other person fill in the gaps.

In the silence often comes the wisdom.

The priest's self-honesty unsettled me. I wondered why he didn't load me down with all the regular Catholic teachings, but he probably guessed that I had already been well indoctrinated at The Most Precious Blood Academy.

"Will you," I asked, "say . . . the rosary?"

"Now?" He had not expected that request.

"No," I answered.

Then he understood.

He reached out, the back of his hand touching my cheek. "Of course I will."

Tess would tell me that I'm simply covering all my bases.

I was tired by the time she arrived in the afternoon, hair akimbo, looking very distracted.

"Things aren't right with Cassie. She's insisting that I cook every night and gets frustrated that I can never remember how to use her food processor. That's new stuff and my brain doesn't respond well to new tasks. She's pushing me to drive my car more, even though my eyes aren't right yet. I don't understand what's going on."

I could see that Tess felt very uneasy. Cassie had been her savior. Maybe it was like a Mama bird pushing the fledgling out of the nest.

On and on Tess talked, letting off steam. Then abruptly she stopped and said, "I talk too much. I need to shut up and listen to you." She folded her hands and studied me as if I were a student come to discuss a term paper.

I had already talked myself out with Hawk and Father Esperance. What I wanted from Tess was simply the smell of her, the touch of her hand, the taste of her lips.

"Well," she said into my silence, "you asked me the other day what I think happens at the end? See, I remembered." She was very pleased with herself, as memory had become a real problem for her.

I waited.

"And I shut you up because I didn't want to talk about it." She added, "That wasn't right or kind of me."

I waited some more.

"I don't know," she said.

"Seaweed . . . king," I prompted.

"I haven't thought about him for some time. That's progress. Okay, he gave me a choice whether to slip into the deep or come back into my body."

That's not the choice I've been given.

Tess was trying to work it out, thinking aloud. "It could have been short circuits firing in my brain, making him up, but I don't think so, Sonny. I think there must be a place where we all go, that our stories don't end with death. Life is a journey, so why shouldn't death be one too? A different one where the body is no longer the container of our soul. You know what Meggie, Dr. O'Connor, told me the other day?"

I suspect she told you to stop running away.

Tess continued, "She said that the current thinking in psychology is that we don't have a singular self but rather a repertory company of selves within each one of us. That we create a fictional self to maintain a sense of predictability for others. That maybe all selves are contextual or that there is a Self beyond the many selves."

Tess furrowed her brow. "I like that last idea best. I think that must be our soul. What do you think?"

I was too tired to think, but I lipped, "Interesting."

"Sonny, if she's right about that, then who am I? Who are you? What does it mean when we say we love each other?"

Love is, Tess. All these questions matter little in the spotlight of love.

"Come here . . . Tess."

It must have been the way I said it, because Tess stopped all her intellectual meanderings and climbed into bed next to me. She lay there, her cheek against mine, her lips buried in my neck, her breath matching the pattern of the ventilator.

In the silence comes true wisdom.

Chapter 43

•◆•

WHEN WE GOT HOME from the hospital, a police car was sitting at the top of the driveway. My heart jumped.

Maybe Imp has been found!

But no dog appeared at the car window. Only a man in his early forties, who stepped out of the car to greet us.

"Detective Swenson. I assume that one of you is Cassie McDermott?" He addressed Cassie while looking me up and down.

"That's me," Cassie said, appearing decidedly nervous but gracious. "Come in, come in," she said. "Would you like a cup of coffee?"

"Yes, Ma'am, that would be kind of you. I hate to bother you, but I have some questions."

"Have you seen my missing Sheltie?" I asked, not willing to let go of the possibility that this was about my dear pal.

"No, I'm sorry. It's about Natalie Hagen," he said, stepping into the kitchen nook.

Cassie rolled her eyes at me. "She knows nothing," Cassie said, nodding at me.

"I'm innocent," I replied, playing along with Cassie's weird sense of humor.

He turned intense blue eyes upon me. "Innocent of what?"

With her back to us, Cassie muttered, "Well, maybe not so innocent."

His eyes traveled to my bare ring finger. He lowered his six-foot muscular frame down upon a chair and took off his hat. His dark brown hair showed streaks of white at the edges.

Cassie barked at me. "Well, don't just stand there. Get down the ginger snap cookies." She was keeping herself busy brewing the coffee.

I hustled to the cupboards for plates and cookies.

Meanwhile, Cassie snorted, "I really don't have much to say, never having met the lady, Detective Swenson."

"It's less of a mouthful to call me Charles." He smiled at me as I placed the plate of cookies in front of him.

Out of his view, Cassie grimaced at his familiarity. It was clear she didn't want to get cozy with any cop.

Why is she so anxious? He seems nice enough to me.

"This was her house, was it not?" He took a cookie.

"More like a mansion I would say," I replied, hoping to spare Cassie having to answer all the questions.

"I gather she must have been a very wealthy lady after her husband died. Your husband knew her, didn't he?"

Cassie poured the coffee into a newly chipped coffee mug and brought it to the table, black and bitter. "Yes," she answered, placing the mug in front of him.

I thought she was on the verge of being rude, so I asked, "Would you like some cream or sugar with that?"

He studied Cassie's face and silently shook his head.

"What kind of relationship did they have?"

Cassie snorted, "Well, it sure wasn't a business one, if that's what you're driving at."

To spare her, I jumped in. "They had a long-term affair about which Cassie knew nothing; isn't that right, Cassie?"

Cassie, her back to the detective while she poured herself a cup of coffee, only nodded her head. She then spun around and addressed me. "Tess, this doesn't have anything to do with you. Detective Swenson here wants me to answer the questions."

My cheeks reddened.

Why is it so hard for me to keep quiet and let others do the talking?

Still, I wasn't going to leave Cassie alone with the detective. I busied myself by pouring another cup of coffee, this time for me.

Cassie sat down at the kitchen table, facing the detective.

"I apologize about having to ask you such indelicate questions," he said.

"Then tell me why you're here," Cassie replied.

"Certain questions have risen as to the manner in which Natalie died and her involvement with your husband," he said, then added, "And you."

"Is there any evidence of a crime having been committed?" Cassie was not going to be passive in the interrogation.

"The coroner stated that she died of a broken neck, the result of a fall down the stairs. She was discovered by the cleaning woman the next morning. There was no evidence of alcohol or drug intoxication in her system."

Cassie looked straight at him. "Accidents do happen, Detective Swenson. When my husband learned of her death, he plunged into a deep depression. I, of course, didn't understand why and assumed he was having business difficulties."

"Was he having financial problems?"

Cassie sighed. "I should have been more aware of all that he was carrying on his shoulders, but he thought to protect me by keeping the troubles all to himself. Only after he died did I learn of the business debts. I guess he kept thinking the economy would turn around and things would get better."

"Where was he the night Natalie died?"

"Devin was no murderer, if that's what you're thinking. It's painfully clear how much he loved that woman. He was away at a conference in Chicago while Natalie was here. I'm sure you could substantiate that fact. Besides, why would he kill his mistress?"

I knew how much it hurt Cassie to acknowledge the affair.

Detective Swenson gave away nothing in his facial expression. "He certainly stood to gain by the inheritance of her property."

"But he didn't know about her will."

"He fell to his death too, didn't he? Off a bridge. Hit his head on a rock and drowned."

Cassie turned away her face. "Yes," she said, very quietly. "I was there when that happened."

She never told me that!

"Could it possibly have been a murder suicide pact between them?" he asked.

Cassie whipped her head around. "Just what are you implying?"

I could hear the anger brewing just beneath her words.

"Perhaps they felt their love affair was doomed. Sometimes, love only survives in the forbidden zone. Here were two people, supposedly happily married, having an affair that spanned years. Then one becomes a widow, unmarried. She's available, but it would mean he'd have to extricate himself from . . ." Detective Swenson leaned forward.

Cassie exploded. "Devin would never have left me!"

He sat back. "Precisely."

I couldn't keep quiet any longer. "You mean to say you think Devin and Natalie cooked up their own deaths?"

Cassie stood up. "I don't believe that for a moment. Natalie fell to her death because she wasn't looking where she was going. Besides, she was a woman."

Both Detective Swenson and I frowned in puzzlement.

Cassie explained. "No woman is going to be stupid enough to be the first one to go in a double suicide. What if the man chickened out at the last moment? Nope, you're barking up the wrong tree, mister."

Detective Swenson obviously knew he had pushed Cassie as far as she was going to cooperate. He asked and received the name, date, and location of the Chicago conference that Devin McDermott was supposedly attending when Natalie met her unfortunate end. He stood up, ready to leave.

Cassie busied herself cleaning up the coffee mugs while I ushered the good-looking man out the door.

"Are you Mrs. McDermott's daughter?" he asked.

"No, I'm simply a homeless, unemployed, about-to-be-divorced lodger in the charity of her heart."

He stepped back and took a second look at me.

"I know," I explained. "I look and sound normal, but I'm not. I was in a terrible car accident. Traumatic brain injury." I tapped the side of my head.

"I'm so sorry," he stammered, having lost confidence in the conversation. "I don't know what to say."

"At least I didn't fall down the stairs and break my neck."

He nodded. "Yes," he said, "It kind of puts things into perspective, doesn't it?"

When I returned to the kitchen, Cassie was emptying the dishwasher in rough fashion, banging the cups together, slamming shut the cupboard doors, throwing silverware into the drawer.

"This is just the beginning shot across the bow. First there are the questions, then the insinuations, then the gossip among the locals. 'Did you know that Mrs. McDermott's husband cheated on her with Natalie Hagen? They all died in mysterious fashion, first Mr. Hagen, then Natalie, then Mr. McDermott, bang, bang, bang, and she got all the goodies. Wonder how she managed that?'"

"Cassie, how could anybody think badly of you?"

She was not about to be comforted. She stormed out of the room and up the stairs, then stood at the top. "Maybe I should jump too. Wouldn't that give the little biddies in town something to talk about?"

"Cassie!"

"Oh, don't worry, Tess. I'm not the suicidal type. And Devin was not a murderer. Unfaithful yes, a liar to boot, a failure at business, but a murderer? No. That double suicide murder theory is a bunch of crock."

"Perhaps," I ventured, "Natalie did kill herself. Perhaps she demanded that Devin leave you and he refused."

The suggestion stopped Cassie in the middle of her tirade. "Maybe," she said. "I rather like that idea."

"You know," I said, continuing in the same vein, "gossip can flow both ways."

Cassie stood up a little taller, as if looking in a mirror while sucking in her gut, then expelled her breath. "To be suspected of a crime or pitied as an unloved woman—those are my choices? This place is feeling less and less like home to me."

She retreated to her bedroom.

Sonny

Chapter 44

• ◆ •

ACCORDING TO TESS, an intransigent cold front was descending from Canada. The moon had bleached from a golden harvest moon to a pale specter of itself, a rocky outcrop orbiting in dark space. No rays across the ever-lit hospital floor. Tess described the expectant stillness of the chilling air, but in my sterile room, I sensed no such thing.

I knew that, outside my prison walls, people were ramping up their furnaces. The damp cold in Chicago had taught me how people hunkered down in the dens of their homes when the North winds arrived.

But nothing ever changes in hospital spaces. Death is held at bay.

I looked at Tess. "October . . . 31st," I said.

"No," she answered, "It's only the 25th." She checked the date on her Velcro-strapped digital watch.

"The day . . . of the . . . Dead."

"Huh?"

"Hawk says . . . when the veil . . . between . . . the worlds . . . is . . . thinnest." It was an effort for me to say so much.

"October 31st?"

"Yes."

"Okay," Tess said.

"A good day . . . to die."

Tess's eyes widened in alarm. "No, no, no." She looked around as if to call for help, then returned her gaze to me. "You're okay, yes?"

"No," I answered.

She touched my forehead. "But there's no fever."

How could I tell her that the mind often knows before the body what is going to happen? The infection is still there. The fever is simply awaiting another curtain call.

"On my . . . own terms."

She shook her head. "You can't. I won't allow it. I need you here, Sonny. Who will I talk to about all my problems? Who will listen? Have you seen the hospital psychiatrist?"

Then she stopped and asked, "How will you do it? You can't take pills or hang yourself or shoot a gun or even stop the tube feeding."

She followed my line of vision to the ventilator, then backed away from it, lifting her hands in protest. "If you think I'm going to be the one to turn it off for you, well it ain't going to happen, Sonny."

I smiled at her.

No way will I ask you to perform that task.

"Hospital . . . staff."

"They can't do it. The Hippocratic oath. Nope, you're out of luck." Tess said it with a definitive air as if all discussion were closed.

"Comfort . . . care." Again I smiled at her, wanting her to know that this was my decision, but that I understood how hard it was for her to hear it.

Tess grew more agitated by the moment. "I'll be back," she said, disappearing from the room. She had gone to ask the staff what could or couldn't be done about my decision.

During her brief absence, Father Esperance entered the room. "How are you today?"

"October . . . 31st," I answered.

He paused but a millisecond. "Okay. I'll be here. You sure about this?"

"Yes."

Tess barged into the room, then balked upon seeing the priest. "He isn't a practicing Catholic anymore," she barked.

He ignored that remark and put out his hand to shake her hand. "I'm Father Esperance. You must be Tess."

She backed away, then pointed to the ventilator. "Do you know about this?"

The priest nodded.

"Well, isn't it a sin to commit suicide?" Tess was pulling out all the stops.

Father Esperance looked at me, then at her. "He loves you, Tess. He knows you're hurting."

God bless him for speaking the truth.

"No, I'm not hurt. I'm angry," she said. "At both of you for accepting what I cannot accept."

"Tess," I said, "Come . . . here."

She reluctantly inched her way toward me, not letting herself get anywhere near the priest, whom she probably saw as a co-conspirator.

"What?" she asked me.

"Closer."

She bent her ear close to my lips.

I whispered, "I love . . . you, Tess."

She put her lips close to my left ear. "Then don't leave me, Sonny."

A hot tear fell on my ear.

"Please," she begged. "I know you hope to find Mama Dora, but it may not happen. I'm real, alive, flesh and blood, Sonny. You have me here. I'm not a hope or a dream or an illusion."

"Tess . . . so hard . . . Gonna die . . . soon . . . Help me."

Father Esperance stood up and left to give us privacy.

Her delicate fingers wiped a tear off my cheeks. She inhaled her grief and anger, then exhaled in a loud sigh. Tess was coming around.

"You want me here on October 31st when they disconnect the ventilator?"

"Yes."

"Do you know how hard that will be for me, Sonny?"

"Yes."

"I love you, Sonny. I would do anything for you."

"I know."

"But I have a favor to ask of you."

"Yes?"

I would grant you the world if I could.

"Come back from there in another form or whatever to let me know that you're okay. To let me know you still love me."

I winked at her and said, "I'll be . . . your . . . guardian . . . angel."

She cradled my cheeks with her warm hands, lowered her face, and kissed me. "You already are, Sonny."

Hawk arrived during the early evening hours. I let him know of my chosen date with death.

"I'll sing you Across," he said.

Without argument or question, he understood and accepted my decision.

Already the fever was returning in the night's encroaching darkness, the infection creeping out of my rotting body into the only part of me that remained sensate. Slowly, I could feel my thoughts grow fuzzy with the swarming, languid heat. Soon, my consciousness would bank down, overwhelmed.

"Thank you," I muttered to Hawk, wanting him to know how much I appreciated the way he was helping me move onto the next phase of the journey.

I don't think he heard me, as he was working on me with his eagle feather, trying to infuse me with enough energy to keep me alive so that I could depart this life on my own terms.

As much as I had wanted to spend my last days on earth in a highly conscious state, it was not to be. The fever was a flood that rode over me and into me and through me and I was but a floating particle buffeted in the swirl and whirlpools of the body's final defense.

As I began sinking into its depths, I heard myself call out, not the prayer of a man who makes dignified, courageous choices, but the cry of a little lost boy.

"Mama, help me."

Tess

Chapter 45

· ◆ ·

CASSIE HAD ONE LAST CHORE to do before settling into the house for the evening. She had made an appointment to see her lawyer and it was clear that she didn't want me to go with her.

I waited until she had left before collecting my keys and heading to the car. I knew the visit by the detective had really unnerved her. A week was up by my calculations, and it was time to confront Spenser Mudge. He was obviously the source of the detective's fishing expedition.

The winery was about to close its doors when I arrived. One look at my face, and Mr. Mudge released the last employee. That left just the two of us in the tasting room.

I picked up a display bottle of the winning chardonnay and pulled off its award medal. "I'm gonna hang this around your neck."

He wagged his hand like a dog's tail. "Now, now, let's not get upset here. I've been thinking about what you said."

"Yes, and who sent that detective up to the house as a warning shot at Cassie?"

"What detective?"

"Oh, come off it. You know. Swenson, Swanson, something like that. He had a whole lot of questions to ask about the death of your aunt, insinuating that maybe it wasn't an accident."

"Honestly I didn't . . ."

"Already, Cassie sees people looking at her in a different way. It's a small town, Mr. Mudge, and if you can't keep your suspicions to yourself, well then neither can I. Only mine aren't concocted out of thin air. I have receipts to prove what a phony you are."

I knew my eyes were slitted like a snake about to strike. I was furious, raging at a lot of things—the accident, Sonny's decision, Nick and Sandy, but most of all, at this slime ball of a human being.

How dare he deny the obvious?

His puffy cheeks reddened as he gasped in protest.

"I didn't do it!" he shouted.

That stopped me.

"Well then, who in the hell set that bulldog detective on Cassie?"

"I think I know."

I waited to see how he planned to squirm out of this situation.

"After you came by last week, I went to see my attorney. I wanted to know how much damage you could do to my position here at the winery. He told me that if you had proof to back up your claims, then I might as well kiss this job goodbye. I'd be finished in this community."

"Precisely what you are now doing to Cassie."

"No, I swear, I've not said anything to anybody but the attorney."

"And he is bound by attorney-client confidentiality," I said.

"Yes, I'm sure he said nothing to anyone, but . . ."

"But what? The proverbial fly on the wall?"

To my surprise, Spenser Mudge nodded. "His office is in a very old building, one that is not truly soundproofed. His secretary, a lovely woman, has been known to share a tidbit or two that she's overheard."

"If that's the case, why doesn't he fire her?"

Spenser Mudge again wagged his hand in the air. "It's a delicate situation between them. She's a very attractive woman."

"And he's a married man."

"Yes. You do understand. I think she is the source of any innuendos. I truly am sorry that I brought up any of this business. It's better to leave well enough alone. Agreed?"

"Oh, but the cat is out of the bag now. You want me to keep quiet while Cassie is being skewered in public opinion? Not what I would call a fair deal." I rattled the medal against the bottle of "Leelanau" chardonnay.

As if to catch me off-balance, he asked. "Where did you get those receipts and from whom? Oh, don't answer that. It was that bitch, Sally McGovern, wasn't it? I could get her for theft of business property, you know."

He was trolling for a bargaining chip. I did owe Sally McGovern a lot.

A scuzzy smile emerged onto his face.

"You're such a scumbag," I said.

"I've been called worse. You leave me alone; I leave her and that Cassie woman alone."

"Well, at least I understand one thing," I stepped closer to the winery door.

"What's that?"

I opened the door and turned back to look at the pudgy, puffy Spenser Mudge, dressed in a tweed jacket, trying to look the part of a well-heeled country gentleman. "Why your aunt passed you over in her will. You were never worthy of Hagen's Heaven."

The clashing temperatures of summer and winter blasted through that night, shaking down what little foliage was left on the trees after the freak snowstorm. From the outside porch, I looked out onto the fragility of leaves and the ferocity of the wind, swirling first this way and then that way.

All the voices of the forest hushed before the roar of the cold wind. No bird calls, no raccoon squabbles, no coyote chorus, no distant motor boat on the water.

As I stood outside, my tears fell fast and furious. I wasn't weeping for the end of fall, for Sonny's imminent death, for Cassie's troubles, for the state of my bruised brain. No, I was weeping for Imp. I could no longer maintain the fantasy that she was roaming about nearby, chasing moles and chipmunks. I had to accept that I would never see her again.

"Imp, I love you!" I shouted out into the gale. "I will always love you!"

If only my heart could go into hibernation and wake up to a warm, embracing spring day and she was back in my arms again.

Chilled to the bone, I turned back to the front door, clasped the solid handle, and entered. Cassie wasn't downstairs. I set about preparing a simple meal as she had taught me. When all was simmering on the back burners, I climbed upstairs to her bedroom, expecting to find her taking a nap.

Cassie was not asleep. Instead, she had gotten out her two biggest suitcases and was slowly emptying her drawers.

"Cassie, what are you doing?"

"As soon as this storm is over, I'm going away for awhile. Don't worry. I've arranged with a caretaker in town to come whenever you need help with anything."

"But I can't stay here alone, all by myself."

Cassie straightened back up. "Why not? You can cook and you can drive. I need you to be here to watch over this place. Invite that McGovern woman to come live with you."

"But I can't afford this place anymore than you can."

She smiled. "I've been working on that and will leave you some instructions. I'm not going to disappear, Tess. I'll return. I don't know when, but you have my cell phone number. You can always reach me that way."

It was childish, I know, but I was overwhelmed by feelings of abandonment. Nobody—not Imp, not Sonny, not Nick, not Cassie wanted to stick around. It was like I was some toxic poison to those I loved.

I quit Cassie's room, annoyed at her lack of empathy for my situation, and retreated into my bedroom downstairs for a good cry.

Nobody loves me. Damaged goods.

Then, damn it if I didn't hear Meggie's voice speaking in my head. "Time to say goodbye to the judge. You are doing the very best you can right now."

Sonny

Chapter 46

⋄

IN AND OUT OF THE FEVER, *I come and go.*

I saw or thought I heard the crying of Tess, the rosary from Father Esperance, the whispered prayers of Hawk, but I was too deep into the fever to either acknowledge them or respond. Sometimes, it was simply a blank slate. Other times, snatches of dreams emerged.

I arrive at the house again, walking straight up to the front door. Inside, the house is big and drafty, echoing voices from times past. There is nothing of the future present. I hear a low moaning, a bass voice singing about the river Jordan, then an a capella choir of sopranos and altos resounding in a big, cathedral-like space. The wind soon rises and blows away all human voices. The house creaks and shakes in agony. I am alone in the darkness. I am surrounded by ghosts. Nothing really makes sense. I wait for the light to come. Any light will do.

I woke up scared.

Will my death simply be an entrance into the big void, where only the wind speaks and the past is washed away?

I yearned for Father Esperance to come and comfort me with thoughts of Heaven, redemption, and resurrection.

Can I back out of my decision, change the date, keep on going until there is no more going?

I feel like the groom who, upon the eve of his wedding, suddenly thinks it's all wrong, that this isn't the woman for him, that it's all a big mistake. Surely there are those who put a stop to the onrushing ceremony, but probably more, like me, who have made a public announcement of intention and are afraid to disappoint the crowd.

It will be okay for Tess. She will rejoice if I back out now. Father Esperance will go with whatever I decide, but what will Hawk think? Not what will he say but what will be in his heart?

Yes, he will know the truth of my disbeliefs and that I am chickenshit.

I let the fever obliterate everything.

My death will come soon enough.

Tess

Chapter 47

● ◆ ●

I COUNTED THIS as the second worst week in my life, the first week having stretched out for forty days and forty nights. The natural storm, having thrashed its way across the lake from Wisconsin, soon wore itself out on the resistant fabric of land. The inner storms of fear and anxiety, however, kept me spinning in constant disarray, despite the smile I pasted on my face. I asked Meggie to see me twice a week until I could get my bearings.

The first departure was that of Cassie. "I'm heading south," she said, "and I don't know where I'll land. I'll come back when I'm old news and the gossip has turned to another target." She packed up her Subaru, gave me a kiss, and said, "I promise I'll call you. I left the name of the handyman and a document giving you power of attorney over Hagen's Heaven on my bed. Now be a good girl and continue with your rehabilitation program. I'll check in on you from time to time."

With that, Cassie drove away. I watched her car turn the corner and waited until I could no longer hear its familiar sound.

I couldn't believe my savior would leave me like that. "Damn that Spenser Mudge," I growled, heading indoors where it was warm and cozy. I fixed myself a cup of coffee, called up the rehabilitation program, and announced I was taking a day off. I deserved a good sulk.

Then I remembered that Cassie had said the document was on her bed, so I headed upstairs.

When I first read it, it made no sense whatsoever. I had to read it two more times before I realized that Cassie had not given me the power of attorney over Hagen's Heaven.

No, resting on her bed was the deed to the house and property of Hagen's Heaven inscribed with my name. She had transferred it all to me.

It hit me all of a sudden.

Cassie wasn't planning on ever coming back.

I slumped down on the side of her bed.

Cassie, whatever am I going to do without your help, your advice?

I should have been grateful, but I wasn't. I was terrified.

A sealed envelope slipped to the floor from the pile of documents. It was addressed to me in Cassie's handwriting.

Dear Tess,

So now you know that I have no plans to return. It was a lovely fantasy, being the owner of such a beautiful place, but the ghosts of Natalie and my dear husband have haunted me from day one. Mr. Mudge's accusations only intensified my uneasiness in living there, but you have no such associations

to the place. I've watched you walk around the property in awe
of its beauty, and I thought to myself that if anyone should own
Hagen's Heaven, it should be you.

Perhaps that was the design of the universe in the first place.
Heaven knows why we land where we do, but your appearance
in my life was a gift. I was lonely, and I felt your love. It gave
me the courage to do the right thing.

I ask of you but one small favor—to speak to no one of what
I am about to tell you and to burn this letter after you read it.

I don't know why or really how Natalie Hagen died nor do
I really care. In the long run, she made Devin happy and he
never stopped loving me. I know that may be hard for you to
understand. I would have wished he could have found everything
he needed in our relationship, but that was not to be.

What I have the most trouble with is forgiving myself in
regard to Devin's death.

As you recently learned, I had followed him when he started
walking toward that high country bridge in a deep depression.
I didn't know at that time about Natalie or her death. When he
climbed over the bridge railing, I suddenly understood what
was about to happen. I emerged from the cover of trees and
yelled at him, "No, Devin!"

Surprised, he looked at me and leaned out from the bridge,
one hand grasping an iron railing.

I ran to him. "Why, Devin?" I grabbed his shirt, then his
belt to keep him from jumping.

"Let me go," he said. "I've been unfaithful to you all
these years."

"But I love you," I answered, unable to believe what he
was saying.

"And now she's dead," he said.

At that moment, it suddenly dawned on me. He wanted to kill himself out of grief for another woman.

He let go of the railing, but I still had my hand hooked in the back of his belt.

"I need . . ." he said, the words piercing my heart, "to be with her."

And then I did a terrible, unforgivable thing, Tess.

I opened my fingers.

The letter stopped there. No signature. Nothing. Almost as if Cassie were the one who'd dropped off the bridge.

Now I understood why she had to leave. Smudge had gotten too close to the truth.

I read the letter over and over, then put it in the fireplace and lit a match. I watched her confession crinkle up, as if in agony, then turn black, before crumbling into gray ash. She was right, of course.

Only Heaven knows why we land where we do.

The second, looming departure had a date—October 31. Sonny was holding fast to his plan to have the ventilator turned off. Inside, I nurtured the hope that he, like me, would be able to find his own breath. I planned to spend as much time with him as possible before that date.

Sonny didn't cooperate with that plan. The fever kept him mostly down and out. When he did awake, I quickly told him of Cassie's departure but not of her reasons. It barely registered with him.

The nurses kept chasing me out of the room, speaking in hushed voices. It was like everything was rushing to the finale.

"You need to return to the rehabilitation program," said Meggie at our next session.

"Why? What's the use?" I was feeling really sorry for myself.

"Because this is your work, and if you don't continue, your brain won't make the necessary reconnections."

"Cassie's gone. Imp's gone. Soon, Sonny will be gone. And Nick and my colleagues in Cambridge . . ." I was shoveling deep into the landscape of self-pity.

"Gifts of the heart," she said, tapping her chest.

Not quite what I had expected her to say. I had wanted some good old-fashioned sympathy.

"Now it's time to complete the circle of all that love," she continued.

"Yes," I said softly before great, heaving sobs shook my frame.

It was then that Meggie O'Connor moved to my chair and put her arms around me. I soaked her shoulder with my tears.

"Self-pity is like a tar pit that can swallow you whole, Tess. Grief is something quite different. It honors the gifts they have given you. You have been well-loved. You will carry that always within your own heart."

"But Sonny . . ."

"You will have to love him back, Tess. You have to respect his choices about life and death and that means letting him go."

But all I can see are Cassie's hands opening and letting Devin fall to his death.

Sonny

Chapter 48

. ◆ .

THE LAST DAY. It came so fast, in a blur, as the fever had put me down hard. But this morning, October 31, I awoke without the fever, a small blessing in disguise.

If I am going to die today, I want to be conscious. I want to say goodbye with my eyes open.

The hospital staff informed me that I had to wait until the team of doctors and nurses assembled in the mid-afternoon. They had to review the protocol and the medicines.

One last visit by the hospital psychiatrist to determine what I truly wanted and whether I still intended to go through with it.

"Yes," I said on the exhale of the ventilator. "I am . . . tired . . . of this . . . unnatural . . . life." I scanned all the tubes and equipment keeping me on life support.

I guess he ascertained that I was of sound mind although not of sound body.

Tess arrived early and claimed the nearest chair as hers. When no one was in the room, she reached over and gave me a long and lingering kiss, caressed my cheek, and then washed my face with a warm washcloth. She stared into my eyes as if trying to fathom my decision, but she didn't try to argue me out of it.

The nurses shuttled in and out of my room. I couldn't help but feel like an object of curiosity. They wished me good luck and bon voyage and told me they would miss me, how much they had enjoyed working with me. Some even acknowledged that they thought I was making the right decision.

Part of me wanted to sleep into death.

Saying goodbye is exhausting. That's probably why there aren't many people who choose the date of their own death.

"Would you like a sedative before we turn off the ventilator?" asked one physician.

"I don't . . . want . . . to be . . . asleep."

He nodded and said that it would be a gentle sedative, something to put me at ease.

I agreed to that, fearing a last minute attack of anxiety and regret.

"After the ventilator is turned off," he continued, "you may find yourself starting to gasp. We will immediately give you enough morphine to let you be comfortable."

We both knew what that meant.

The day wore on, and I was beginning to fray. I enjoyed the attention, but I was scared and wanted it all over. Why did death have to be so formal?

Hawk arrived. His hands did one last scan over my body while the others looked on with curiosity.

Tess kept one hand against my cheek.

Hawk then nodded and asked, "Are you ready?"

"I will . . . be," I answered.

He moved to the far corner of the room, unwilling to join the circus of visitors.

Jane Smith came in. She leaned over and whispered, "I reserved a space for you at Grand Traverse Memorial Gardens, as you requested, next to your mother."

"Thank you."

"They'd only do it if you agreed to a cremation, and I said you were all right with that." Jane was double-checking to make sure of my wishes.

"Ashes to . . . ashes," I said.

"Dust to dust," added Father Esperance, appearing by the side of the bed. He again asked if he could perform the Sacrament Rite of Anointing the Sick, but I said no. Saying "Hail Mary" was as far as I could reenter the Catholic rituals.

The area around the bed was getting crowded. Tess was not willing to relinquish the hand on my cheek.

I appreciated her touch.

My last lifeline.

Finally, the team of doctors entered the room, loaded with syringes, vials, and a grim determination on their faces.

I tried to smile but it came out more as a grimace.

Hawk moved to the end of my bed and spoke to me and to the others. "When the ventilator is turned off, I will begin singing the Lakota prayer songs. Sonny, pay attention. In this passage to the next dimension, there will be someone there to help you across. The songs will be the last thing you will hear in this dimension and the first thing you will hear in the next."

The team of physicians and nurses now arranged themselves on both sides of my bed, near the ventilator, near the intravenous line. They had their needles of morphine that they could not legally give me until after the ventilator was turned off.

Without taking away her hand, Tess moved so that she was solidly in my field of vision. She mouthed, "I love you, Sonny." Her eyes glistened with tears, but she refused to shed them.

Father Esperance began slowly to finger his rosary and softly intoned, "Hail Mary, full of grace. Blessed art thou among women. Blessed is the fruit of thy womb, Jesus."

"Do it," I commanded.

The nurse turned off the ventilator.

Hawk began to sing, "Kola, lecel ecun wo!"

Everything went still.

My mouth opened to take in air, but nothing happened.

I saw the doctors inject the morphine into the line.

My vision began to swim.

Last image:

Tess giving me a thumbs up sign with her free hand.

Last thought:

Tess, Tess, Tess . . . I love you.

Tess

Chapter 49

• ◆ •

IT WAS THE BEST OF TIMES; it was the worst of times. Words were useless, and only touch would do. I refused to yield my hand to anyone but held it to Sonny's cheek. I would not abandon him. I would not burden him with my tears or despair, so frequently I had to turn my eyes away from him.

It was a carnival of people trooping in to say goodbye, and I resented each and every one of them. I yearned for quiet solitude with him. I wanted him to gift me with some precious last moments of wisdom, but he was preoccupied, acknowledging everyone making pilgrimages to his bedside.

Oh Sonny, don't go. Please change your mind.

But he was too busy holding court to read my mind, to give me comfort. Occasionally he would lean his cheek against my hand, a slight pressure to remind me that he knew I was there for him.

I wondered if the Jesus image had finally infiltrated and sunk beyond the mask into his soul. There he was, his body lifeless, awaiting the sentence of death, neither stoic nor serene. He had questions, I knew that.

What comes next? What comes after? Will God forsake me?

He knew fear but kept that bottled up inside. He experienced doubt but the decision was final. Thus doubt became irrelevant. He was on a train moving lickety split, faster and faster, speeding toward the dark tunnel. He wasn't going to turn back.

My finger reached out and wrapped around a curl of his hair and gave a gentle tug. For a brief moment he shifted his attention toward me. Soon, all too soon, that would no longer be possible. I would reach out and there would be no cheek, no hair, no face, no smiling eyes to welcome every day. The afternoon hours would collapse back onto me for definition. I hid my face so he could not see what I was feeling.

I felt two eyes watching me and looked up. No, not Father Esperance whispering his repetitive chant about Mother Mary and avoiding my icy reception. I would not yield my place to him. No, these eyes came from across the room and belonged to that medicine man, Hawk. When he saw me returning his gaze, he looked away.

Such sadness in those eyes. Like me, he knows that words are deafening at the approach of the mortal hour.

Our eyes met again. He tipped his head to acknowledge what we both experienced, the fragility of the human condition. I suddenly understood why Sonny took to this man. A slight smile emerged on his face, but his eyes, his eyes spoke of what could not be said.

Meggie O'Connor was smart to have married that man.

Finally I could stand it no longer. I had to leave the room to go to the bathroom. I deposited my jacket, my pocketbook, my book on the chair, silently daring anyone to try to usurp my place.

I held it together going down the hallway to the bathroom, into and out of the stall, until I saw my face in the mirror. I began to sob. My face reddened. Despite clutching my sides, I could not stop shuddering, and a moan that was more animal than human escaped from deep inside. Only when another human being, a middle-aged woman, entered the bathroom, did I turn on the cold water and splash my face. I did not want her to know of my grief. I wanted no questions, no explanations.

How can I spell out the imminence of death? How can I talk about choice and dignity and love all muddled together into a test of endurance?

I will be strong for Sonny.

When I stepped into the hallway, Hawk was waiting for me. He took my hand and said, "Yesterday, he told me that he had left the hospital bed to go exploring. A house, he said. In the kitchen of that house, he found his mother. Or maybe the truth is that she found him. He especially wanted you to know that behind the attic door, he heard a small dog barking."

Imp.

I bit my upper lip, my lower lip, my cheek, but I could not hold back the cracking dam.

Then this quiet and reserved medicine man did the most extraordinary thing. He wrapped his arms around me and I cried, not giving a damn who heard me in the hallway, his shoulder shielding me from curious looks.

"Sonny plans to come back, to let you know that he made safe passage. You must be open to his signals," he said.

I nodded, exhausted by the flood from the ever-replenishing well of grief.

He whipped out a yellow bandana from his back pocket and gave it to me to dry my tears.

I started to apologize for my loss of control. "My brain doesn't function like it used to."

He nodded. "It's funny how an accident can make a person much more open to things of the spirit."

I didn't know if he was talking about me or about Sonny.

He tipped his head back toward Sonny's room. "He's waiting for us."

I nodded. "The sentinels."

A puzzled look crossed his face.

"We are the ones who stand there with lit torches, sending him on his way into the darkness."

"With song and prayer," said Hawk.

"And love," I added.

The relief on Sonny's face at our return was palpable. I sat down on the chair and placed my hand on his cheek.

His lips quivered with the memory of our kisses or with fear.

His gaze wandered to Hawk and the tension left his face.

The hospital team began to gather in the room.

Sonny whispered in my direction. "Okay . . . Tess."

Then I heard him give the command to the staff. "Do it."

As the priest mumbled in the background, I shifted position so that I could see Sonny clearly and he could watch me.

The physician moved to turn off the ventilator. I looked at Sonny and gave him a thumbs up sign. My lips silently articulated but one word: *Love.*

I will be strong for you, Sonny.

He stared at me and smiled.

The wheezing sound of the ventilator fell off and Hawk began singing the Lakota prayer songs.

With his eyes still fiercely latched onto mine, Sonny briefly gasped for air.

The physicians injected morphine, the sweet poison of sleep, into the intravenous line.

Sonny's eyelids drooped.

I whispered, "Take care of Imp, Sonny. She's behind that door, waiting for you."

But I don't know if he heard me.

And then it was all over.

Sonny had found his way home.

Tess

Chapter 50

• ◆ •

It is April 30, six months after Sonny crossed over.

A lot can happen in six months. At first, I was totally lost, adrift without anchors—no husband, no dog, no guardian angel like Cassie, no one with whom to spend my afternoons and occupy my thoughts. I would be lying if I didn't admit I was scared.

I worked like the devil at the rehabilitation program, mainly because it gave me a purpose, a daily schedule, an order to my life. They tried their best to teach me to cook. I kept to a simple, limited menu, one without too many steps. At long last, I remembered how to season the food and that a cup of wine in any sauce makes things taste better.

Thank you, Edward Hagen, for your well-stocked wine cellar!

Finances were another matter. I no longer seemed to have the ability to work out a sensible budget, especially with such a grand house. There was always something that needed fixing, whether it was a leak in the roof, the automatic generator failing to fire, or the driveway to be plowed. Luckily, Meggie's husband, Hawk, proved to be a godsend in that area. We worked out an arrangement whereby he would be the handyman on call.

Meggie said that as long as I could offer him home-baked cookies and freshly brewed coffee, he would come cheap. Not only did he respond to middle-of-the-night emergencies, but he also offered me friendship and sound advice.

Hawk told me that Sonny was making a journey in the next dimension from the West to the North, East, and finally the South.

"And it's from the South that new life comes," he added.

"Reincarnation?" I asked.

But Hawk just smiled.

I'm sure if Sonny gets to choose, he sure wouldn't come back looking like Jesus.

Meggie continued to see me twice a week, until I got my feet on the ground. She arranged for me to meet with an accountant who helped me understand income flow and apply for social service disability payments. Nick made good on the court-ordered payments and even checked up on me from time to time to see how I was doing. We even got to the point where I felt free to tease him.

"Isn't it scary to live with someone who can hear what the Spirits have to say about you?"

He laughed. "Well, yes, but Sandy is diplomatic and tends not to share with me what they're saying."

After the divorce was finalized, he called me to announce that he and Sandy were getting married the next month. He didn't want me to find out about it by reading the newspaper.

"I hate to say this, Nick, but she seems to be a fine woman. I hope the two of you will be happy." Then I paused and added, "But not as happy as we were in the beginning."

Nick chuckled.

The new me tends toward being bluntly honest, not out of self-confidence or a sense of irony, but because my brain no longer seems capable of subtle communication.

I rather think that Nick likes parts of the new me better than the old me but still not enough to leave Sandy.

Meggie O'Connor and I worked hard on my letting go of Nick and any hopes for reunion. I will always feel sad about the divorce, but I accept that life keeps offering these inevitable changes.

"Transitions will happen whether you like them or not," said Meggie. "But it's your choice as to whether they become transformations as well."

She loves to say things like that, provocative statements about which I have to think a lot.

I can say it a lot simpler, and I do. "Shit fertilizes."

I've decided to keep Natalie's furniture and southwest colors. They're warm and suggest a different landscape than a cold, wintry Michigan. I did, however, sell all the family portraits and photographs to Spenser Mudge. I think he suspected that I might blackmail him if he didn't buy the lot. That money will cover the property taxes next year.

I thought about returning to Cambridge for the Christmas holidays and reuniting with my old friends, but I got a surprise call from Cassie saying she planned to come and stay for the holiday week. That was a relief to Meggie who was afraid I'd get depressed by revisiting my old life in Massachusetts. She was still trying to solidify the "new me."

"Tess, the accident and trauma to the brain have made you much more emotionally labile than before the accident."

Of course, she's right. I tend to explode with petty annoyances, bureaucratic hassles, physical clumsiness. I don't seem to have as much patience as before. Meggie says I need to continue to learn how to develop "self-soothing" behaviors.

"You have to slow your breathing, tell yourself that things are going to be okay, and be more forgiving of yourself. The brain takes a long time to heal."

She made sure I was on anti-anxiety drugs and a small dose of anti-depressants, but truth to tell, I find a glass of wine every night does wonders. I don't ever dare drink more than one glass, as I'm afraid I could get addicted to the sweet relaxation and mind-numbing effect alcohol has on me.

In a moment of weakness, I asked Sally McGovern to move into the big house with me. She gave the idea ten good minutes of thought, then gently turned me down.

"Good friends don't always make good house mates."

What she didn't say was that she and Spenser Mudge had somehow made up and were seeing each other again. When she did tell me, I let her know it didn't bother me. That really wasn't the truth, as I think she deserves better, but as Sally once said, "Better here may be never."

The snow didn't really start to fall big-time until January, so in between the smaller storms, I continued to scour Hagen's Heaven for the remains of my little pal. I never did find her bones. I had to settle for the image of her barking behind the attic door, urging Sonny to come her way.

Cassie returned in her old Subaru five days before Christmas. I didn't hear her car rumbling up the driveway. She let herself into the house and yelled up the stairs, "Tess, I'm home. Come on down and greet the old gal!"

I flew down the stairs and into her arms. She looked tanned and healthy, having lost weight and trimmed up her figure.

"You're looking good too, Tess," she said. "You doing any better with that cooking?"

I shook my head, and we both laughed.

"Well, I best get to work helping you some. Tess, my bags are in the car. Will you get them for me?"

"Oh," she added as I headed out the front door, "I left your Christmas present on the back seat. It's not wrapped, but that's okay." Cassie—the woman of mystery.

I bounded out the door and down the porch steps over to the familiar car. The windows were steamed up, but it looked like something was moving inside the car.

I opened the back door and there, wiggling from head to toe, was a gorgeous little Sheltie puppy, strapped into a seat belt harness.

"Why, hello little guy."

A mahogany male Sheltie, about three months old. His tongue flashed out and licked my face as I unhitched his harness. As soon as he was free, he leapt into my arms and covered me with kisses.

Cassie appeared at my side. "I see the two of you are getting acquainted. I'll get the bags. You take him inside."

His body was all motion. He snuggled into me, licking my collarbone as I headed up the porch stairs. As soon as I placed him on the floor, he piddled in excitement.

"Oops," said Cassie, coming up behind me. "You've got some housebreaking to do with him."

"You mean . . . ?"

"Well, sure. You don't think I want to put up with another dog? He's your problem."

Cassie couldn't have given me a better present in the whole world. I watched that little guy during all day and named him "Rascal" that evening. It fit his mischievous personality. Since then, I've discovered that Rascal is a master paper shredder, hole digger, and gull chaser. He has yet to distinguish gulls from eagles, wild turkeys, and airplanes, but he waxes enthusiastic about every chase.

In truth, Rascal has given me a reason to live. Suicide is no longer an option. I have responsibilities to this little guy.

"You wouldn't really have killed yourself?" asked Cassie.

I think she was feeling guilty that she'd left me so abruptly. I wasn't going to let her off the hook.

"The days were pretty dark after Sonny died and the nights even more so."

"I had to go, Tess."

"How long will you stay?"

"I will be gone before the New Year," she said. "I'm moving permanently to San Diego."

"San Diego?"

"Where the difference between summer and winter is only eleven degrees."

"But this is your place, no matter what the deed says."

Cassie shook her head. "No, it's not. It belonged to Natalie and now it belongs to you. Besides, I've got a job waiting for me in San Diego. I'll be coordinating volunteer services at a hospital there."

Something else had been left unsaid. I waited for Cassie to say more.

"There's also an old friend of mine who lives there."

"Now the truth comes out."

"He's asked me to come live with him, to try him out, so to speak."

"What did you say, Cassie?"

"At my age, it doesn't pay to linger in one's cautions. I agreed. We'll see what happens."

I felt like an old grandma cautioning her. "Well, if it doesn't work out, you can always come back here."

She patted my cheek. "And put up with that rapscallion who is right now chewing on my left foot?"

I looked down, and sure enough, Rascal had the entire toe of her left shoe in his mouth.

Cassie did indeed leave before the New Year to try on her new life. As far as I can tell from our weekly phone conversations, it's working out okay. Reed Clark is his name. He sounds nice enough on the phone, but I suspect at their respective ages, it's taking a bit of adjusting to fit into each other's life.

Cassie promised to bring him up to Michigan for my stamp of approval in the summertime, but I had to swear I wouldn't mention the saga of Edward, Natalie, and Devin to him.

"That's old history best forgotten," she declared.

I've begun to form some new friends and to meet more of Sally's teacher network. They ask me a lot of questions about the private school in Cambridge and express envy of the freedom given to teachers there. Public schools apparently demand much more uniformity in subject matter.

At first, I thought I might be able to do some substitute teaching, but it never worked out. I no longer had the patience or skills to settle down a noisy classroom.

Meggie O'Connor suggested that I contact the Big Brothers Big Sisters program and take on a one-to-one mentoring relationship with some struggling girl. I plan to do that in the near future, but right now I feel more comfortable volunteering at the local animal shelter, especially since they allow me to bring Rascal.

He gets to socialize with other dogs while I clean the cat house and shovel manure from the horse stalls. I can only manage about three hours a week before fatigue takes over. At least, it's a start back toward a working life.

In the meantime, Rascal makes me laugh every day. Although Shelties aren't water dogs, Rascal loves to splash in Lake Michigan. We run up and down the beach for exercise. At night, before the full-length mirror in the bedroom, he drops down on his front legs, begging his image to come out and play. He stalks sticks and pounces on ants as if they are prey.

He is a good student, and he learned "sit," "down," "come," and "stay" with great ease. With some concealed hand gestures, I've taught him to drop down on the floor and roll on his back when I ask him, "Would you rather be a Republican or die?" That trick always produces a polite but uncomfortable chuckle amongst my Republican neighbors.

All throughout the winter, he leaped high into the air to catch snow flakes. Now that it's spring, the smells of the burgeoning, blossoming earth enchant him. Squirrels and chipmunks taunt him with their chatter and lead him on futile chases.

As for me, I've discovered that spring on the Leelanau Peninsula is magical. New life, new possibilities are carried in the soft breezes that waft off the big lake.

Last week, that police officer who had questioned Cassie in the fall called me.

At first, I thought he was scouting for more information on her. I wasn't about to reveal her new location, but he told me he wasn't calling on official business. He cleared his throat on the phone, a nervous gesture, and said, "Actually, I wanted to know if you would like to go hunting with me."

What a bizarre, backwoods request.

"I don't like killing of any kind," I answered.

"No, no, I understand," he said. "I mean hunting for morel mushrooms."

"Oh."

"You have to know what they look like because some mushrooms that look like morels are poisonous. You don't need to worry about that, because I know morels well."

"You're a poet," I said.

At first he didn't get it, but then he replied, "Well, is there a fungus among us?"

He sounded as brain-injured as I in humor, so I said, "Yes," remembering how handsome he was.

I only hope he likes dogs because Rascal and I are now inseparable.

That accounts for about everything in my life.

Except Sonny.

He promised to come back and give me a sign. Well, I waited and waited for such an appearance after his death. I'd peer into the dark of the night or look into the face of the moon, half expecting to see him emerge out of the shadows, walking with arms open to give me the hug he never could give me in this dimension.

But he never came.

I even yelled into the night at him, exasperated at his no-show. "You promised!"

Then I confessed my anger to Hawk.

"It may not be his problem," the medicine man/handyman replied. "You may not have developed the capacity to hear or see him. Or it may simply be that he doesn't yet know how to come back through the veils between this and that dimension."

Everybody is always counseling PATIENCE to me.

Finally I gave up the struggle to make connection with Sonny. I miss him terribly and recognize that I tend to give more weight in memory to the courageous side of him rather than the fearful side. It helps me drum up more fortitude in myself.

What the dead have to teach us.

After April comes May comes summertime tripping into the peninsula. The tourists and summer people will soon crowd the streets, basking in the warmth, the water sports, the Sleeping Bear Dunes National Lakeshore, the gin-and-tonic afternoons. More of the stores will open, but here at Hagen's Heaven, I can still retreat into the quietness of the land, apart from people, with the animals and Rascal.

Right now, he's sleeping on top of my bed under his own blanket. He snuggles against the curve of my body, and I like to hear the comforting sips of his breathing. His little white paws twitch to some imaginative dream where he is chasing shadows.

I look toward the window. It is a night of a full moon, and the beams shine straight onto the polished wood floor. I am wide awake, no longer scared but rather in awe of life. I've come to understand how tragedy burns all of us in time, how beauty and love can eventually emerge from the ashes. We lose people we love, but we can honor the memory of each and every one through the gifts they have given us. They also pave the way for us when it's our time to cross over.

I hope Sonny will be there to welcome me and be my tour guide in the faraway future.

"Thank you," I say to him, a prayer offered up with no expectation of answer.

But this time, in the translucent moonlight, as I turn back toward the bedroom, I catch the shadowy sight of myself in the full-length mirror with another image coalescing behind mine, unambiguous, borne not of hallucination or desire, but of the opening of spirit. It is Sonny, smiling at me. I spin around to see if he is truly by the window behind me, but only moon rays dapple the empty space.

Quick, so as not to lose him, I turn back toward the mirror. He is still there. He raises his left hand, palm up, and blows a kiss into the room. His image dissipates as rapidly as it appeared, but not before I feel the gentle breath of love coming my way.

The End

Recommended Reading

Denton, Gail L., Ph.D. 1996. *Brainlash*. New York: Demos Health.

Stoler, Diane R., Ed.D. and Barbara A. Hill. 1998. *Coping with Mild Traumatic Brain Injury*. New York: Penguin Group.

Both these books contain excellent resource sections. There are also multiple sites on the internet for learning about spinal cord injuries and traumatic brain injuries as well as sites for assistive technology such as:

www.Getatstuff.org and www.Bindependent.com